Either Side of Winter

Benjamin Markovits

First published in 2005
by Faber and Faber Limited
3 Queen Square London WC1N 3AU

Typeset in Palatino by Faber and Faber
Printed in England by Mackays of Chatham, plc

A CIP record for this book
is available from the British Library

ISBN 0–571–22665–5

2 4 6 8 10 9 7 5 3 1

FALL

A Thanksgiving Visit

I

She cried in bed every night after turning the light off, unless Charles Conway was staying over, in which case she didn't feel any happier but didn't cry. With the light on – a desk lamp she'd taken from the school balanced on her night stand, a restaurant-sized tin of tomato sauce – she read magazines until her eyes got tired and stung. This didn't take long and usually happened shortly after nine o'clock each night. Unless Charles was staying over. But if not, she turned over in bed and turned off the lamp and turned back. When it was overcast, she could see the light of Manhattan caught in the cloud outside her window. By the time the first blackness of the change in light had softened to the coloured dusk of a city evening, she had bent her chin against her chest and begun to blub. In the dark, as if no one could see her then; as if she couldn't see herself. And might not notice how unhappy she was, because if she did, she'd have to give herself a talking to, since nothing much was wrong and she couldn't go on like this anyway.

They first got to the apartment at the end of August, after collecting the keys at the school reception. A hot day, somewhere in the nineties and wet as a dishrag. The air-conditioning was down in Bertelmeyer Hall, and because the teachers were still on break, out at Fire Island or walking the dogs or whatever it was they did, and more importantly the department heads and the vice principal still sitting on their porches in Westchester County, nobody had raised a stink about the temperature. All there was was a table fan blowing this way and then that in reception; you waited for it to come your way, you felt it, not so much a relief as something to feel other than the heat, and you heard it turn away again. Her dad, cooped up in the car all day, had a loose tongue getting out, and said to the birdlike Irish woman at the black phones, how good it felt to be back in the city after thirty years and God did he wish it was him. Amy noticed him saying it then and remembered it later. At the time she felt that slight overflow of emotions of various kinds, which she thought of as excitement then but had since realized was much too mixed up with other things for it to be anything that simple. She got it or something like it every morning the first two months standing in front of a classroom, and then again after lunch when she had to go back and do it again. The best you could do was ignore it since it didn't mean much.

She put her head against his armpit when he said it and her arms around him. He smelt slightly of ill-health or middle age, she couldn't tell which, a sour smell like the rind of old fruit. He'd put on weight since she went to college; and whenever she came back home on the holidays he ate a bowl of chocolate ice-cream before going to bed, sometimes two while watching television. And now a lump of flesh – though she thought of it always as what it stood for or what she thought it stood for, dissatisfaction with himself – hung over his belt. The line hung in her memory over the next few months and sounded more and more like a reproach, as if the words, like food left in a cupboard, could change smell over time. 'I guess I hoped to get her at home a year or two after graduation. We've got a boy as well, sophomore this fall, though he went out of state too, out west. Kids these days got to live their own lives I figure; I know I did.' And then, 'It sure feels good to be back in the city after thirty years and God do I wish it was me.' Later she decided that he didn't really mean it, or if he meant it it was only something he'd planned to say when they got there – planned it over the thirty hours in the car from Indianapolis – and maybe by the time he actually got a chance to say it (and he took the first chance he got) it may have lost some of the feeling, or may not have been true any more. It couldn't be true: nobody could want to live like she was living a second time.

The first thing she did when she got to the apartment was push open the windows. There were three of them in the sitting room and one in the bedroom, all looking downhill towards Manhattan, each containing it seemed to her a different piece of the view. From the bedroom window, if she stuck her head out, she could just about see the modern extension to the school gymnasium, a glassy structure built against the angle of the hill on which the campus sat. The kitchen window – or what she thought of as the kitchen window, since it opened out over the sink at the end of the row of cabinets and countertops that included a small fridge and the oven – looked out on the tattoo parlour and the pizza parlour across from the entrance to her apartment block. Shops stood on the low side of the street and the hill sloped away behind them. Beyond those, and above them, she could make out the trees of Van Cortlandt Park and a strip of flat green just above the rooftops. There was a futon backed up against the rest of the wall, with the other two windows behind it. If you kneeled on it, you could see the park of course and the raised subway station at 242nd Street and beyond that the first warehouses of Inwood across the river, and beyond them the occasional spires of downtown New York. She spent hours in the next few months kneeling and looking, leaning her elbows against one of the sills.

Her sweating palms were caked in dust when she pushed open the windows; she dried them on her denim skirt and saw the marks they made. She couldn't decide whether to shower and change first – she stank from eight hours in the car in any case – or do something about the dirty screens blurring the view behind the windows. Her dad had got himself a glass of milky water from the sink and sat down. She said, 'I can't get these out can you give me a hand.'

'Why don't you turn on the air condition?' he said.

'There isn't any.'

'There's a unit in the bedroom that might get through to us.'

'I'd rather have the windows open. We always have the windows open back home. I just want to get rid of these screens.'

'Let me just drink a glass of water sitting down and I'll help you bring your stuff up. Trust me, they're there for a reason.'

'They're ugly and dirty.'

'They're dirty for a reason.'

She began to wrench one up and down, squeaking, but couldn't get it out of the slots. So she began to open all the cupboard doors to see if there was anything she could use and eventually decided to take off one of her shoes, black and hard-heeled Doc Martens, and bang the heel against the frame of the screen. Her dad at first didn't say anything to the noise. And as it grew louder Amy felt more and more trapped inside her movements, which grew more and more violent and (it seemed) ineffectual. She felt trapped both by the fact that nothing seemed to budge and by the fact that whether she wanted to or not she had to keep hitting the edge of the screen harder and harder with her shoe until one of the facts gave way to the other. When the frame cracked and wrenched out of the slots she began to cry, and was still crying as she pulled the rest of it out and through the window again. By that time her dad had come round and caught her in his arms and they stood there for perhaps a minute while she held the dirty screen in one hand sobbing and he had his hands clasped at her stomach and kissed the top of her head.

'Don't leave me here,' she said. 'Don't leave me here.'

'It's gonna be fine. It's gonna be wonderful.' Then he added a little later, letting go of her, 'I don't want to leave you here. I don't want to leave you anywhere. But I have to.'

She met Charles shortly after that, even before the school year started. There was a function to celebrate the fundraisers and patrons who had recently mustered, each in their separate ways, millions of dollars for the school renovations scheduled for the following summer. The glass extension to the gymnasium was only a prelude to greater things; and the party was held on its brightly varnished wooden floors both to 'open its doors' and usher in the improvements to come. All of the teachers had been invited, but only the new teachers showed up. Amy looked frail in a cotton dress – she never wore dresses – and sandals, her only alternatives to the black Doc Martens. She had always been thin, with thin shoulders and hips, but when she lost weight, as she had after graduation, her breasts diminished and whatever she wore hung loosely over her frame. Short sandy hair cut just past her ears and black-rimmed glasses framed a face that was pretty in youth and might look ordinary afterwards: her cheeks, which had been plump in childhood, retained something of their shape, and gave her an air of good health in spite of her grown-up weightlessness. She had a straight plain nose and narrow chin; and a fund of sexual restlessness that expressed itself in many other kinds of restlessness and distinguished her from other girls caught between pretty and plain with narrow hips and a small chest. Though it didn't look as if it would last her long unless circumstances changed; it might easily have spent itself by her thirties. She looked like a girl who would grow more conventional rather than less.

Charles introduced himself to her when he saw her holding a glass of white wine and not drinking it, but holding it close to her chin as if she'd just had a sip and might soon want another. She thought he looked very much at his ease as she watched him come across the shiny floor towards her in his black shoes, which gave off the same crackling shine as the wooden boards. 'Hi,' he said, rolling up a programme and slotting it under his armpit, taking her glass of wine in his left hand and shaking her now empty hand, still slightly damp from the condensation on the cold drink, in his right. 'I'm Charles Conway.'

'Who's Charles Conway?' she said. She had a way of talking that made her look as if she wasn't listening even to herself: her eyes darted here and there to either side of him, and her lips only wriggled as she spoke.

'I'm one of the famous sons,' he said. It turned out he'd graduated from the school seven or eight years before. As the evening wore on it became clear to her just what kind of character she had taken by the arm: he was greeted everywhere by sudden, and not entirely forced, good humour, and often by the epithet Charles had attributed to himself: 'the famous Conway', people said, and took him by the hand or patted his back or the side of his solid arm beneath his snug black dinner jacket. The head teacher herself called him that, along with the worst-dressed man at the party: a grey-haired stocky gentleman wearing dirty sneakers, a short-sleeved collared shirt, and a whistle on a string around his neck, which he blew at occasionally from time to time and to no discernible effect. Charles was, as he explained to her through the course of the evening, not only one of the star pupils – and a standout on the tennis team, the eight-man crew, and the oratorical society – but also the son of one of the school's more significant benefactors, for which reason he had attended that night. His father, a lawyer, hated such dos and wasn't very good at them, so he usually sent Charles. 'Besides,' Charles said, 'I didn't have anything else to do tonight.' Amy couldn't be sure if he said 'don't' or 'didn't' but the 'tonight' sounded like a late addition in any case.

He had the kind of sandy hair and complexion that blend into each other and suggest an aristocratic air; grainy green eyes which he often blinked; a blond stubble with mineral residues of black and grey in it. He was tall – a good head taller than Amy, who herself was closer to five ten than five nine, even in sandals – and never seemed ill at ease, not even around Amy, who clearly was; partly because he didn't mind if she didn't talk much, which she didn't. When he asked her what she taught, she said, 'Biology' but his only response was, 'I wanted to be a surgeon once, but went off it.' Not that he spent the whole night talking about himself: he had the subtly feminine and quite irresistible charm of a handsome, well-built man who seems to like nothing better than softly spoken gossip. His voice was both languorous and rather abrupt; there were corners slowly taken and sudden halts. Amy found herself standing on tiptoe to put her ear by his lips; sometimes he leaned too far and tickled her slightly: she felt the light waving hairs on her lobe standing on end. He had stories about most of the teachers and told them with the obvious relish of a young man who has not yet outlived his schooldays.

Amy could drink with a will when the occasion demanded, and she rose to it that night. She tended to drink the same way people get in cold water: tentatively then suddenly; and it didn't take much to get her blood going – for that inarticulate though not unpleasant suspicion to overwhelm her that a great deal was happening or about to happen, more than she could possibly take in at once, though she wanted to try. White wine came and went in her glass, which always seemed half empty, regardless of how much she drank. When Charles began to kiss her on the brand-new concrete balcony by the door opening on to the hillside falling away at their feet, she said to him, in a voice louder and thicker than her own, 'I don't know anybody in New York so why don't you come back to mine.'

He said, 'Can we walk there?'

'Sure we can walk there.'

'I don't like the subway round here and I'm too drunk to drive.'

'Sure we can walk there,' she said again. 'Five minutes.'

He stood for a moment in reflection, with his face bent towards her cheek and his mouth open. 'Did you notice how the concrete under these lights looks like it's got moonlight on it?'

'Isn't there a moon?' she said, looking up.

'No, no moon.'

She called him 'Charles Conway' all night, and thought of him that way even after they'd been seeing each other for several months. She called him Charles Conway in the staff room, too – an L-shaped room curled around one of the bathrooms, some said carved out of the stalls. It stank like it too in hot weather, because the windows wouldn't stay open any further than you propped them, and all anybody did was stick a textbook in to wedge them up. One of the older teachers, Mr Peasbody, had taken her under his wing. He was a slenderish, elegantly dressed man from Connecticut, with an incongruously heavy and pock-marked face and large sad eyes. 'What's the young lady doing tonight?' he'd ask, crossing his legs and swivelling his desk chair round at the same time. 'I'm bored with myself these days. Cheer me up.'

'Charles Conway is taking me out to dinner in Manhattan.'

He became something of a joke and a symbol – of all things gallant and rich and metropolitan, and well above them, unless you were young and pretty. In short, of the kind of people they taught every day, the kind of lives their students would lead, which they could not quite aspire to themselves.

When they woke up together the next morning, Charles surprised her by having nowhere to go. She got up first, plucking a towel from the top of the bathroom door and wrapping it round her. He propped her pillow behind him, stretched out elaborately, and clasped his hands behind his head sitting half up. He was sitting like that, looking cheerful and sleepy, when she came out of the shower: her thin brown hair grew wispy and pale in the wet, and she folded another towel round her head to hide and dry it.

'I'll get you a towel,' she said, hoping he'd leave her to dress alone, but he answered, 'Don't bother, I'll shower when I get home', and didn't move. There'd been rain overnight to wipe the slate clean, and the sun was up in a clear sky and streaming more and more fully through the window as noon approached. It caught his face, or rather specks of his face – his stubble, the grain of his eyes, his teeth – which glinted in the yellow band of light as he squinted against it. She gathered an armful of clothes and changed in the bathroom. It was

Tuesday morning, she had a bad head, and her first day of school was Wednesday. When she got out again, dressed except for her wet feet, he was flicking through her stack of magazines.

'I wouldn't mind writing for one of these outfits,' he said. 'They're all the same: cosmetic compositions, in both senses. Like abstract art – composed of elements rather than figures.'

'Are you hungry?' she said.

'What d'you got in the house?'

She considered for a minute. 'How about we go out for breakfast?'

'Sure, I don't mind.' And he got up naked in front of her and carefully put on his clothes from the night before: the black trousers, which he'd folded and hung over the back of her desk chair, white shirt (from a hanger in her closet), cuff links, laid next to his watch on the tin of tomatoes. Only he left the bow-tie untied and loose around his neck. 'I know a little place around here', he said, 'I'd like to show you.'

That in fact became a characteristic of their relationship. Charles Conway showed Amy Bostick around town. Everywhere they went he knew 'a little place', and as often as not the proprietor there would greet him by name or by taking Charles's paw in one hand and holding Charles's elbow in the other and shaking both at once. The place he took her to that morning was a kind of Mexican greasy spoon, a 'short-order joint' Charles called it, named Rosarita's. At least that's what someone had painted in pink and blue on the white board above the awning. They sat at one of the round unsteady tables on the pavement underneath it and when Amy complained about sitting out of the sunshine and getting cold – she wore only a plain white T-shirt, linen shorts and Birkenstocks, and goosepimpled lightly – Charles called out, with patrician good humour, for someone to roll up the awning. A narrow-shouldered, dark-skinned man with a heavy moustache promptly attended them. He moved in the jerky almost brittle fashion of a skinny man whose skinniness has outlived his youth. As soon as he saw Charles he called out his name and put his hands around his neck, then bustled in and came out bearing two peach-coloured drinks in large wine glasses on a tray. Amy was more touched than she had any right to be and felt herself falling under the spell of the sandy young man in a dirty tuxedo whose stains showed up bright and dusty in the sunshine.

She was still somewhat drunk from the night before, and the peach-coloured liquid suggested at least that it was going to get better before it got worse. Charles it seems had decided to let her talk. He ordered some kind of huevos and ate them hungrily and without great dignity when they appeared; leaning forward to get low to the plate and looking up at her from under his thickening eyebrows to show he was listening from time to time. Amy said something about looking forward to the football season, that being the one thing about the start of the school year she always looked forward to: the leaves drying up on the trees, the first norther coming through to knock them off, and Notre Dame. She hadn't decided yet who to root for now that she'd transplanted herself. Her alma mater, Amherst, was pretty much a wash-out as far as football went. And she figured she'd spent enough time on the East Coast now not to beat against the prevailing winds any more – she might try pulling for the Giants.

Charles said, 'So you're one of those girls who makes a point of liking football.'

She almost bridled at that: she had been trying to impress him. Charles didn't seem to notice and, somewhat abashed, Amy made a confession she'd been hoping to get to at some stage in any case. 'I guess I've always been something of a Daddy's girl.' That set her off, though she probably left as much out as she included – saving it for later, perhaps, when she needed something vulnerable to expose for the purposes of conversation. Her father, also named Charles as it happens, though he went mostly by his middle name Jack, treated her like a boy from the start. To the point where, when her younger brother Andy came along, being that much younger and blooming later as a boy, he couldn't hope to keep up and turned out something of a disappointment in that respect, and concentrated on what she wouldn't compete with him at, like painting. Jack had a try-out for a minor-league ball club after college, which when he didn't make it he ended up in law school. Played the hot-shot lawyer in New York for five years, till Mom came along and they went home to Indiana to raise kids. They were both from Indiana, that was part of the appeal: but Amy guessed he kind of took out his ambitions on her. Not that she minded at all: going to state in softball her senior year was probably the most etc. of her life. And so on.

But, as usual, she edited less than she had intended to. And certain phrases cropped up now and again: I guess I was always the lucky one, I totally see why he resented me. These indicated what she had wanted to indicate in any case – that she was a favourite child. However much she told herself that it was ungenerous, and worse, to bring these things into the open, that they should be the unacknowledged solace of her lonelier hours. Still, the truth insists on being told. She was blessed by the preferences of love. The natural choice of affections. The darling of hearts. The inheritor of her parents' dreams. The one to bet on.

Though as for that, even Amy couldn't be sure how much of it was true any more, if it was ever true. It's always hardest to edit out what you have begun to doubt. Her brother, in his sophomore year at Pomona, had begun to get his cartoons – his graphic art – published in some San Francisco magazines. He won a sculpture prize, including a thousand-dollar cheque, on the strength of which he spent the summer backpacking through Mexico. Aunts, cousins, old college buddies, were always ringing up her parents to say they'd come across his work or his name on a website somewhere. You couldn't go home without seeing some magazine page tacked on to the fridge or the living-room mirror, most of it too strange or horrible to look at. She had quit the softball team her freshman year and the word she used for Amherst football was really the word that summed up how she had begun to think about the four years after high school: they had proved something of a wash-out. Nothing had changed, least of all her, except that everything she used to like about herself had gotten a little dusty.

Her relations with her mother Joanne had always been somewhat prickly, on her side at least. They just didn't get each other for a start, besides which there was no way Amy wanted to end up like Joanne: sweet and condescended to, as Amy saw it. Not that her father seemed so happy these days. Another source of guilt. Arthritis in his knees meant he couldn't even play softball any more, and he spent too much time in front of the couch watching the TV. Two years before he had had his teeth out (after Andy left for college): the thought of that plastic smile sitting in the glass on the shelf above the bathroom sink made her want to cry. He was forty-seven: already he had the artificial cheeriness of an old man to whom no one pays any real attention. Cheaply renovated, that's what he looked, with the hair he had left brushed back along his neck in thin strands that reminded her of her own wispy scalp after a shower. She should have moved back home after graduation, for a year at least; only, for whatever reason, and the fact surprised her as much as her parents, she hadn't. When she told her father she was moving to New York, he said, 'That's the right kind of thing for you to do. Though I can't say I didn't hope you'd come back home. But you always used to take things on head on.' She puzzled over that 'used'. Maybe he thought he didn't know her so well after four years at college. Maybe something else. She got the sense he was sending out a delegate to live the rest of his life – the life he should have lived in New York, when he ran around with a 'pretty fast crowd' and didn't have kids. (That hokum 'pretty' gave the game away when he said it.)

Amy knew herself well enough to realize this account of events was only partly right. She needed to think of her life as important. It didn't seem so any more. Charles, she already suspected, practised some editing of his own. 'I guess I better push off,' he said after breakfast, hopeful of contradiction perhaps; though when she asked him what he had planned for the day, he adopted a brisk tone. 'Buddy of mine's trying to set up a company,' he began, and swallowed the last of her drink. 'I won't bore you with the details, but I'm lending him a hand.' And then added, after signalling for the bill: 'Financial and otherwise.' As he had guessed, perhaps, that stopped Amy's curiosity short. All she said was, 'Do you get summers off?'

'That's not how I work,' he said.

She watched him from her window after he saw her to the lobby. Kneeling on the futon and straining out, she admired the way he seemed to have somewhere to go but no hurry. His dinner jacket trailing off a thumb over his shoulder; the pleasant downhill swagger of a light hangover the morning after, his feet loose in his shoes. But the road dropped sharply and he disappeared behind a bend in it on the way back to the school where his car was parked. She didn't get a look at his car. She thought, I hope I get a chance to before it ends.

Now that he was gone she didn't seem to have so much to do, and her apartment didn't have any answers. Not since high school had she fallen in love, and wasn't sure how to go about it any more. It used to be easier – this wasn't hard work, but she felt she could go either way and didn't want to have to choose. Already the thought presented itself to her: I suppose it depends on how lonely I get teaching, what I decide to make of this whole thing. And then she wondered what about Charles Conway gave her such grounds for confidence the choice was hers; that's when the first shadow of doubt fell across her, and an ache ran along a vein in her temple. Just like in college, she told herself: by the time you decide you are where you are where you are, it's too late. And: I hope he calls; I'm not sure I have the guts to any more.

She hardly thought about him Wednesday, that's how she put it to herself at night, aside from a single embarrassment. There seemed so much for her to worry about, running hot and cold all day. By the afternoon the combination of her intermittent sweat and the air-conditioning had taken its toll: she stank slightly, and wished she'd worn a cardigan over her T-shirt to hide the patches under her arms. The problem she thought would be to keep the children quiet. In fact, she couldn't get them to talk: row upon row of fourteen-year-olds, asleep or terrified or sullenly resentful, appeared before her; and she guessed in retrospect that she should have waited them out. But at the time – how could it be otherwise, given the restless, eager, dissatisfied current to her nature – she buzzed and flitted around them, playing the fool or the prim miss as the occasion demanded, confusing them and herself, desiring alternately and with an instant passion that surprised her to be each of their best friends or never to see them again. By eleven thirty she was utterly beat. She sat in a stall in the teachers' WC and cried. Then composed her face, and walked out across the baseball field on a bright clear September day whose sunshine it seemed couldn't touch her as she shivered in it regardless, heading for the cafeteria. The sight of all those children talking at once and eating appalled her. Already she suffered from a kind of persistent stage fright, convinced she would be called upon to remember a name or chastise a delinquent. So she held her head up in a blind way, certain that everyone could see what a miserable fraud she was. Filled a tray with food she was too nervous to eat, and sat in the far corner at an empty table by a window overlooking the concrete balcony on which she had first kissed Charles Conway, the famous son, two nights before.

Other teachers joined her, muttering do you mind if we? as they sat down. Amy sipped a mug of black coffee while picking indiscriminately from a paper plate heaped with tuna-fish salad, cottage cheese, carrot sticks and chocolate doughnuts. A headache danced circles around her eyes, but she began to talk in spite of it. 'My throat's so dry, I can't spit enough to eat,' she said.

'After day one I always feel like I've been to a rock concert,' declared a bulldog-faced man with his elbows on the table. And added, 'I'm in computers.'

Mr Peasbody, stroking his tie, looked round elaborately and said, 'At this point, my dear, you're closer to their age than ours.' They shared a table in the Biology office and had already been introduced. He had made a point of explaining that he was far too old for her, being gay besides, and that he intended to call her from the first what she clearly was: a dear, a darling, etc. If she didn't mind. She couldn't read him one bit, and at first she attributed this to the fact that she couldn't read anybody in this strange new world, anybody at all. Add to that, his being gay, a Connecticut blue-blood, and so on. Most of her relations with older men were driven by the worries over whether or not they wanted to get her into bed. Later, she decided that he was odd; a deliberately closed book.

'It doesn't feel that way,' she said.

'Not to you, perhaps. Not yet. They'll grow on you. They are not as strange as they first appear.'

'Look at them. Eating.' She gestured at the children through the glass partition between the students' hall and the faculty dining room. The teachers were outnumbered and some basic quality of that fact could not be ignored: the mass of vital energy was on the other side of the glass wall, and against them.

'*Growing*, I often think, brings out terrible manners.' This from a gentleman in a bow-tie, a pleasantly filled-out figure, with silky cheeks. 'Stuart Englander.' She had seen him in the hallways outside the English department; a stack of leather books between elbow and rib, a couple of girls in tow. He had a reputation for being particularly patient with girls. Amy was young enough to feel his charm: the charm of an old man's contented curiosity, directed at you. Just a half-smile suggesting that not much changes over time, after all. He took her hand.

'I'm Charles,' she replied; blushed and added, 'but you can call me Amy.'

So the thought of him hovered over her first day, but rarely alighted: a slip of the tongue waiting to happen. She had decided over the summer to finish her grading and her preps in the office before going home; but when the last bell rang she filed out with the rest of the students into the baseball field and walked along the row of yellow buses towards her apartment. A backpack hanging off her shoulder, sandals over her feet: a figure indistinguishable from the students pushing their way past, apart from her loneliness and silence, and the slight respect they accorded her, making way, for being one of those people who had already gone through what they were going through and couldn't do so again.

She ate supper kneeling on the floor with papers spread out across the futon. When she awoke with her head by the plate, she got up, leaving the dish there and her cup on the floor, and took off her clothes on the way to bed. As soon as the lights were off, she began to cry but it wasn't long after that she fell asleep.

II

Amy's father called, some Saturday afternoon in October, to say that why didn't the whole family come to hers for Thanksgiving, if she didn't mind. From that moment she stopped at least two or three times a day in the middle of whatever she was doing to look forward to it. And after that there was Christmas and after that she could always stay in bed and refuse to go back East when the New Year came. The thought of Charles Conway, of never seeing him again, barely troubled her at all from this imagined retreat; nevertheless, she phoned him at once to tell him the good news, and turned off the Saturday cartoons, and let her dad's old army blanket slip off her pyjamaed legs and when Charles said, why don't you come downtown and we can make a real day of it, she answered repeatingly, 'I want to see you. I just want to see you.'

Charles had already heard a great deal about the charms of Jack Bostick, but he was, among other things, one of those talkers who had so many afternoons to draw out that there was nothing he couldn't hear twice or three times and with interest too. They sat together against the hedge of the roof garden at the Met, sharing a cup of tea, and twisting from time to time to get a look at the Park behind them: the wind laying a flat hand over the trees; autumn's untidiness, the seams picked at and ravelling, litter and leaves scattered against the green. 'I'd very much like to meet your old man,' he said. 'I have a feeling the two of us have a lot to say to each other.'

Amy noted a slight resistance in her to such an assertion, the bristle of the trees against the wind, contrary, but felt too much carrying her forward, forward, to pull up short. The tea got cold in her hand as she explained herself: a familiar explanation she had almost grown tired of repeating by the end of college, the words worn out; but she ventured upon it fresh now, with a new listener, and a rising and irresistible sense that whatever view of herself had been true before could be true again, regardless of the disappointments and disillusions of her college life. These were simply an interruption. She was, had always been, Daddy's girl: a bruiser, healthy and virulent, blunt with happiness and a confidence in her own talents that the frailty and uncertainties of the girls around her had justified all too often. Her father being the root and source of everything she believed in and acted upon and excelled at. From the beginning she had belonged to him, a daughter to rival any son, star of softball and debate teams, both of which her father had coached in his brief spare time, the object of every adolescent crush. 'You know,' she said, 'how there's always one dad the girls get stuck on.'

'I had hoped and imagined that to be the case,' Charles replied.

'That was my dad. Even after he had his teeth out, he was the kind of man who could bring it off. Make a joke of it, you know, but not look like an old-timer. He had a good body, too, wasn't anything to be ashamed of with his shirt off. So when he took the girls rafting over the summer and took us out on the water bare-chested – hairy enough to set him apart from the boys we knew but nothing gross – I always caught my friends checking him out.'

She added, conscious of using the past tense, to make up for it, 'He could have played baseball, too, maybe, if he wanted.' And again, drinking the cold tea, 'It's not like he drove us, either; so when I quit the softball team after freshman year, he was right behind me.' And roused herself, aware of tailing off, ending lamely: she had suspected before that everything began to go wrong then and that her father's tame acceptance of the fact had included a more general acknowledgement of her family's failure to be anything out of the ordinary. 'My friends at college used to say' – this coyly, sidelong – 'I was too in love with my dad to fall in love with anybody else.'

Whether or not it was true, she had already guessed that it was one of those insights into ourselves that, kept clean by constant repetition, takes our eyes off other dirtier revelations. Though even Amy couldn't quite forget the misery of her first two months in New York by repeating, 'I am happy, and loved, and the all-American girl.'

'I can't wait', Charles said, 'to take him on the town when he comes.'

Again, that slight bristle of resistance; the tree bent forward under the wind, ready to snap back.

Charles had a place on Fifth Avenue, a rather grand one-bedroom looking down on 79th Street, and, at an angle, south along the Park. Prints of hunting dogs ranged along one wall, papered deep maroon. A mini-bar lay between two windows, tall as doors, which opened on to narrow fretwork iron balconies. Flowers in terracotta pots banked high against the black paint of the rails. Amy always had the sense when she came in of stepping into an expensive dirty secret, and refused to sleep over, even on Saturday nights. It looked like the flat an older man might keep for a high-class mistress, and she didn't want to be a part of the son's inheritance – a pretty young thing to play with at home on weekends, a part of the idleness and the languorous curiosity and the great unacted ambitions of Charles's world. It seemed an easy way to be happy, and she did not want to be happy easily. And she guessed, rightly perhaps, that Charles quickly grew bored of anyone or thing that gave in to him.

An element of family pride prompted her resistance, a puritanical unwillingness to live on borrowed riches and glamour. Something of the same had persuaded her father to leave Manhattan behind, his life at the firm; some urgency original to her mother to forswear baubles, an argument won before Amy's birth, repeated from time to time in her parent's marriage, and won again and again by Joanne. 'Your mother's right,' her father used to say, about a boat for the lake or a swimming pool in the backyard or a new car. 'This isn't a thing we need.' One of the few prejudices she had inherited from her mother: a sense of the honour in making do, as a matter of taste. She had been taught living within her means, and over time the phrase had come to include cutting back on what you could let yourself hope for, out of propriety.

Besides, she wished to cut short any jokes about 'Mrs Charles Conway' in the teachers' lounge, any eager, envious curiosity into the life they led. 'Not much' was how she answered questions about the things she got up to on her nights and weekends; though this was hardly true. There were restaurants and bars she couldn't afford, private parties in lofts and roof gardens, once a helicopter ride and a weekend in the Hamptons. But Amy refused to have her head turned, and clung to a kind of middle-class faith not unlike the religious, part of an argument about what was real and what wasn't real, what mattered and didn't. Almost to her surprise, Charles followed her tamely back (when she let him) to her place on 246 $^1/_2$ Street after a night on the town. She would sleep against him in the subway car; they would stagger out together at the last stop and sweat off any leftover drunkenness climbing the hill to her apartment block; then the next morning she would send him home. Amy suspected from time to time that the root of his 'patience' with her (that's the word she used, some of Charles's friends talked of forbearance) lay in a groundwater of unhappiness not unlike her own; but this insight into her lover required the same insight into herself, and for the most part she was willing to attribute his attentions to gallantry and affection.

Even so, it made plain good sense when her family came at Thanksgiving to give them her flat and stay over at Charles's place. But she wanted to make a point about families, and mucking in – to flaunt her own inheritance in front of him.

'This is what I'm really like, around these people,' she hoped to show him: this is who I am. Not simply to prove her independence, but to preen herself, confident of looking at her best in their affection, at her most desirable, playing the role of golden girl she thought was hers in the family play. In their three months together, Amy had never met Conway *père*, and made a point of not insisting on it. She met his older brother Robert only once, at an alumni function at the Yale Club. He was a lawyer downtown, and rather charmingly spent the evening getting drunk in a corner with her, complaining about the party and disparaging Charles – who was flitting through the crowds and could be seen from time to time, when they parted, emerging from an embrace, or pushing his way through the packed hall, a drink in each hand spilling over.

She spent the afternoon of their arrival, the Wednesday before Thanksgiving, growing increasingly anxious. Charles had slept over the night before, since her holidays began that morning. His life was all holiday, to an extent he left purposefully vague, but he had rather charmingly caught an enthusiasm for Amy's that outran her own. He brought her eggs in bed, cooked in a way she disliked, along with the papers, which he read, elaborately at his ease beside her, picking at her plate of unfinished food, and fresh squeezed juice, somewhat watery, with the pips in, and only a cup of coffee for himself. Occasionally uttering, in an offhand way, such things as, 'I once thought I wouldn't mind taking a run at politics, but then there's the plain fact of living in DC or God help us Virginia.' And, 'I might turn my hand to the greenhouse question, before I'm through. If only to annoy my father.'

Amy eventually grew fed up with his laziness, what she sometimes called his timelessness, the way nothing pricked him to move on; and she kicked him out of bed at last, and out of her door, claiming the hundreds of things she had to do to prepare for Thanksgiving, and including, in the rush of her scolding, 'I don't know why you stick around here you get on just fine on your own and never miss me once', when he complained that he wanted to hang back to meet her folks, etc. The sentiment snagged in her thoughts, she hadn't meant to go so far, and even the recollection of her saying it and his heeding it later surprised in her a thrill of fear. She watched him loping beside the current of leftover rain running along the kerb. Rags of blue sky were torn from the clouds. She didn't want him to go; such an ordinary and pleasant afternoon might have stretched before them if it weren't for her insistence on spoiling everything; and the corollary of these thoughts struck her for the first time: she didn't want her family to come.

Most of the morning was spent in a hurry that took her mind off the main event. But when the turkey had been got, and everything else in the fridge left on the counter to make space for it, and the cans of candied yams stacked neatly on top of the shelf. When the bags of stuffing, two kinds, had been stuck behind the cereal boxes, and the sack of potatoes, despaired of, pushed to a corner of the floor. When she had bought not only a blend of fresh coffee for her dad from the toniest deli in her neighbourhood but a coffee-maker to brew it in from a warehouse appliance store in Inwood across the Harlem River; and hauled two six-packs of beer up the walk-up and slid two bottles in the freezer to ice them for his arrival. When she had stripped her bed and laid on fresh sheets and a duvet for her parents, and piled a tidy heap of covers beside the futon for herself and her brother. When she had got in a real sweat, in spite of the rain overnight and the opened windows, which turned into a temper; and begun to be overwhelmed by a sense of consumption outstripping the heartiest appetite, of the leftovers to linger week-long in her fridge, kept under saran-wrap on a fatty platter as token and evidence of her family visit, then discarded at last, with a heart as cold as the turkey.

Then she sat down and waited for them to come.

She had fallen asleep in front of the television when the bell rang, some hours late, and she thought, not yet, not yet, before waking up and buzzing them in. A trip to the sink to wash the sleep from her eyes, and even so she had time to look round her quiet apartment and count the seconds, before she heard heavy steps coming at last up the stairs, the shuffling gait of a man with bags. Amy had left the door open a crack, and her father pushed his way in and set down two pieces of matching initialled luggage she had never seen before, and said, 'where's the bathroom?' before her mother, pale with lank hair, came and gave her a hug that smelt of the airplane. 'I'm sorry we're late but let me tell you, you wouldn't believe . . .' she began and sat down on the futon. 'I need a drink of water,' she said with her hands on her lap.

Already Amy felt a slight constriction around her throat at the clutter, not only of bags but of people. Her mother had set a handbag at her feet on the floor, between the futon and the chest from home serving as a coffee table, which Amy stepped over to sit beside her and give her a glass, slightly clouded from the tap. Her mother looked at it once, and said nothing, and drank. Her dad came out and laid his coat, a greasy Burberry, over the two bags in the hall. 'Look at this, look at this, look at this,' he said, rubbing his hands in a complimentary fashion. He had lost weight and looked well on it, in spite of the long haul and the early start. There was an animal satisfaction to his movements, a directness, pleasurable in itself like a clear style. His hair, thin and dull the last time she saw him, had been cut short, and bristled slightly where it stood – and now purringly resisted the rub of his hand across his scalp. 'I'm going to make myself at home,' he said, looking in the fridge, and her heart went out to him, gratefully, in answered faith. Her mother looked fretfully across at him and called out, 'I wouldn't mind some juice if there is any', holding out her glass for him to fetch. The resentment, Amy thought, a woman feels that her body ages more shamefully than a man's.

Her mother wanted a nap but Jack was eager to 'hit the town' as he said, and since she didn't like to be left out of anything, she thought for a minute and decided to come along. Amy felt already she had been muted slightly, turned down almost imperceptibly in volume. She hung back, as the day wore on, more and more with her mother – they both laboured somewhat under the awkward burden of the man's vitality. Amy had suggested they walk to the school grounds and there was a coffee shop where she often . . . but Jack cut in that he'd like to 'get out of the sticks' and when her mother chided him, Amy, reddening slightly, insisted she 'didn't mind at all what they did she was so happy to see them both' to gloss over any suspicion of injured vanity, not entirely successfully. But it was still at that point in the day when she felt closer to her father than her mother, and she didn't want to let him down in front of her.

This in fact became the pattern of their afternoon. Amy wanted to show them the roof garden at the Met, since the day was windy and sunny in equal measure while it lasted, and the Park looked wonderful in the quiet of being above it. But Jack said he couldn't stand the crowds there, it was more of a supermarket than anything else, and what he used to do on a free afternoon in New York was get a bag of lunch at Zabar's and take a book to Riverside Park. And so on. They spent much of the afternoon looking for places he'd been to thirty years before though he couldn't quite remember the cross street, etc., if it was there at all any more. In any case, he said, there wasn't a better way to see the Upper West Side than getting lost in it, a phrase he had every opportunity to repeat. Amy scarcely knew the neighbourhood at all. Charles Conway lived east of the Park, and she knew Manhattan mostly according to his habits and haunts. All she knew of the West Side was the cross-town bus at 86th Street, next to the subway stop. She pretended at first to a certain amount of local knowledge, and looked deliberately perplexed at any question she couldn't answer. Then gave up, and tagged along behind him with her mother. It was nearly four o'clock before they had lunch on a dirty bench in the flowerless gardens of Riverside Park. And then Jack had an idea for coffee and there was a bookshop he used to love.

In the end it was something like desperation that made her lure them round to Charles's apartment. She hadn't planned to introduce them till Thanksgiving itself – had made in fact a great fuss about wanting them all to herself for the first day and he shouldn't mind if she didn't call him. But as they were walking through Central Park, just at sunset, the light, cold and liquid, leaking around and soaking the few leaves and bare branches of the trees, her father got muddled about the east and west and they found themselves out at Fifth Avenue. Her mother, who had been complaining steadily of the cold and her feet for the past half-hour, said, 'At this point and without any interest in arguing the matter, I need somewhere to sit down.' Jack stared up and down the turning paths and muttered, 'Hold on a bit, I just need to get my bearings.' And, after a silent minute, 'I can't figure that at all. Always look south, they say, always look south.' Her mother had begun to repeat herself – 'As I said before, and without any interest in . . . '– when Amy interjected, 'Let me just see if he's in', and walked off towards the glimmering street lights of the intersection.

God, I hope he's in, she thought. Let him be in. And didn't look round to see if they were following.

Something subtle had shifted, from the moment the doorman greeted her with, 'Evening, Miss Bostick' and ushered the three of them, footsore and cross-grained, into the mirrored splendour of the elevator. They stepped out into Charles's flat, and he was at a little side-table by the window, writing letters it seemed. He wore a white shirt, open-necked, and as he strode across the room towards them the collar stood up around his ears exposing the clear firm lines of muscle sloping down either side towards his shoulders.

'I expect you both could use a drink,' he said, stooping to kiss Mrs Bostick on the cheek and taking Jack by the hand, 'if you've been chasing after Amy all day trying to find her way in the city.'

'He teases me for living in the Bronx,' Amy said, conscious of playing a game in tandem – aware that he realized whatever it was that had worn them out wasn't her fault but it might be easier for all to pretend that it was. 'He says I can't find my way in town without a taxi.'

'I didn't know you were a taxi-taker,' Jack said, surprised to find his ill-humour lightening.

Charles stood at the little bar between the windows cutting lemons. 'If anyone here is interested,' he called over his shoulder, 'the small room for private contemplation on diverse subjects runs off the bedroom. Amy, why don't you show your mother the way.'

'Charles!' Amy protested.

'He's quite right,' Mrs. Bostick said.

'I have a mother myself,' Charles explained, turning slightly round. 'Gin and tonics all round, will that do?' he continued, when it was only himself and Mr Bostick in the room.

'You've got some fine things here,' Jack said, staring at the walls with his hands clasped in front of him, not quite knowing where to sit down. Charles put a drink in his hand and sat down himself, at one of the two silk-cushioned couches facing each other under the chandelier. He set his sweating glass on the naked cherrywood of a side stand, and kicked his loafers off and crossed one leg underneath him. 'Take a load off.'

Jack sat down opposite. 'Mind if I do the same?' he said, hoping the phrase sounded comfortable and easy in such quarters, dimly aware he was only imitating the younger man, his host. After stooping carefully to untie the laces, he wrinkled his toes in their socks and lay back. 'God that feels good. I forgot how tiring the city could be.'

'That's right.' Charles leaned forward. 'Amy tells me you used to practise downtown.'

This set them off, and by the time the 'girls' came back, Jack could happily declare to his daughter, 'Don't worry about us, we're already old friends.' And Charles could leave it to his guest, to get to his tired feet and do the honours for the ladies, handing them each their drinks from the little bar.

That evening was perhaps the high point of their visit, as Amy at least considered it, looking back – before the shameful and rather embarrassing conclusion to her parents' stay, which affected her far less than she might have imagined such things would. Even at the time she suspected a trajectory at work, whose progress could easily include a sharp downturn and temporary collapse. Everything was going well in a way she hadn't envisioned; a portion of her life usually neglected had been included or acknowledged in the course of the day. And while she had expected to feel something along those lines when her folks came, a touch of heat from her old real life, the reverse, rather, had proved the case: her new life (and lover) had revived the old.

Charles said they could order in or go 'out on the town' (a phrase her father repeated), but that he hadn't got the equipment to cook up anything in house. Jack, pink and refreshed, declared he had itchy feet and wanted to get out among the lights; but Mrs Bostick complained she couldn't go any further without something inside her and they may as well stop where they were seeing everything was so nice and comfortable. 'You can look at the lights from here.'

In the end, Charles offered a kind of compromise and assured Joanne, taking her by the arm, that they wouldn't go far and hardly needed to put on coats. Nevertheless they brought what they had with them, stepped into the elevator again and out at the lobby. A brisk cold walk along 79th Street, the glow of the traffic running against them, the homeward bound. Amy thought of the overwhelming number of private errands and destinations required to produce such a large conjuncture at the cross-town road running into Fifth

Avenue: all those solitary purposes commingling, the inevitable coincidences. Obscurely saddening: everyone with some place to go to, such a mass of resignation and relief at the end of a day. The crowds themselves a symbol for the crowd of days ahead facing each of them: 'one of many' was the rule behind each thing.

They turned left on Madison and almost immediately turned again as an usher in black-tie held open a glass door for Charles, who led them into a low-lit restaurant, done up expensively in bland grey leather and pale wood. The maître d' pointed them to their table, and pulled back the chairs of the ladies. There was no menu, no cash register; everyone called Mr Conway by name. The currents driving most public relations and transactions had been wrinkled away or got rid of altogether: money, anonymity, choice. Charles's aristocratic affability often appeared implausible to her, too good to be true (and consequently neither good nor true). He seemed lost or lonely, suffering painlessly the drift of his life. But for once Charles looked not only at ease but at home. Amy remembered it later as an entirely happy dinner, and remembered little else. Wine was poured, drunk; food brought, eaten. The bright litter of a leftover meal stained the plates: saffron, pomegranate husks, fig rinds, fried flowers. Mrs Bostick, a woman both weak-minded and stubborn, for once tried everything on the table – never complained that 'food was one part of her life she never felt the need to experiment in' and drank two glasses of red wine, regardless of the fact that it 'made her acid'. Amy, tipsily, repeatingly asked, 'Doesn't he look handsome, like a man in a magazine? Doesn't he look just like a magazine?' She felt full of love for Charles and her new life; and some reflected glory fell on her father, as she pinched Jack's stomach to see how trim he'd got, and declared, 'I've got all my boys about me.'

'Except your brother,' Mrs Bostick said.

'Yeah, well.' And added, as she thought of it, 'You can't

have everything' in an offhand way that surprised her and which she didn't much like.

When they were finished, Charles stood up and wished several good nights and asked the doorman to get a taxi for the Bosticks. Nobody paid and nothing was said about the bill. When Jack tried to get the wad of his wallet out of his back pocket, Charles touched him by the elbow, surprisingly womanish, and assured him obscurely, that it 'got sent up'. They were in the cab before Jack could protest, or Amy could ask him to come back with them or stay behind or kiss him good night. She looked back at Charles waving and receding on the pavement of Madison Avenue suddenly heartsick at his absence and frightened at the return of an older order whose comforts she had for the first time in her life begun to doubt. Perhaps the Bosticks weren't as happy as she thought they were – a reflection that should not have surprised a woman who had been miserable for months. Jack began to worry as soon as the cab door shut: first, that he should have insisted on giving Charles some money, and later that the meter wasn't running, and he knew what that meant in New York City: they were being taken for a ride. The worries got mixed up in each other in contradictory ways: Charles should have let them get the subway; it wasn't his business to push expenses on to them; he should have let them 'give something towards the meal'; maybe they should get out now (on a dark cold night in Harlem) or have the cabbie drop them at the West Side where they could take the red line up. Jack even raised his arm to knock against the glass, getting his courage and his dander up, when Joanne, stubborn as she always was in her comforts, took him firmly by the soft inner elbow and told him 'he didn't dare', a phrase Amy noticed but did not remark upon.

They crossed the Harlem River in rather magnificent silence, surrounded by warehouses and water, the glitter behind them, the dark rise of the Bronx in front. They got out at last against the slope of 246 $^1/_2$ Street, climbing awkwardly from tired haunches in the deep-set car. The taxi drove off before Jack could get his money out. 'Charles must have paid already,' Amy said.

'He's a good kid, but I should have insisted,' her father began, his mood lightened in spite of himself by the free ride. And even Joanne's rather cryptic remark, that he wasn't 'in a position now to insist on anything' couldn't bring Jack down again. Amy let it go a second time.

Andy flew in on Thanksgiving. He'd caught the red eye from California and showed up almost two hours late sweaty with travel and light-hearted as only the sleepless are, arriving. Joanne had been leaning out over the futon, looking down for a cab to pull up, for almost an hour. It drove Amy nuts. 'He'll come when he comes,' she said, looking at her father. 'What's watching going to accomplish?' But Jack for once only responded, 'Let her look if she wants to', and couldn't sit still himself – stared out across Van Cortlandt Park feeling the cold outside in the window against his nose and brow. He was waiting, too; and Amy regretted her insistence that she could manage on her own, though the turkey was in the oven by noon, and a spread of vegetables lay cut across the counter-top and ready for the pot. Nobody had anything to do but worry about Andy; and when he rang at last Joanne clapped her hands together and kissed their tips, but refrained from getting to the buzzer herself, conscious in some way of offending.

'What took you?' Amy said, when Andy hauled self and duffel into the crowded sitting room, smoothing his long lank hair over his shoulders with a free hand. 'Was the plane delayed?' echoed Joanne.

'No, not really,' and he left it at that. The two missing hours remained unexplained, an irritating puzzle that ran through Amy's head during the course of the day like a bad song.

Andy had changed, and had been changing some time; his sister could not put off acknowledging it any more. Skinny and pale as a teenager, he had grown, certainly not fit, or fat, but weightier at twenty; an accumulation of mass at his shoulders, his cheeks, his neck, his belly, almost in spite of himself, signalled the gravity of manhood. Amy had only got skinnier and weaker since quitting softball; her breasts had diminished from hanging pears to nibs of loose skin pulled from her chest. She often wore T-shirts without a bra around the apartment on weekends, in a manner that rather tiresomely aroused Charles, since she had rarely felt sexually so unripe, so green. Another way boys had it better, their bodies announced their coming of age forcefully and unembarrassed – not the first eruptions of adolescence, but the second slower onset of manhood. She now looked her kid brother squarely in the chin, and could smell him too, the smell of a man's body, creased, neglected, carelessly used. He hadn't shaved, and rubbed the flat of his fingers against his resistant cheek.

But he'd grown in the essential, too. She had last known him well four years ago, in high school, where his obsessions with graphic art, anti-heroes, alternative worlds, cult subversions began. A not altogether unhappy boy, only rather friendless, earnest, confined to his imagination and the corners of school life. Which he shared with a diverse set of outcasts, who matched his indifference to strangers (indistinguishable from shyness), and, rather more worrying, a subtle suspicion of girls that approached distaste. College suited him; the corners were still corners, but belonged to grander halls. He encountered the like-minded, and learned the first most powerful lesson of success: that the world would serve his purposes, and he did not have to discredit its judgements – a habit he'd acquired in high school and quickly dropped. Success, of course, of a limited kind: the friendship of people he admired, the occasional publication of his art, a little money. Even a small following on the web. The renewed pride of his parents, the envy of his friends.

He pulled his hair into a ponytail, and fixed it with a rubber band kept around his wrist. 'Can I get anyone else a glass of water?' he said, and when no one answered he filled one himself, clouded and top-heavy from the tap, and drank long and loudly. An expectant air surrounded his silence and his arrival. He took off his oversized denim jacket and laid it carefully on the duffel bag by the door. Amy guessed the pleasure of the prodigal returned; typical, that Andy show up late on the day. 'I was once an all-American girl,' she thought – before she began to doubt the place she would make in the world, and, stranger still, the place she would make for herself in her own personality. 'I was telling Harry Edwards about you,' Joanne was saying, 'and I was saying I didn't know anything about . . .'

'You remember Harry Edwards?' Jack cut in. 'Our friend at the Indy Record?'

'Anyway, I showed him one of your pieces and explained that it takes some getting used to. At least it did for me but once you do . . .'

'He said you should send some of your work to the arts desk there. He said it's a long shot but you've got quality and they might take a second look at a local kid. He said . . .'

Amy stopped listening, and Andy glanced at her, raising an eyebrow. She was dropping cut potatoes in a pot of cold water, one by one, watching them drop and noting the splash of each, absorbed in the rhythm of the repeated act. Andy came through the arch of the kitchen and took her by the neck and side of her face with his large long-fingered hand. She felt a ring at her cheek as he said, 'I got you a present, big sis. I don't know if you'll like it. Something for a windowsill maybe. A little odd.'

He turned to root through his duffel and brought out a strange wooden figure, often handled and well oiled, as tall perhaps as the bone between his elbow and wrist. 'Artists use them, but I found this at a market.' He spoke in short sentences; had the slightly unnerving controlled air of a boy who has decided to refrain from excess, and with the enthusiasm of youth, extended the dictum to all, even the least, parts of his life. 'From the twenties, they say. I've got one myself. I just like the look of them, so light.' How brown you've gotten, she thought, in California – not quite healthy, he'd always been so pale, but unwashed-looking and slightly moly. The kind of boy who doesn't mind where he sleeps. His vanity lies elsewhere. 'For putting up with us this weekend. For putting us up.'

She noted that 'us' as she set her gift under the window by the oven. It stood superimposed against the brick of the apartment opposite and the thinning trees above, the brown and green of the leaves losing way against the brown and green of the park coming through behind them. The figure was composed of segmented limbs, jointed at ankle, elbow, knee, wrist, each adjustable, so that it could assume and hold any variety of pose. A thin steel rod rising from the centre of a wooden base supported it from the bottom, so his feet (and the shape suggested a man), didn't need to touch ground, but could perch as they pleased on air. His legs, for example, were now spread wide in a bow-legged swagger; one arm hung back by his side, and the left reached out in front as if leading a charge. His face was a blank, a knob; his torso, split into three unequal caterpillar segments, could be twisted as required. 'We use it to get the proportions right. Only it's got no gravity, so things come out a little light-footed. I think they're pretty.'

'We met Charles,' Joanne said archly, folding her hands between her knees where she sat. 'A very nice young man.'

Jack stood up, warming up. 'The thing about class is that it is what it is. There's no point pretending that it isn't.'

'A looker, I would say, if that's a word the girls still use nowadays. A real looker.'

Amy for once didn't mind their teasing. I've nudged them a little bit more my way, she thought; a little way in my direction again.

Charles couldn't make it to Thanksgiving dinner. He had an 'engagement in town'; but that dinner passed as it always does, in a great sweat and hurry at first, and a slow sweat and languor afterwards. They teased Andy about his girls. 'Every girl I know wears boots,' he said, 'up to here', and struck his fist halfway up his shinbone. 'And rubber belts. It's like they're preparing for the Day After.' No one had met these girls, and Amy explored at some length the possibility that Andy made them up. 'Who would make girls like that up?' Andy felt peevish, flattered at once. 'Why would you want to?' Just embarrassed enough to make it matter; sometimes it's a kindness to blush. 'Believe me, I can make up better.'

'Yes, I know,' Joanne declared, rather archly. 'I've seen them. Rather too much of them, dear.'

'Besides, there isn't anyone . . . specific,' stopping short at the word he meant to use, subtly twisting its tail end, and suggesting a more general complaint. No, it's true, there isn't anyone specific. Each of them considered the strange phrase, weighed it up, examined their friends in its light. 'That's not really what I mean,' he said at last. 'You know.'

Amy had slipped into an old habit: her family. What she needed was not to think about everything. What she needed was to do *this* without worrying too much if everyone was happy; she never used to care if they were happy. What mattered, what counted for the family, what held it together, ran infinitely deeper than happiness – seemed grander and pettier at once, bore the same relation to happiness as a place to weather. Constantly affected by it, of course, but enduring in spite of, regardless of, its vagaries, its surface troubles. It was only recently that being happy counted for much in their conversations, in their thoughts about each other. As far as that went, it was only Andy who seemed happy; certainly not she herself. Maybe Jack now, he might have come through to the other side again, after whatever it was the two of them went through when Andy left for college. Joanne was always Joanne and only Joanne; in any case, nobody ever asked how she was doing. After dinner she put on an apron and 'made a start' on the dishes; and the rest sat down to watch football.

Charles called that night around nine o'clock. Amy answered and immediately switched the phone to her other hand and ear when she heard who it was, drew her knees up, spoke softly. 'Happy Thanksgiving,' she said, attempting to convey in that phrase a world in which they always said such things to each other, the holiday greetings, the casual meaningless repetitions of shared life. 'I miss you,' she said.

'I'd like to stand your folks some drinks at the Yale Club tomorrow night if they'd care to come. Bring along your brother. I'd like to meet the famous brother. What shall we say, around six o'clock? And we can take it from there.'

'I miss you,' she repeated, and added quickly, to break the silence, 'have you had a good day?'

'Yes, I've enjoyed myself. I look forward to seeing your lot tomorrow night.'

When he hung up, she felt a line had been let loose, and it was only the tension of that line, holding her against the winds, which had kept her in place. Without it she felt nothing, she moved with every gust or flaw, and offered no resistance, which might have bruised her, fighting the currents.

She shared the futon that night with Andy. They had often split beds before on family holidays, though not in years: they hadn't been on a family holiday in years. The bulk of him moved her to reach out and pull him back at the shoulder towards her, as she might with Charles – if only to feel the gravity of flesh, its satisfying weight and traction, its concentrating force. She lay on her back and waited for him to say something, his long back running against her side. He didn't; perhaps he was shyer than he seemed these days, more alike and unlike his old awkward self: that's often the case, the changes in us awaken outgrown uncertainties. Amy guessed he had a girl in California, or had had girls, and knew what it was like to lie in bed beside them now, and forbore from turning over as he might have done before because he had new habits to repress. Back in high school, they might have stroked each other by the back or arm and talked; so she broke the silence at last.

'Dad looks good.'

Andy grunted – perhaps he'd only been asleep – and rolled over. 'What?'

'I said, Dad looks good.'

'I bet he does; he got fired.' His voice heavy, certain, rehearsing familiar facts, not only facts, but conclusions: attitudes reached after some consideration.

'What do you mean?'

'Made redundant, whatever you want to call it. What do you think the deal is with all that golf.'

He raised himself on an elbow and looked at her – his long face, thickening with age at the cheekbones, around the eyes, not handsome in the least, but attractive to some perhaps, intent, more and more assured of other virtues: something had happened to him that had been delayed in her. He knew his mind; had no one left to please but himself.

'Why didn't they tell me?' The thought, which had been threatening all day, formed at last. She felt the words in her throat like the warning of a cold: why do they treat me like his kid sister? Why do I feel like his kid sister?

'I don't know. They didn't think you were happy. And you know what you're like with Dad. I guess he didn't want you to find out – I don't count as much. And he hoped to take care of it all before we came.'

'Did he?'

'They couldn't pay for me to fly out. But I sold something the week before, and managed to hitch a ride to the airport. You know, bus to Penn Station. Subway up.'

'Is that why you were so late?'

'Partly.'

'When were they going to tell me? Should I bring it up?'

He looked at her in the half-light leaking in from the city sky. 'I don't know, Sis,' he said at last. 'Do what you want to do. If it were up to me –'

'What?'

'Why not? I mean, does it really affect how you live any more, one way or another. Honestly?'

'Andy Bostick. When did you get to be so cold?' She pressed her knuckle into his forehead, slowly, but with growing force and twisting a little this way and that. He didn't budge, still looked at her. And she gave up in the end, rolling her back towards him.

She didn't mention it. Not even Saturday night when she might have done harmlessly enough; but by that point, somehow, there seemed to be a general assumption that she knew. And Friday turned out to be a wonderful day, quick and light, cloud and clear air sharing the field of the sky, exchanging sallies. Autumn bluster among the trees lining Fifth Avenue, the drifted piles in the Park. Colour and shape picked out, lifted, almost too real; threads of sunshine unravelled from them. Drinks at the Yale Club turned into supper at Jean Georges. Jack and Charles arm and arm, making plans. Even Joanne somewhat drunk, hailing a cab to take them back to the Conway pad, where she wanted the WC. Jack discovered a box of LPs, and began to go through them recklessly. Music jumped out of the speakers hidden in the bookshelves. Horns turning slow corners, the traffic whistle of trumpets, pedestrian drums. Charles and Andy mixed cocktails, experimenting. Amy didn't know what to think any more. All that was over. What was left was terrible excesses of love. She would wake with a sore head and heartache.

Charles had invited Jack to get in a game of golf with him Saturday afternoon; he had a regular three ball with some fellas from his father's firm, and why not make it a foursome. Amy protested, coyly: she wanted Dad to herself. Secretly glad to watch him go. Everything would turn out OK; her life in New York seemed less foreign to her by the hour. She didn't have to choose, one or the other; a phrase she repeated to herself all day unexplained: she didn't have to choose, father or lover. And whatever Andy said, Dad looked tip-top. He hadn't been so skinny in years, so ready to laugh, so happy to lie and talk big, and make plans. From this moment on I will be happy, she thought, high spirits growing and rising in her like the butterflies she suffered every morning before teaching class. Conscious that everything the past few days had been building towards that revelation, and also vaguely aware that it wasn't the kind of insight likely to be true if ushered in by such a fanfare of feeling. Nevertheless, she repeated it silently to herself, that Saturday afternoon: From this moment on I will be happy – as the three of them went shopping at the second-hand stores around St Mark's Place. And waited for Jack and Charles to meet up with them for supper in town when they finished their round of golf.

'I can't believe it's already your last night,' she said, holding her mother around the waist, and stepping awkwardly to keep stride behind her.

Joanne turned round and took her daughter's face in her hands. She gave Amy a hard look. 'You won't miss us. I know you girls. And such a nice young man.'

'It means so much to me to hear you say that. I don't trust anything I think when you're not here.'

'I know you girls,' Joanne repeated. 'You've got a real nice set-up here, if you don't mind my saying.'

It wasn't quite what Amy expected to hear, but close enough that she could ignore the difference.

It was pretty clear from the start something had gone wrong. First of all, Jack and Charles were almost an hour late to the restaurant, a small French bistro somewhere by Gramercy Park. Andy had drunk two glasses already from the bottle they ordered, and seemed quietly detached. Amy finished the basket of bread and asked for another. They came in at last looking worn out, though Charles put on a better show and kissed Joanne before sitting down. Perhaps, Amy thought, they've had a fight over something, or one of them lost badly, embarrassing both. But if anything, they seemed rather com-

Joanne cut in. 'What happened between you two today?'

'Nothing much. We lost a little money out there, that's all.'

'How much?'

'About twenty thousand dollars. Not much, split two ways.'

Nobody said anything for a minute. The car had mostly emptied by that point, except for a couple of kids horsing round with a balloon at the far end of the carriage. Occasionally, you could hear it squeak; an awful sound, like a thin knife, followed by giggles. 'Jack,' her mother sighed, 'Jack. I suppose this is another conversation we have to have.'

He was sobbing now himself, all bluster gone, his head against his chest, and his shoulders shaking ever so slightly in a terrible way. 'What's happening to you?' she said. 'What's happening to you these days?'

'I didn't want to say I couldn't play. They pushed me into it. What you have to understand about these people is that they're bullies. What you have to understand is they're better than you because they've got more money, and they know it. They know we don't belong with them. I had my shot at them, I'll say that much. I had my shot.'

'Did he offer to pay your half? Jack, did he offer to pay?'

Amy had never felt so cold towards them in her life, these people, for whom money was a moral duty, pleasure was a duty, everything reduced to what was good and responsible and nothing left over. Her mother, prim-faced, purse-lipped, sniffing at bad luck like a dirty word; her father, weak-chested with sobs, giving into her, again and again, her version of events: the sin of the game, the weakness of his will, all that foolish showing off that never proved anything about any man worth his salt, worth his family obligations, worth the name of man; all that winning, that blood-lust for winning, and the high life; where had it ever gotten them? where had it got Amy? when the best any of them could do was quit when they were behind. Now they could see for once who was right; now they could see for once who kept the family together. All those years.

In the end, she was glad when they left her – to clean up after them and prepare for school in the morning. A desultory breakfast, that awful waiting around for cabs, half-speeches begun, interrupted, neglected. Jack had an air of muted apology Amy hated to see in him. As if he'd been caught out at last and the game was up and there was nowhere left for him to go. Joanne, prudent, prudish, kept him busy, almost out of kindness. Andy had long ago retreated into those reserves he'd always possessed. When the car came – Joanne, looking out over the futon, saw it first – and buzzed, the relief was palpable. They had a minute again in which to breathe and speak freely of things that mattered; it was OK, the end was in sight. Jack took his daughter in his arms, and in spite of everything, she felt the muscle busy under his shirt, smelt his new-found animal health; he wouldn't let go of her, and then, detaching himself, said, 'I won't let go of you. I won't let go.'

Joanne, on tiptoes, hugged Amy briefly, and whispered, 'I think you know what we think of your young man.'

Andy ushered her out and kissed his sister on the brow. Goodbye, goodbye. Amy waited a minute till the echo of their steps had faded down the stairs, then walked to the window and watched them load the car up. Watched it pull out. Nobody looked up or waved.

She spent the next hour walking down to and up from the laundry room, carrying baskets of sheets and towels, underpants and socks for the week ahead. She began to sob with her face in an armful of wet cotton as she prepared to heave a bundle into the open door of the drier. At the relief of it all, to be on her own again, and realize that what she had put her faith in had failed her – and she was free to live by lesser lights. A minute with her face held in the sweet cleanness of washed sheets.

Charles rang that afternoon, just when she had begun to get

bored. In fact, the sound of the phone reminded her she was sitting in the half-light of a grey day, and had been sitting like that for about ten minutes, and the spell was broken. She needed something to do. She needed to get back to work. Neither mentioned the night before, or ever mentioned it, except obliquely. He said, 'I'd like to see you. I'd very much like to see you, if I can.'

'Yes, of course.' The phrase came out of her, unplanned, unironic. Of course, he *would* like to see her. 'Maybe I could come to you tonight. And get the subway up in the morning. Maybe that would be all right.'

She hadn't felt so settled in years, so sure of herself. So sure of a boy. Charles took her out to a nice meal, and she accepted a glass of wine, only one, she didn't want a headache in the morning. They went to bed about ten, ten thirty. If he didn't want to wake her up every night, he'd have to get used to her hours. Very comfortable; she could just make out a corner of Central Park, the heavy hand of a tree, under the blinds, from where she lay. Only Charles said, before she drifted off in his arms, 'Sometimes I think I'm losing it. When the money doesn't mean anything to me any more, it scares me how quick everything else follows.' It was an apology, perhaps. She thought of the little figure Andy had given her, propped still against her kitchen window, those weightless limbs, their exaggerated gestures. She pictured her father, she pictured Charles, in its poses. If she nudged them at all, they fell down, again, again.

WINTER

Second Chance

I

He had never been a coward with respect to habits, and could break them when he chose. Even so, Howard Peasbody had his routines. On Tuesday mornings, his first class began late, at ten thirty, but he woke up at seven anyway and went for a run through Riverside Park. He did not enjoy it, but suffered it rather in grudging concession to the demands of his ego, which was unwilling to live without a certain modest level of creature vanities. His stippled face, scarred by acne, had been somewhat smoothed over by age; his thin hair looked least bad loose on his head: a comb seemed to take twenty thousand dollars a year from his social status. Still, he was tall enough and ran to fat only around the hips. There was something of the gentleman in his manner; he had the kind of natural wit and fine feeling that turned every imperfection into an expression of subtler character – a refusal to join in. When he came back, consciously virtuous and sweating vaguely into the neck of his Harvard sweatshirt, he woke his lover for breakfast. This was the single morning of the working week Tomas sat up for him – still sweet with sleep, stretched out yawning in his loosely girdled bathrobe. He picked at the newspaper Howard brought up after his run; sniffed a cup of coffee. It was too early for him, almost a quarter to eight; but he endured the desultory chat for the sake of Howard's company, for the plain fact of his presence: a something extra given once a week before the day drew them apart again and set them among strangers.

Tomas flattered himself that it was mostly for his sake the 'old guy' did his bit to keep in shape. But Howard liked to feel the muscle in his limbs aching into growth – enjoyed the pleasant sense of something difficult done with. A cup of black tea with a half-spoon of sugar; a toasted bagel, buttered. He had a sweet tooth and usually starved it; the tea struck him as a guilty treat. That five-mile run exhausted, among other things, his power to be dissatisfied. And he never found the company of his lover more comfortable than on these late breakfasts. Our bodies, he thought, are easier to please than anything else. And they didn't have to talk much. Tomas was usually fond of chatter, in which Howard occasionally heard the undertone of reproach: why aren't *we* happy when *I* am or could be, but for you. But these early mornings kept him quiet. And Howard could peacefully enjoy the warm gravity of the younger man's body; which seemed at times the only thing preventing something loose in him from drifting free.

On Tuesdays Howard left late enough to check the mail on his way out; another habit that reinforced his sense of a leisured breakfast. He stooped in the lobby to peer down the brass-walled slot, took out a sheaf of envelopes and magazines, and sorted them quickly into the pleasurable and the professional. Returned the latter, and jammed the rest into the inside pocket of his teaching jacket: sometimes a letter from his widower father, a retired schoolmaster himself, living in Connecticut; maybe a note from a college friend (Howard had remained unseduced by the Internet and continued to correspond by the mail); occasionally, the boon of an early *New Yorker*. Then he bought a cup of coffee from the newsagent and walked to the subway at 86th street; settled onto the relatively empty uptown train and spread whatever he had across his lap and began to read, keeping his coffee between his knees. Most of the time of course there was nothing at all in the post and then he only drank his coffee and tried not to consider the upcoming day.

On the Tuesday after Thanksgiving – a steadily miserable drizzly morning whose only chance at better things was to give way to a light fat snowfall in the evening – Howard got both a letter and the magazine. The letter surprised him: the return address in the top-left corner read 'A. Rosenblum', and offered a phone number beneath the street reference, tacked on in a different pen at a different angle, as if she had forgotten to include it in the letter itself, or had suddenly *worried* that she had forgotten, after sealing the envelope. Or *he* had forgotten. But Howard, with a swiftness in reaching conclusions that surprised him, assumed 'A.' was Anne, a woman he had been friendly with in the first few terms of his graduate course in Biology at NYU. They had parted awkwardly enough at the time, and had not seen each other for the better part of two decades – that is, for almost half their lives. Still, something about the writing must have suggested her to him; for they had exchanged more than a few letters in their day. He had plenty of time to sort through his memories of her, as he bought his coffee and made his wet way along 83rd street eastwards and uptown towards the subway.

Anne Rosenblum was one of those Vermont Jews he used to know plenty of in college, arty and conventional both, well read, and handsome enough in a broad-shouldered way, unless it was only the shawls and cardigan collars banked around her neck. A countrified complexion, good-natured brown eyes, dry curly hair mostly twisted into a bun. He had always liked her: a straightforward girl underneath the rather self-conscious Bohemian wrappings, with a sharp mind and an affable gossipy manner that required none of the delicate insinuating condescension with which Howard habitually addressed most women. (And, he had to admit, most men as well as he got older.) Indeed, something about her struck him as manly – a certain bluntness, or intellectual vigour – and he remembered a phrase he used at the time (to her, in fact) to describe the effect of her company: 'You always take me firmly by the hand.' The analogy upset her, perhaps he intended it to: it suggested the rather hail-fellow-well-met manner of a woman unsure of her sexual charms. He suspected she was cleverer than he (a painful admission), but consoled himself with the thought that she lacked his reserves of discipline, of disinterest, of abstemiousness. Qualities by which he had hoped to prune himself over time into a simpler, more functional shape.

And in fact she dropped out of the Ph.D. programme in her second year to become a writer; a betrayal of her parents' expectations she had spent much of their brief acquaintance worrying over and planning. But she never told him when she packed her bags – he remembered being surprised at the time. Occasionally, and more and more recently, he came across her name in the Science section of the *New York Times*. She wrote mostly about matters relating to genetic engineering (the subject of her aborted dissertation). And though these articles signalled success after a fashion, he remembered her well enough, he supposed, to know that such work fell short of her ambitions. She wanted to write plays – and to spend her literary life trading off neglected studies must have effected a painful coming down in her own estimation. The phrase pleased Howard as he thought of it, suggested to him the careful way we back down an unsteady ladder.

By the time, however, he found his seat in the train, it occurred to him that he must have taught any number of Rosenblums in the past ten years, even an Aaron, an Amy. A few Hasids at Columbia stepped on with their dirty locks and ashy black coats, heading for Washington Heights. It was far more likely that some student, lately gone to college, or indeed the mother of some student, had written to thank him; or rather, to mention some recent success. A number of his kids had gone on to become doctors or professors, and liked to credit him for inspiring them, etc., to go one better than he had. The week after Thanksgiving was just the time you might expect to get such letters: two months into freshman year, or med school, after the first decent holiday, the first chance to reflect. It rarely pleased him, to be honest, such self-promoting gratitude; and it wouldn't, to be blunt, surprise him to hear it coming from a Rosenblum. *They* tended to possess a rather odious sense of the honour of the teaching profession – not uninfluenced by the fact that teachers stood at the gateway of their parental heaven, an Ivy League education for their children. Besides, he knew he was an excellent teacher, *that* wasn't one of his self-doubts. He did not trick anyone into his subject; he didn't set out to charm. (These phrases often ran through his head, word for word, at the end of a bad class perhaps, or at some slight from the administration; and sometimes spilt over into unrelated dissatisfactions, as he sat on the pot in his lunch hour and remembered a spat with Tomas: 'I don't trick anyone, I don't set out to charm . . .' Not quite true, of course: charm was the one attraction he could command. His air of patient irony often seduced others into climbing up to share his view, the thin cold atmosphere of his perch.)

He trusted his own passion for his subject; dry but steady and sustaining. The view opened out at Dyckman Street, as the train ran up the elevated tracks. Broadway looked grim at the top, nothing but discount stores and bad cafés; truant and jobless boys hanging around outside the doughnut shop. Then he rattled past the warehouses – watched a couple of late students slouch on – and over the concrete flat of the river. You need a few people to drum into kids that curiosity is the hardest and not the easiest instinct to satisfy. You need a teacher who doesn't play to the gallery for laughs, who lets the kids come to him and not the other way around. A familiar litany that brought out his least ironic inner voice, the voice of his father's son. 'Honest enough to fail them, to make them win their praise so they know what praise is, the kind of thing you can only earn when you reach the point it doesn't matter any more, it doesn't please you.'

The letter lay in his lap unopened as the train scraped in to 242nd Street. He looked at his watch, just gone nine, and let the kids get off first – he didn't like to hurry in front of his students. The envelope had caught the wet of his walk; the ink had run a little and dried again, and the paper bubbled slightly and crackled under his thumb. He slipped it inside his jacket pocket, surprised that he had already registered its opening as a pleasure deferred. A value assigned without conscious intent. It could only reflect some dormant curiosity about his former friend, who belonged to a very different phase in his life – when he had other prospects, and spent his privacy on other thoughts. The thing would happily trouble him in the course of the day, until he opened it on the subway downtown, when it would surely disappoint. Either way, that is, even if it *was* from Anne Rosenblum. Only when a woman in an orange plastic jersey pushed open the door with a mop and bucket, did he press himself up on his knees and walk out. 'Last stop,' she said, 'we're cleaning up.' Something he had to watch in himself: he had begun to let his reluctance to do certain things express itself in his manner and his actions.

Most of the teachers were teaching, as he strolled into the biology office, took off his jacket, and spread it over the back of his chair. Another minute's relative peace. The letter caught slightly against the seat, so he lifted it from the inside pocket and dropped it on his desk. Amy Bostick, one of those kids they had started hiring fresh from college, said to him – another administrative decision he didn't see eye to eye with, by the way, a poke in the eye is what it was and other teachers felt the same, part of that misguided tilting of the scales towards youth, always towards youth – sidled up to him and said, 'What you got there, Mr Peasbody?', laying a childish hand against his shoulder.

It left him rather queasy, those hands, long-fingered, given to little sweats. She was always rubbing them dry against each other – a terrible sound, like corduroy between hurrying thighs. Miss Bostick was a nervy creature, a real girl, dependent and plaintive. She picked at him steadily all day, to remove a piece of lint from his tweed, adjust a loose button, straighten his tie. Once, giggling softly, she even tucked in his shirt behind. Out of loneliness, of course; that much was plain to him; he had been the object of a girl's father-fancy before, and didn't much like it. This one was rather breathless and inarticulate on the whole; he had determined from the first elaborately to patronize her. Mostly they couldn't tell the difference between charm and kindness: few people could.

'Good thanksgiving?' he said, to put her off. Her hand rubbed the bristle of his neck, absent-mindedly, against the grain of shaving. 'Ach, families,' she said, in a new voice, mimicking. 'Who needs them.'

'Not all of us have the luxury of choosing.' That was a little cruel, perhaps. So that when she persisted, 'What is it?', he answered rather stupidly, 'A letter, my dear,' and added, to make amends, 'from an old lover, as it happens.' Surprised at himself, at his willingness to titillate curiosity with a piece of his own flesh.

'Who was he, Mr Peasbody?' She called him Mr Peasbody, pretending to be one of his 'adoring girls' – 'You have all these adoring girls, Mr Peasbody, mooning over you because they know they can't have you, they can't even dream of having you' – but the name had become a habit with her, and she used it even when she had forgotten to flirt.

'She, as a matter of fact.'

Amy withdrew her hand from his neck, and looked at him squarely. 'Well, well,' she said at last, 'aren't you a bit of a dark horse.' It was a tone she hadn't used with him before; it had the slightly colder air of appraisal.

That phrase ran through his head the rest of the day. Dark horse, dark horse – it didn't seem a very happy thing to be. Yet the image captured something he had always suspected, not without pride, about himself: a sense of veiled powers, of force restrained, obscured. Yes, he withheld a great deal. By necessity, it seemed, in his youth, when he was still unsure of his place in the world, of his rank within it. A hesitation, a slowness to judge which soon turned into an unwillingness to admire, and hardened into habit. His father, George, had always puzzled over that quality in his son: that refusal to mix in. Not that Howard was ever shy. Even in his somewhat spotty adolescence, he wore his looks well, carried himself comfortably, had the wit in reserve to nudge himself a head above his friends. There were always friends, only they seemed to see more of each other than they saw of Howard, and for some reason Howard never minded. Partly, George wondered why the kid never brought girls home: he could have had plenty of girls. He had that way with him, an amiable, insinuating manner, that nevertheless demanded nothing, needed nothing, indeed seemed to want nothing from anyone – which always charmed the girls, George knew. And then it became clear why Howard never brought the girls home, after his freshman year at Harvard, when he brought a boy. An unimportant boy, as it happens, insisted on mostly for the show of it, for the point to prove, and never seen from or heard of again. A flesh-and-blood instantiation of the 'confidential chat' they never had, which spared the need for it. Not that George minded much, after the initial shock, in spite of a constitutional repulsion from the fact of it, from the acts, no sea of love could wash away. At least his mother would never know: she had died of cancer when her son was still a fair-faced, blond-haired, plump-cheeked boy. George was rather relieved, all in all. It seemed a sensible, a specific explanation for a more general failing that had begun to worry him about his son, an otherwise charming and accomplished young man, and particularly pleasant companionship for an old-fashioned and, through force of occupation if nothing else, rather pedantic father. And George began to suspect that his son had always had a much busier private life than he let on, thank God. Though he never saw any further evidence of it.

Howard liked to give off an air of mystery: he found it let him get away with a great deal of little else. He was 'humanly lazy'. That was his own phrase for it, and Tomas had, in the course of their long cohabitation, worked hard to turn the phrase into something worse than an excuse: not entirely without success. Howard had begun to feel the self-reproach in it; and instinctively relied-on little dramatizations, even occasional fibs, to dress up the monotony of his inner life. But he hadn't been lying to Amy about the letter, though perhaps he had painted up the facts a little. One night Anne and he had gotten each other drunk and gone to bed together. A dull day towards the end of January had given way to a drippy snow in the evening, and they caught the cold of it coming home from class across Washington Square. They stopped off at a bar on Minetta Lane to warm up, started with beer and finished with whiskey sours; then picked up a bottle of Bourbon on the way out to get them through the night. Maybe there was some other occasion for it, he couldn't remember. His mother had died shortly after New Year; he was always looking for an excuse, during those short days, to cheer up. Perhaps Annie had sold a story, come into an inheritance; whatever it was didn't seem important afterwards, at least to him. Howard had never been a big drinker, but was given to binges: this was one of them, and he dragged poor Annie along. Both were lonely: they had begun to form one of those deep unsexual attachments that drive out the possibility of more frivolous, physical good times – because of the pretend, the dolled-up fakery sex required, and which their soberer, disinterested friendship put to shame. Then they fumbled at each other, with his back against the wall-heater, on her dorm-room bed prickly with the spines of opened textbooks.

It wasn't long after that she quit school. But something in their friendship had given way in any case, and Howard couldn't say that he minded much. Still it surprised him, over the course of the school day, how much his thoughts turned towards her. She bore grudges he knew, a quality he used to tease her about. It charmed him; she was such a rational, sensible girl in other respects, he smiled to see the imperious, casual way she could cut somebody: an old-fashioned term, which she adopted herself, and which exactly met the case. Annie was perfectly capable of blanking you in an empty hallway if you'd displeased her. Howard put it down to a kind of sexual paranoia: she was a pleasant-looking girl, healthy and quaintly voguish, but lacked that lime's twist of tarter appeal to sharpen the appetite of boys. It seemed a great if commonplace shame, for a stylish girl, that she was born no beauty. And she clearly minded the dearth of it, suspected, often rightly, the honourably pure intentions of her male friends. 'You're just like the rest of them,' she used to complain to Howard. 'Everyone's gay when it comes to me. Don't think you're anything special.'

And yet, in the event, he wasn't quite like the rest of them, was he? Even before that drunken night, she had roused in him a feeling of – well, he shouldn't dress it up as something sexual, because it wasn't simply. It was broader than that, an acknowledgement of human equality, a term diluted by centuries of liberal platitudinizing into a universal truth, when in fact it should designate only a most rare and particular phenomenon, a meeting. He had the sense that she matched him in human force, in vital mass, in powers held in reserve. 'You always take me firmly by the hand,' he used to say to her: and she felt the sting of the phrase, the mockery implied by its masculine challenge, but he meant it kindly, if not more, if not lovingly. With Annie, he did not have to restrain or deflect, or soften with irony. That phrase he used with Tomas, by way of excuse: for staying in, or keeping quiet, or leaving early – that he was 'humanly lazy', had seemed at least at first, in his youth, a gentler way of saying that he was tired of holding back, that there was no one around him who could bear his natural weight. That was what he meant at first; but it was true, as he grew older, that he suspected his own strength, its slackening, he suspected that 'laziness' was no longer a kind way of describing something else, but an unkind way of hitting upon the fact of his flaccidity, his spreading weakness. He hoped it was Annie who had written; he very much hoped that slight pleasure awaited him, on the downtown train after work, of tearing the envelope open with his thumb, and discovering news of her in his lap, after eighteen years. It surprised him, indeed, the weight of pleasure promised, growing at each deferral. Of course he'd be disappointed, there was no question of that; but the curiosity kept him a little warmer through the day, a hot stone in his pocket that would soon grow cold in the open air.

He knew it had come to the point he could no longer hide from himself the fact of his unhappiness, the depth of it. As if he had turned a corner in the road, and come suddenly upon the view, falling away from his feet: miles upon miles upon miles of unhappiness wherever he looked.

The rain in fact *had* softened to snow as he walked down the hill at five o'clock on a winter afternoon. He could see fat flakes of it dissolving in the heat of the lamp lights and dripping away again; but in the colder dark they only touched his brown wool overcoat and stuck, or printed his bent face with hot red spots. It struck him he had not written anything but letters and school reports in years: this was the kind of solitary moment he used to turn into verse, harmless and not quite happy. His father had been Head of English at Groton, and in his youth, Howard had wasted hours on poetry in the way other boys play around with rock bands, only rather more friendlessly of course: there was still a chest full of scribbled yellow notepads in his childhood bedroom in Greenwich. George had little cause to sort things through or throw them away; with an empty house and a dead wife, time and clutter (the two not unlike in their irregular excess) were things he had plenty of room for. Now Howard came to think of it, their literary ambition was another subject that used to occupy his conversations with Annie. Her plays would be performed on Broadway; his poems would appear in the *New Yorker*. 'I know what's going to happen,' she used to say. 'All us writer types. I'm going to make a break for it, and everyone else will stick to real jobs and settle down.' And he remembered some lines he'd read, which he used to quote to her (in his reciting days), about the difference between poetry and prose:

> Sparrows were feeding in a freezing drizzle
> That while you watched turned into pieces of snow
> Riding a gradient invisible
> From silver aslant to random, white, and slow.
> There came a moment that you couldn't tell.
> And then they clearly flew instead of fell.

The image cheered him somewhat, suggesting as it did the ease and completeness of transformations. But he raised his collar against the flakes, to keep them from trickling down his neck; and mounted the iron steps to the elevated platform of the downtown train.

It *was* from Annie, the letter. Just as well, he thought, that he didn't open it at once: the shock of time passed would have been greater. By this stage he had sloughed, at least in his thoughts, some of the years gone, some of the skins worn, since he had seen her. She wrote with a black-inked fountain pen, not a scratchy, stingy one, but full-flowing; and some of the lines had smudged and gone blue at their washed edges from the wet. The words seemed fresher on that account, unset, capable of revision; and he could tell at even a first reading that she had tried hard to say as little as possible, breaking out, briefly, into detail, as if something *had* to be given away, conceded, however insignificant.

Dear Howard,

I thought of writing before, many times, but lacked the occasion. I don't have one now, only the chance to find one seems to be getting smaller rather than the reverse, so I thought, I'll simply begin. I want to see you, I have something to say.

I have seen you, twice as it happens, in the past twenty years: once in the Park, walking two steps ahead of a fair young man; once, shopping, on the West Side. I thought, if you had seen me, I would have come up to you, but you didn't.

There's a coffee shop not far from my apartment, on 85th Street, just east of Second. Called Rohr's. If you don't want to call, meet me there, Saturday? at noon.

Annie

Just like her, he thought, that mix of the sensible and the clandestine. Also, something careful about the choice of words, those offhand repetitions: see you, seen you, seen me. *Exactly* like her: she couldn't write a shopping list without making the ordinary and slipshod into an artificial style. One of the things he found tiring about her. Even so, he thought, I'll have a cup of coffee with her, Saturday; and it struck him that no consciousness of altered lives could make that seem anything but natural: a cosy drink with Annie on the weekend. Time didn't matter very much: it always looked small next to something human. The snow had stuck and frosted, at least on the cold tops of parked cars, as he stepped out of the subway and walked down Broadway, tacky and bright with Christmas, towards home.

He never mentioned the letter to Tomas, but then, he often kept things quiet till they had to come out. Another habit: it seemed best to him on the whole to keep what you knew in reserve until it was needed. Things said or done had a way of snagging on the world, of taking on more than was meant, becoming hard to untangle. Of course he also knew that anything stored in the icebox had a way of changing colour and losing smell, of denaturing in some way; but generally, he preferred that risk. Even on Saturday he said only, 'I'm going out for a breath of air.' Tomas lay on the sofa shirtless in sweat pants; a little heater blew away at his feet, a steady thrumming white noise. He was running through the TV channels with flickering eyes.

'You know it's snowing.'

'Yes, I thought I'd have a look.'

'There won't be anything to see. Too fat and wet.' Tomas, being German, set himself up as an authority on cold weather. Also, when he was feeling lazy, he couldn't bear it for anyone to do anything, especially Howard.

'Well.'

'Maybe I come with you.' Tomas swung upright, one of his sudden movements, and slapped his hands against his knees.

'No, I'm only going round the block,' Howard said, leaning on the opened door, and gently letting it close him out. In his casual hurry he hadn't thought to grab his overcoat. Instead, he lifted the collar of his tweed jacket, and felt the bulk of his wallet in the inside pocket. A blue turtleneck underneath kept his Adam's apple warm, still a little pink from the morning's shave. Even so, having planned to walk across the Park, he caught a cab instead on Amsterdam. He was late anyway, and somehow arriving by taxi lifted the sense of occasion, suggested a rendezvous. Tomas was right; nothing stuck, except the traffic on the cross streets; but the pavements and roads looked dirty and dark under the crushed wet. He felt a little raw all round, scraped, as if for once he might feel the sting of what touched him: a pleasant sensitivity. He had smoothed a handful of cologne across his face after shaving, and could smell it now, in spite of the cold of the cab, the sweet intimate odour of his own skin.

Rohr's stank of coffee and wet wool when he walked in, stamping his feet. Nothing more than a hole in the wall, with an old-fashioned glass front, and jars of beans stacked above the counter. She wasn't there. He bought a cup of regular from a girl still wearing her woolly hat (the red bobble swung side to side around her neck), and added just a shake of sugar from a sticky pot. The littlest sugar rush was how he thought of the coming reunion, a light squirt of quickly used-up pleasure. A bookshelf held a jumble of travel books and detective stories, with an aquarium perched unsteadily on top: a goldfish flicked his tail through green gloom. Other than that, there were rugs laid over each other on a linoleum floor, and wicker chairs lined up against a bar, looking over the street. Someone had spilt coffee on his newspaper, the *Post*, and left it behind. Howard unstuck it to read the front page, and sat down. He hated waiting, an impatience he also disliked in himself; it disappointed him. Only, a sense of his own importance clashed with his conviction of being on his own anyway, of always biding time – and trumped it. He tried to concentrate his attention entirely on the front-page stories, about a killing in Queens, about the Knicks, but kept looking up.

And then when she came he didn't recognize her. A short-legged swaggering young man pushing his way out the door, coffee in hand, shouted something at someone coming up the street from Howard's left. He turned his head, and saw a dark-skinned guy wearing a yellow tie and a baseball cap and sunglasses against the low winter half-sun break into a kind of dance step with his arms held stiffly out. The pair embraced. 'Man, look at you, Tariq,' the first said, taking a burnt sip of the coffee. He ran his words into each other, and let them stick together, like something chocolatey. Howard could hear him through the glass. 'You look like the most guido Pakistani *I* ever met.' Then someone tapped him on the shoulder, and Howard turned and said, 'Yes?', taking her in in a stranger's glance, before he recognized her. 'Annie, Annie,' he said. She bent down and kissed him on the cheek, then reached over to hug him awkwardly across his shoulders. He swung an arm around her waist, but a sense of falling short, of not having done their greeting justice, lingered for the first few minutes of their conversation. 'Let me just get a cup of coffee,' she said and turned away.

He had expected expansion of some kind, plumpening of feature, loosening of hair, perhaps even another layering of shirts, cardigans, shawls; also, the mark of added burdens, twin weights at the hips, shortness of breath. He thought by this point in life she'd be well and truly frazzled, she always had so many seams coming undone even when he knew her. In fact, the reverse had happened; she had if not retracted then at least pruned herself into more manageable quantities. She had never been fat, he had never thought of her as fat, but she had in her youth a sort of breadth, a physical generosity; and now even the bones of what he had considered her essential shape had proved to be pliable to time and, no doubt, her own will. Her hair, cut short, had straightened into a bob. He saw this when she hung her coat, brown knitted wool lined and hooded with fur, on the hat stand; and she was wearing only a black T-shirt underneath, a charcoal skirt, stockings and leather boots. Half as tall is what she seemed, and narrower too, as if caught in the corner of a wide-angled lens. Her chin came to a point; her cheekbones, it seemed, had drawn closer to her eyes, making a pink triangle, frosted and chapped slightly, by the cold. Even the hook of her nose had sharpened a little – she had a sharp face, prettier, more boyish, than he remembered. She seemed to move with tiny, tidy deliberations: ordered a cup of French roast, black; waited without shifting or turning for her mug; snapped open her purse and counted out the change; thanked the girl in the red hat. It struck him how small she was; how much smaller than he; that he doubled her, that she could not have resisted him that night, if he chose.

'Thank you,' she said, sitting down. Their stools both faced the street, but she had space to prop her feet on the crossbar and turn entirely round to face him. He could only turn his head. 'My guess is you don't often venture east; but I have to get back to the apartment soon. I've only just come round the corner and can't stay long. The fact is, there is someone I left at home who's dying to meet you.'

'I can't think why.'

'I'll get to that in a minute. First, I just wanted to say: hello, how ya been.'

She had caught him off guard: she had such directed purpose; he expected to lead the reminiscences. 'Much as you see me. I don't change,' and added, with a laugh, 'if I can help it.' She cocked her head at him, in a way he used to hate. She used to knock on his forehead with a knuckle and say, 'come out, come out, wherever you are' – a piece of foolishness that always left him *stumm*, like he'd been set up. How can you expect anything but silence at such questions? 'I've seen your name, now and then,' he said, 'in the *Science Times*. Anne Rosenblum. Old Annie Rosenblum.'

'You must have laughed,' she said. 'Who would have thought that stuff would get me my breakthrough.' Again, not quite what he'd expected; he'd almost been hoping for a confession of failure, of blunted purpose. She seemed to guess something of that, and went on, 'Well, I do all right. I hear you're teaching?' Just the sort of question he had feared: what you'd ask any acquaintance. There was a little more of that, on both sides. He didn't mention Tomas. She didn't mention whoever it was she had to get back to. A delicacy, he supposed, they both employed in case the answer was only loneliness on the other side; and yet, they'd always been jealous friends, and the habit of it had a strange persistence, in spite of everything.

'You know, Annie,' he said suddenly, 'it was a month before I found out you'd quit. I forget who told me: certainly not you. Nobody knew what the hurry was. We had a few guesses –'

'What did you guess?'

'That you found some sugar daddy in the city; that you sold a script to MGM; that you got pregnant, married. Well, it's . . .'

'What did *you* guess?'

' . . . twenty years ago. I don't know what I guessed. I suppose I missed you, mostly. I felt –'

'I called you every day for a week. I knocked on your room. I left –' He preferred her like this, unsmiling, insistent. Her nose had a red streak on the tip, like the mark a bandage would make, pulled off at a stroke. She used to get cold sores there, and whenever she was hot, or ill, or insistent, a faint red stripe appeared where the blood burned through. This was a thing he remembered, something preserved.

'Fairly wretched about that night, and more than a little confused, on several counts. You never called.'

'Two or three times a day. I left notes under your door.'

'You never called. I never saw any notes.'

'Howard, of course I did. Of course you did.'

Perhaps she had. It had occurred to him before that he might be capable of suppressing certain facts, for the sake of his balance, his steady course. He considered the possibility, in a detached way: That, while he thought the great trouble of his inner life was his need to exaggerate, to puff himself up for even the faintest of emotions to register and give off a little heat to the world, the reverse might be true. That only the carefullest containment prevented all kinds of passionate outbursts, that he had a great store of emotional fuel, burning inwards and building up warmth. That the least thing could upset him, spill him; that he lived in fear of that chance. It didn't seem very likely; and only a certain pressure to conform internally to the accepted view of these things, of repression, suggested the idea to him at all – apart, of course, from moments like these, when someone gave him reason to believe that his own view of the world might have consistently misled him, even to the point of inventing facts.

Then she said, 'I was pregnant. That's why I left. I wanted to have the child – I got what I wanted. She's at home now, my daughter, waiting for us. Drink up: I said we wouldn't be long.' Then she continued, as though reciting a difficult declension, learned by rote: 'Our daughter. Your daughter. About to turn eighteen, and I thought –'

'Good lord,' he said, surprising even himself, by his lightheartedness, his casual astonishment. He might have said 'good lord' the same way if she'd told him she had sold a book for a million dollars. It occurred to him, suddenly – in regard to that little scene he had witnessed, between the young swaggering Italian and the 'guido Pakistani' – that it was the greeting itself that delighted them, the form of it. Those wide comical steps and the heavy embrace proved to be the purpose of their encounter, rather than its introduction – proved to be the proper occasion for joy, rather than the no doubt desultory conversation that followed it.

'Oh, Howard, don't look so peevish. I could never bear that pursed look you get when you're trying to sound pleased.' He almost bristled at the injustice of her remark: he thought he'd never felt so easy in himself, so well feathered, so buoyant and dry. But it occurred to him once more that he might be looking through a distorted lens: himself. And then Annie apologized.

'I can't expect you to take it in at one sitting; especially when I sprung it on you like that. The fact is I feel guilty, at my silence, in the first place. Which wasn't all my fault, as I said. You were a difficult man back then to spring bad news on. But if I'm honest I have to confess I got what I wanted, and one thing I didn't want was to share. But more than guilty, I feel –' and here she cocked her head up and sideways and looked out the window. Anyone passing by would have thought she was unhappy, or that they were strangers, or, even worse, lovers who had nothing left to say to each other. But she was only searching for the right word; a characteristic gesture. It surprised him how well he remembered it, how fresh the irritation was – at the ridiculous purity she aspired to in expression, the exactitude: a selfish virtue it seemed when she let the rest of the world run happily to waste and imprecision. Or perhaps he was only envious, conscious of being outdone. 'Tremulous,' she continued, 'unsure, but eager, at the thought of adding you to us. Of being filled out, as a family. I can't say how good it is to see you. I don't mean to be sharp; don't listen to me, you never used to. It just seemed to be – I won't delude myself by saying "the right moment", because we both missed that moment years ago – a chance, that's all. Her last year at home; God knows where she'll end up next year, that's another thing I wanted to talk to you about. She never tells me anything about her college applications; and I had heard, from a friend of a friend, that you were teaching, and thought, maybe you could advise her. And then, you know, she seemed ready to me – ready to meet you, without making too much of it or too little. I'm running on. You always had a way of making me talk. But we should go back now; it isn't far. Francesca's a tough kid but she's human, in spite of her parents, right?, and I'll bet she won't say it, but she must be on pins and needles.'

They stood up, and he took her coat from the hook and helped her into the arms; and with her back to him, she said, 'The fact is, of course, I was losing her anyway. There isn't anything left for me to lose; she's going away. So I don't mind sharing now.' She kissed him quickly on the cheek. 'You're being very good, but you haven't said anything. Do you mind? Is it very terrible, having a brand-new daughter?'

'No, no, of course not. I don't know what I think yet. It seems so', he laughed lightly, 'unlikely, all things considered. Wouldn't you say?' Perhaps that offended her a little; perhaps the laugh was a little too much, too casual; perhaps he meant to offend her a little. After all, he'd suffered greatly, it seemed to him, at her hands: or rather, there was a possibility he had suffered; he couldn't be sure yet, how much he had lost. Even so, as they walked down Second Avenue, into the cold wind blowing up from midtown against the traffic, he felt easy, elaborately leisured, as if he'd been asked back only for another cup of coffee, and to look over some holiday snaps she'd forgotten to bring. Francesca, a pretty name. He felt very well feathered indeed against wind and world; buoyant; dry. And there was still plenty of time for him to work out a line to take about the whole thing.

Annie led him through two glass doors into the lobby of her apartment block, done up in the shabbiest manner of the Upper East Side: threadbare pink carpets ravelled over rubber steps, scalloped lighting softened against cream walls, tall mirrors bookending the elevator. Each suggesting a faded gentility that never was. And it didn't surprise him, after all, to discover that Annie had sacrificed comfort and style, in the end, to what her kind liked to call 'a good address'. The elevator clanked to a halt in front of them and shuddered open, a half-foot out of place. 'Mind your step,' she said; they'd fallen mostly quiet, and continued so, as the lift ascended by imperceptible increments to an indeterminable floor: the fifth, he noted, stepping into the corridor. 'Penthouse suite,' Annie muttered, making a wry face; a little embarrassed, he thought. No doubt at dusting off an old line mostly reserved for strangers, at treating *him* like a stranger and falling back on 'conversation'. Turned out to be true, though, he noticed on his way home: the fifth was the top floor, and she may have reddened a little at her slight but irrepressible pride in that fact.

Frannie, as her mother called her, was sitting down as they came in. The bathroom door stood open in front of them – revealing dirty grey tiles and a dripping bath tap, and Annie moved quickly to close it. That was her bedroom, he supposed, to his left; then a corridor ran the length of the flat to his right, and Howard could see his daughter sitting in a club chair against the back window, reading the newspapers. Francesca turned and saw them, stood up and sat down again: just giving him time to note her dumpy figure and bright bohemian layers, a shawl, a cardigan, two heavy bunches of beads falling loosely across her spread breasts. Less pretty than her mother was and had been: less susceptible to refinement. Something spoilt about her, overfed; she had the look of a girl who hadn't often been refused, and wasn't accustomed to denying herself. He had a wide experience of such girls, particularly prevalent among the only children of the shabby genteel, and, dare he add, among Jews. Disappointment shamed him; if he'd had a choice he wouldn't have chosen her. So this is the stuff he was made of.

'You'll forgive me,' Frannie said, standing up again, 'if I

don't indulge in any emotional reunion. I can't say I've missed you: I didn't know you. But I gather that's not your fault. Still, I must say, it's good to have you on board: Mom was beginning to drive me nuts on her own.'

She strode towards him, her various swathes shifting and resettling, with a plump red hand outstretched. He almost shrank from touching her: she had moved too quickly into fact, with all the unimaginably banal particulars that transformation entailed: breath, warmth, smells, an accent more heavily soaked in Jewish New York than her mother's. Annie grew restless beside her; excess of pride and worry had nowhere to express itself in her trimmed-back figure, and turned into nerves. 'Can I make some coffee? Do you want anything, Howard? Something to eat?'

'Why don't you bring out those chocolates?' Frannie suggested; and she turned to Howard. 'I gave them to her for her birthday. Some have cream inside; some liqueur. You feel sick afterwards either way, but you can't help wondering which you'll get next time.'

'Coffee is fine,' Howard said; to his own surprise, he felt conscious of his daughter's weight, and instinctively resisted her indulgence. He took the club chair for himself now; mother and daughter sat opposite on a delicate orange sofa propped up on one side by an old phone book. Annie had pulled off her boots, and sat on folded legs with her hands across her lap. Francesca lay awkwardly back against a heap of cushions: she struck him as the kind of girl uneasy in her shape, but unwilling to admit it. A door on his left opened on to another bedroom. No doubt his daughter's. There were various boots lying bent-necked on the floor, among clothes, bedsheets, even a packet of tampons (it was very much *girls-only* in the flat). The mirror over the unmade bed revealed the corner of a desk, the textbooks on it (poor kids, he thought, not for the first time: what *burdens* we make them bear for their *knowledge of the world*), and a window, streaked with stickers peeling in the cold.

He looked round him. It was obvious the only thing Annie could keep tidy was herself. There were books everywhere: some caught in the act, as it were, suddenly neglected and frozen in their latest gesture like the citizens of a library in Pompeii – bunched open, or fluttering on their spines. Books being used: serving as coasters, paperweights, dessert plates (covered in orange peel), props. There were books embracing other books as bookmarks. On the shelves constructed out of bricks and boards against one wall, books stood two deep, or lay squeezed in sideways. On the orange sofa: half swallowed by the cracks between the cushions. On the armrest of his chair – *Hamlet, Jane Eyre* (Frannie's school texts, of course) – sprawled, balancing on their open faces. On the glass coffee table: loosely barricading a vase of dead white roses, whose petals lay scattered across them. On the dining table pushed into the corner underneath the hatch to the kitchen: stacked like chimneys around an open laptop. On the wooden cover for the air-conditioning unit next to the couch. Annie now set her mug there, next to another mug, long cold no doubt and forgotten, ringing another book.

What wasn't covered with books was covered with newspapers: Saturday's *Times*, but the *Post* as well, the *Wall Street Journal*, a slipped heap of *New Yorker*s spreading across the kelim rug. A store of papers waist high stood in the corridor, waiting to be taken out. Her apartment looked like student digs, only older, richer, more spacious; and he thought: she hasn't given up, she hasn't become less curious about the world. She still had a few posters on the walls, framed now and hung on nails rather than stuck to the paint with blue tac. He noticed in particular, above the dining table, a playbill for the Stethoscopes, an a capella group formed by some of their medical school friends at NYU. The date was November 25th, 1979: it was their Thanksgiving concert, Howard had just turned twenty-three. Who could have guessed how little would happen in the next twenty years?

As they talked, he got the uncomfortable sense that he was

watching an elaborate advertisement for a family. Though whether they were selling themselves to him, or simply preening, he couldn't be sure. It occurred to him that he was only an occasion for their preening: they'd brought him in at last to prove how well they got along without him. Well, let them, he thought. And yet, there was something about the clutter of the apartment, about the density of life, that moved him, drew him inwards, by force of gravity. An unpleasant sensation: the way we give in, in spite of ourselves, to the simple mass of other people, their answering weight.

'Mom dresses so corporate these days,' Frannie declared, appealing to Howard, to start an argument. (Perhaps it was only his silence that spurred them on – to fill the terrible quiet of their ignorance of each other.)

'I do not. It's just that you get to a stage in life when you realize you're only one cardigan or shawl away from looking like a bag lady.'

'Thanks for that, she rejoins, heavily ironic.'

'What? I wasn't talking about you.'

'If you can't see the implicit criticism in that then you're more deluded than I thought you were.'

Howard put her down as one of those girls, who, believing she's come to terms with the mediocrity of her looks, thinks she can't be fooled by anything any more. He got such girls from time to time in his classes.

'You like to talk,' he said at one point.

'Oh God, please don't tell me that I verbalize everything. If there's one thing I can't stand, it's people telling me that I "verbalize", as if that were the strangest thing in the world to do to your experiences. Everybody else just talks, somehow whatever I say is *verbalizing*.'

'All I said was, that you like to talk.'

'Don't worry,' she said, considerately, 'it's not your fault. It's just something I get a lot, believe me.'

He wasn't sure that he liked her. Growing up alone with his father, a distant and correct man, had spoiled him: he hadn't needed to get along intimately with anyone. Something about the phrasing of his thought made him stop short. But then his daughter said, 'Mom used to be more expansive, now all she does is retract. I'm expanding for both of us. I can't bear the way she pinches herself every morning in front of the mirror: thinking, a little less of this, a little less of that. Some here, some there. All right, I'm only seventeen years old, but I've figured out that getting bigger with age is the least of our worries. Only expand, would be my motto. Let everybody else shrink around you if they want: more room for us. It's not just the weight with her, it never is: it's the way she dresses, the way she looks over a menu. The way she eyes me up and down when I pick out another chocolate. I can't stand it: all it means is she has fewer and fewer choices. I know what it's like, believe me: every time you eat you ask yourself, do I need this? Pretty soon you can get by without anything at all. Pretty soon you don't *want* anything. I ask myself: do I want this? And pretty soon I *need* everything. I can't tell, I'm too subjective: maybe we're each as bad as the other. But you should know: she didn't used to be like this.'

'No,' he said, warming to his daughter. 'She didn't. She used to be more like you.' He couldn't be sure he hadn't offended. And he thought: now Annie's more like me.

As he was going, Francesca said, 'Peasbody. That's a strange name.'

'My,' he began, then stopped himself and resumed without particular emphasis, 'your great great grandfather, the story goes, was something of a drunkard, and came through Ellis Island a little the worse for wear. The "s" is what's left of his slurring. The immigration officer wrote it down and the name stuck: Peasbody. That's the story at least. My mother always thought we should get it changed, that three generations of Peasbodys were enough is enough. We were just the kind of people, she said, to stick by a mistake for a hundred years, too lazy or too loyal to correct it. She thought we needed a new start; and tried to take us in hand herself, but couldn't see the job through. She'll be sorry never to have met you. After she died, well, several years after, when I was your age, I thought about changing my name, to please her. But I was always too lazy, or too loyal. So year by year goes by.'

He wasn't used to confessing so much to strangers; it left an unpleasant taste in his mouth, like a lie. And in his confusion, he kissed first Annie and then his daughter on the cheek, and said, 'I hope to see you both soon, very soon', as he shut the front door behind him, and fled. In spite of the weather, he walked home across the Park. Specks of flakes, like tiny white distillations of the cold, fell around him and disappeared in the asphalt paths, in the dirt, in the grass. A second chance: he had been given a second chance to make something other than solitude out of his life. Here was proof: that he bulked so large, even in the corner of his own thoughts, that these could not contain him, that part of him was exposed to the world, and snagged on it. That he cast seeds about him all the time; and he wondered less at the fact of the fruit than at the seeds themselves. It occurred to him, of course it did, that such sophistries were only his way of seasoning the amazement, so he could stomach it. He had a daughter; God, there was work for him to do if he had the heart for it. The prospect appalled him, like the thought of moving house. He had lived so long and so deeply off his memories that he had begun to doubt the truth of them; and now who could say where his own life ended and where it would begin?

II

Tomas gave off an air of innocent greed; big-chested, he ran slightly to fat, regardless of the hours spent happily under a bench press. There was something that would not be trimmed about him, reduced to the needful, measured; the excess, the vitality of him sometimes struck Howard as rude and bludgeoning, a refusal of fineness and the shelter it demands. Pale faced, he wore his light-blond hair piled high and loose on his head, cropped round the sides; and was big in all joints, elbows and knees and hips, so that a kind of mechanical exuberance and imprecision often caused him to break dishes or catch old ladies by the shoulder with a strapped bag. His father was an American soldier stationed in Germany who had had an affair with a Czech-born nurse. She raised him alone in Hamburg, without bitterness, ran through boyfriends, never married – and regarded the accident of her son's birth as the only thing that could have brought her such steady and equal male companionship, given a nature more inclined to spontaneity than duty. The misery he left behind, like unwanted clothes, surprised her into a sudden sense of her age (forty-three) when her son broke out of university to come to New York. But she kept her tongue, and he settled there on the strength of his American passport, and worked his way quickly through various menial jobs at a documentary-film company to his present status as production manager.

Tomas's company often made films with what their various directors considered to be a scientific edge. Science, particularly genetics, was in the news; and Howard had some old college acquaintances working in production, who called him in when they needed someone to explain their prefabricated accounts of this or that evolutionary phenomenon. Howard was easy and fluent in front of camera, and didn't much mind what the directors made him say. His doctorate, after all, concerned genetics; but, being only a school teacher, he had little stake in sticking by the complications of truth or an original and professional point of view. The fact of appearing on television flattered him; it made him seem less lonely to himself. Or rather, it made his loneliness take on a greater, more public significance: he knew things other people needed to know. Occasionally, he even suggested slight changes to the script, which tended to make his explanations not only truer but more interesting. And the directors learned to trust his interventions, and called him in on projects only distantly related to his expertise. These television appearances touched him faintly with a schoolyard celebrity, which did him no harm in the classroom, or the headmaster's office, for that matter. Though his fellow teachers, especially in the Science department, occasionally sniped, with unembarrassed jealousy, that he had sold his soul to the television devil; and addressed him, with mocking humility, as 'the geneticist, Dr Peasbody' over their cafeteria lunches.

Tomas was working as a runner when they first met. Howard teased him by asking for ever more elaborate sandwiches from ever more distant and specialist sandwich shops. He liked to see the boy work up a sweat; Tomas at this point was still twenty-three, and breathless with the heartbreaking energy of youth. Wore shorts through the thick of winter; and high socks to keep the wind off his ankles when he biked. His skin always flickered between rose and pallor, depending on the animal heat expended in his last exertion. He finished off, unabashed, whatever sandwiches, potato chips, chocolate chip cookies were leftover from his lunchtime runs. And spoke in a rather innocent staccato, gently accented by the inevitable Teutonic suggestion of the military. Once, Howard even asked Tomas to flush a toilet he'd forgotten to attend to himself; he was busily going over the script with the assistant producer and didn't like to think of the thing festering, etc. Tomas burned red at the shame of it, though when he got there the bowl was clean; perhaps the man was playing with him, and he dropped the lid and sat down head in hands, feeling the heat of his face; and trying to work out whether he was simply angry or also flattered (successfully teased, tested in some point) by the unusual mark of attention.

After they first made love, Howard insisted their relationship remain an 'open' one. Tomas was heartbroken, but said nothing. The one-year anniversary of his arrival in New York approached: he had a job, he had a lover; he had done well. Spring had come; the air had that washed, wrung-out feel of a cloth about to expand again and take on moisture. He remembered it from the previous April: it was his first answered memory, his first echoed season. It seemed he had to cut his nails every other day; and the trees, even in Harlem, on 154th Street where he lived (above a fire station – 'Only security you'll ever need,' the agent told him) had broken into petalled green, tough fresh cuticles no bigger than fingertips. Even the dogshit smelt sweeter in the sun; baked slightly when the sunshine caught the angle between the apartment blocks just after noon. Newspapers blew lighter along the cross streets. Awnings opened out again on the avenues. After two weeks he said to Howard, when they lay in his broad bed at the edge of sleep, 'You're the only thing keeping me here', but it wasn't quite true even then. And by the summer, when Howard answered him at last – 'You're the only thing keeping me here' – it was hardly true at all, though Tomas was deep in love. And he couldn't work out why Howard had answered him in those terms, how much, what exactly he meant by it. 'But you've always lived here; you've got nowhere else,' Tomas said, a phrase that sounded narrower, more dependent than he intended. When what he really meant was, you don't need me for this to be your home. Howard blinded himself on his lover's pale back, in the dent between backbone and shoulderblade. 'You're the only thing keeping me here,' he repeated. 'You're the only thing keeping me here.' Conscious, of course, of being misunderstood; of intending a greater depth of misery than his buoyant young lover could plumb.

And it was Tomas who took other lovers, by that first fall. Howard raged at him, inconsolably, when he found out. Not that Tomas proved shy in confession; he had a natural, easy way with experience, and a faith in his love for Howard that couldn't be shaken by events or decisions, his own included. By this point, indeed, their first passion (never very fiery on Howard's part) had cooled in any case; and Tomas's sense of their growing companionship delighted in the fact of having news to tell. And such news: he felt obscurely that he had done as he'd been told to do; his reward being that the task proved more pleasant than he'd anticipated. (It was a barman from a hole in the wall on Avenue A: a kid from Tennessee who wanted to design stage sets, and sidelined as a lighting assistant at a nearby bar/theatre called the Nuyorican Café. Both had had military fathers and suffered for it, a conversation, now painless from repetition, they approached with feigned tenderness, remembered soreness.) Tomas had been a good boy; he wanted Howard to know how good and loving he had been. And in spite of his anger Howard almost laughed at the way Tomas, like a dog with a bone, laid his little infidelity at the feet of his master. No doubt that insight stoked his fury further: it reassured him he could grow cruel as he liked and the boy wouldn't turn away. Perhaps inconsolable isn't the best word for Howard's reactions. His vanity rather than his affection had been touched. He remembered this clearly, thinking, I can't believe that ugly dumb kid has the balls to cheat on me, to think he can go one better. The thought made him sick at heart: to be reduced to such crudity.

He gave the boy one terrible night and then reconsidered: better policy by far would be to show how little he cared. It was only jealousy, the habit of jealousy. And he wasn't a coward with respect to habits: there was nothing in his emotional life he couldn't master, and bend to his own will, to express what he wished it to express. He had learned over time that emotions were only a means of expression, a means most of us handled clumsily. But if we took pains to determine just what it was we wanted our emotions to *say*, we could adjust the manner of expression to match the meaning – over which we exercised a strict control, lying as it did within our will. He simply adapted the old question, What exactly do you want to say? into What exactly do you want to feel? and corrected his emotions accordingly. He did not want to feel jealous of Tomas; he knew that if he concentrated, and applied suitable thought to the matter, he would no longer feel jealous of Tomas. He did not feel jealous of Tomas.

In fact, for several months that fall, as the leaves banked against the railings of Tompkins Square, they used to go to the Nuyorican Café, even on a school night, to take in a reading, or a show – dreadful performances, mostly, and to be honest, both of them were more or less grateful when Tomas decided to drop his recent acquaintance. Apart from anything else, the journey home across town and up proved to be a greater nuisance than the thing was worth. But Howard congratulated himself on the precedent set: Tomas had no reason now not to confide his little flings to his real lover. And he made a point of taking lovers of his own: casual, mostly uncomfortable one-off affairs, which he never told Tomas about. Howard knew he couldn't have kept the ugly, preening boastfulness out of his lips and voice, which would have been particularly unpleasant, for both of them. Tomas, for his part, managed with remarkable innocence and charm to gossip about his lovers like any other news. A strange but somehow undeniable testament to his good character, his generosity. In any case, Howard rather enjoyed the secret knowledge of his own few affairs; the mystery bulked them out, if nothing else. And they were something to turn to, if he ever felt so jealous again, so compromised and dependent.

Even so, long after the words had become nothing but a habit for Tomas, Howard used to answer his good-night pledge with his own more passionate assurance: you're the only thing keeping me here. You're the only thing keeping me here.

But all that was years ago, and Howard's sense of dependence had grown more and more irksome to him; he wished to shrug it off if he could, and stretched himself various ways, testing the strength of the attachment. In part, he was merely bored. His life had little enough variation in it. He needed little variation, but sharing such a meagre ration of vicissitudes with another soul seemed to rob him of his austerity, his purity. By this point, for all his native unwillingness to be disappointed, Tomas had got the measure of his man – such a steady reckoning was hard to miss. Howard, in short, could no longer flatter himself by the image in his lover's eyes: there was no flicker left in it. Nothing to satisfy Howard's innate sense that his life was unusually grand, in substance if not in scope; that he was noble, that his very nobility doomed him to the terribly ordinary course of his days. If pressed (and to be fair, he often pressed himself), he conceded that his distinguishing virtue was hard to put a finger on; honesty, perhaps, came nearest the mark, but he wasn't exactly honest. Simple truth telling certainly fell more easily to Tomas's lips than his own. By honesty, he meant rather an undistorted sense of the value of life, of its illusions: he possessed a clear vision of the neutral, loveless landscape in which he found himself. Nothing flowered around him or underfoot; so he walked without hesitation in straight lines. And trampled on phantoms in a fashion that often seemed cruel to others. It seemed to him a worthy tragedy, that just those natural gifts – his wit, his subtlety – which might have allowed him to make a name for himself in the world, had in fact dictated the terms of his deliberate and rather joyless mediocrity: nothing, he saw, was worth putting your name to. The fact that he'd stuck by his lover for over seven years seemed to him a kind of lapse in discipline: he'd let himself fall into bad habits and hadn't the heart or the courage to break free of them. Fear of his own nature, left entirely to itself, unbuffered by the necessary decencies of shared life, played its part. With each passing year, he grew more and more terrified of what he would do to himself if left alone, the logical conclusions he would reach.

Shortly before the letter from Annie Rosenblum arrived, he stopped for a drink at the Irish bar outside the subway station below the school. Tuesday before Thanksgiving, and even he felt the gentle relief of absent duties, cleared space. Night had fallen already across the broad parkland at the foot of the hill; star and moon grew stronger between the bluster of the clouds. Tomas wouldn't get home for another hour or two; in any case, Howard realized, nothing in his mild celebratory mood inclined him to see his lover. He wished rather to draw out the hours of their separation. Let him worry a little when Howard came home late. Carved wooden booths ran along one side of the bar; generations of drinkers had cut names or mere lines, depending on their patience and sobriety, into the dry-fleshed wood. As Howard waited for the barman to pull a pint of Guinness, someone called his name, and he turned to find Benny Kahn, a colleague from the middle school, a short, pillow-chested man, with rimless specs pushed up against the bald patch in his curly hair. Howard joined him for the first beer, and offered him another. He could feel the tension mounting in his colleague – hear it in the little stutter of his voice, the clipped phrases, the slickness in the man's small fingers as they ran through the back of his semitic curls. Howard recalled certain rumours that Benny used to 'take a *shabattical*' from his wife from time to time, with some boy or other he picked up downtown; the wife and he had, apparently, come to a kind of understanding. Howard never paid much attention: he didn't believe most of the gossip he heard in the cafeteria. The teachers were just as bad as the kids; worse. Howard, for his part, felt very little nerves, only the slow softening of drunkenness, moving down his face, his hands, his feet.

After two more beers they took it in turns to hit the john. Benny was waiting when Howard pushed into the booth. It didn't last long and then Benny came out first and Howard waited a while on the toilet seat, happy to have a minute alone before flushing. Quite sober now, and being sober, sick of himself. He hadn't done that kind of thing in a year; he wondered why he bothered, it seemed so unlike him, just another habit he'd picked up from other people, and would really rather do without. He thought, if nobody told you you needed it, you might never find out. Perhaps he'd forgotten what it was like to be fifteen; the enormous nights, the way solitude expanded around you as intimately as the space around lovers, the sense of accompaniment one's body offered, the dialogues possible. He had known all of these things at the time, and suffered too, but suspected even then that they tended to be exaggerated. Flues and fevers produce similar distortions, but people forget them as soon as health returns. And the sentiments of lovers obscure many unpalatable acts that nobody in their sober selves would admit to. His desire for such things seemed slowly to have separated from the rest of his desires, such as they were; he might now discard it without fuss or pain. The bald fact of the unpleasantness had struck him particularly in this last encounter, for a number of reasons. Thank God that awkward nervous little man had gone by the time Howard came out of the john. Nevertheless, he stored up the memory of it, on the slow train home; another dirty little secret to keep from Tomas.

When he got back from Annie's place, Tomas had fallen asleep in front of the television: a loose hand pushed his shirt up to the first of his ribs. The heating pipes clanked, quickening, in the radiators. Such violence seemed surprisingly upsetting; a real invasion of the niceties. Howard was reluctant to wake his lover up: he didn't want to have to talk. That walk across the Park had chilled him to the bone; he couldn't quite feel how cold he'd become. And now, by contrast, the close heat of the apartment left him breathless and rather worried; he sighed deeply, again and again, to take in more air. Tomas stirred and roused himself, and blinked, happy as always to find his sight filled with Howard: proof of an instinctive affection Howard instinctively wished to disappoint. 'What was that all about? You left without your coat.'

'I wanted to get some air.'

'I would have come with you.'

'Look at you. You're not going anywhere.'

Tomas sat up, pressing his palms downwards against his brows, as if he wished to commit something to memory. Howard could smell the sleep coming off him; the shirt unrumpled again over the little puddle of his gut. Tomas closed his eyes and swung both arms from the elbow in towards his face – the gesture of someone inhaling a scent of broth from a hot pot. Only he said, 'Come here come here come here come give me a kiss.' Howard obeyed, hanging his head for shame, and closed his own eyes to blot the shame of it out, as Tomas pressed first one cold cheek and then another against the heat of his neck. 'Don't think I don't know,' Tomas said. That boy never needed to shave: he had the kind of snowy skin no blades of stubble ever broke through. Howard thought how young it made him seem, how boyish still – though by this time the gap in their ages had grown thoroughly respectable. Cradle-robber cradle-robber cradle-robber, he thought; then the word shifted, took on its new, more appropriate application; he felt the pinch of tears, then the sticky mess of them, bad as blood. It wasn't fair what had happened; what she had done to him, the extent of life she had committed him to. 'Don't know what?'

'Don't think I don't know you. I know you. I know you feel cold and bad lately; and then you think, I'm a cold bad man. I know better. Don't think I don't know better. I know what a pussy-kitten you are.'

Howard dried up: he was still capable of being surprised by Tomas, and surprised at the poverty of his own privacy, its transparency. Surprised at Tomas's fine feeling. Only the boy always went too far; and Howard could not repress, even from this mark of real sympathy, a slight aesthetic recoil. And he guessed rightly what was coming, he had heard it before, and heard it now, warm with the breath of the boy in his ear: 'The trouble with you is you don't trust anybody; I know because you don't even trust me. You have to give more to get more. I only want others to see what I see, how special you are, how much you have to give', etc. And yet, it isn't that Howard's vanity didn't tally with such an insistence on his rarity. Only the tone of it seemed low, common – it degraded him, to have fallen into such company; worse, to have chosen it, to have proved faithful to it. And behind Tomas's frothy truisms lay the boy's terrible, smug assurance, which he could never resist putting into words: 'I know you better than you know yourself.' A notion against which everything in Howard screamed revolt. In spite of the fact, which Howard helplessly admitted, that Tomas *did* see some things more clearly than he could himself; had guessed how close Howard had been to tears, had deliberately provoked them. He sat up now, awkwardly, pressing his hands against the boy's broad chest to get a purchase on balance; then recomposed his face, till it looked bored or numb – till he thought it looked bored or numb, though he couldn't be sure. It occurred to him, if he wanted to put a sting into that kid, he could tell him the news.

It did sting, of course, Howard's involuntary betrayal, the roots he had planted, without knowing it, in another life. After the shock, Tomas recovered quickly, eagerly – wished to meet her at once, them, lover and daughter both. But Howard insisted, understandably perhaps, that a new father was enough for the girl to take in for the time being. Introducing her now to his young gay German lover might be considered 'gilding the lily' – a phrase he guessed rightly Tomas did not understand, especially in its current ironic application. He hoped it would distract him from that curious mention of the kid's ethnicity, which had little to do with the matter, after all; and Howard couldn't say why he had included it, except to fill out a list. A long list is always more persuasive than a short one. But what exactly was he hoping to persuade him of?

In practical terms, however, his new daughter proved a great comfort to Howard. Whenever he wished for a minute's peace, a minute's respite from, among other things, his own dependence on the younger man's enthusiasms, he said, simply, 'I'm going to stop by the Rosenblums tonight.' Then he might stop by, or he might not, depending. The mere fact of his new daughter gave him a trump card in all the little negotiations of love – those skirmishes over plans and priorities, jealousies, affections. 'I'm going to stop by the Rosenblums' became his coded way of saying, I need you less than you thought, I have a richer *outer* life than you imagined. Which was true, after all: Francesca involved him intimately, relentlessly in the world outside his own head. And Tomas had urged him again and again over the years to venture out of that elegant confinement.

And then Christmas came, and Tomas, a good and homesick German, insisted first plaintively, then tenderly, then angrily, that the Rosenblums come by on Christmas Eve for glühwein and carols. 'They're Jews,' Howard said. 'Well, they can be Jews as much as they like on Christmas Day like the rest of America. I want to meet her.' The snow had fallen too early that year, drifted and cluttered the parks, where it survived, ugly and icy, in banked white streaks under benches, along the sides of cross-town roads, in the ripples of half-buried rock. Everywhere else pavement grit and crowded feet had browned it and ground it into puddles, which leaked and spread on to the doorsteps of the delis, the threadbare shag of the apartment lobbies, the floors of cabs. Winds bullied up and down the avenues unchecked. Everyone had a cold in the nose, drips, streaked voices, unthawed feet. A dingy end to the year, till a warm front blew off the water the night before Christmas Eve. And deposited its white burden of cloud, covering the old in the new – a fresh coat of snow no better than the first but innocent still, still capable of the necessary illusion. 'I want to come,' Frannie had said. 'Makes a change from Chinese food and a bad movie.'

Tomas drove Howard frantic all day getting ready. He woke early, shifted out of bed, and began vacuuming, in sleepy half-consciousness. 'For God's sake, turn it off,' Howard shouted at regular intervals, lifting the duvet from his throat. At nine, Tomas came up with a cup of coffee, said nothing, set it by the bed. There was a kind of silence between them: they had both reached that stage of the invisible contest when questions don't need to be answered, so intimate and sensitive have the lovers become. Howard guessed that he was losing; Tomas had grasped the possibilities at stake. There was the chance of a real future for them now, a growing and changing one, an expansion; even Tomas, greedy, constitutionally unimpressionable, had suffered under the steady retraction of their lives, presided over by Howard's 'honesty' – his refusal to give in to the 'necessary insincerities', even for the sake of happiness. (Tomas had never before considered his enthusiasms to be *necessary insincerities.* The description had an infectious, a deadening persuasive power.) They lived in a large ground-floor studio. The bed lay on top of the kitchenette, reached by a ladder propped against the side of the fridge. And the rest of the room stretched away towards the bay window in long lines of dark wood, broken by couch, coffee table, armchair, and now the Christmas tree, blocking half of the white light from the street. There was a brick fireplace; and Tomas carefully laid a fire across the andirons. It was the awful quiet crackle of the balled-up newspapers that irked Howard most, a little light tickling across his nerves. So he roused himself at last, and climbed down, if only to get himself in the way. Then Tomas began to cook a goose – a desperately messy, sweaty, speculative operation, which took up much of the day, and drew Howard, in spite of himself, in.

Annie and Frannie entered briskly to the smell of roasting bird. They brought enough of the cold in with them to make the shutting of the front door a sweet exclusion; dutifully stamped their caked feet, admired. They had worked each other into a pitch of curiosity through the course of the day. Sisterly by habit, they grew positively girlish. There was such gossipy excitement in the thought of meeting Howard's boy lover. Their lives had been added to, and what was old had been renewed in the process. The sense of novelty included a spice of wickedness: how cheaply mother and daughter had acquired relations. They felt a touch guilty at the ease of it, how lightly the blood-intimacy had been picked up, and free of that heaviness time imbues it with; how easy it might be to lay aside again. And then it was all so strange and painlessly unlike: a studio apartment on the West Side, gay young lives, a real fire. 'Isn't it decadent,' Annie said, with a certain theatrical escalation, not entirely unironic, that reminded Howard powerfully of their old irretrievable youth and friendship, 'here in the middle of the city, a glass of glühwein, these burning logs?' And he recalled what his father had said after he brought Annie home for a 'country weekend' – around Christmas, nineteen years ago. 'I like your friend, son. But I must say, they've never been the kind to hide their light under a bushel, have they?' A test of his sympathetic allegiances Howard refused to answer either way. This was the kind of remark his mother used to put a stop to. 'That's not nice, George; and what's worse, it isn't true.' His father would answer, irritably, 'Well, you know best, dear, you always do.' He meant it too, though – grateful for a correcting influence, a loving margin to his bitterness. But Howard said nothing.

Tomas for once wore a collared shirt, twice unbuttoned,

over his faded jeans; an apron, well wrapped about, brought out the calf-like heft of his shoulders, the vanity in his narrowed waist. He was shy of them both, glad of his duties; and the girl was shy of him. A compound of associations turned Howard's thoughts to his mother – who had been built up over time, in that lonely mythology of widower and son, into an icon of simplicity, sympathy, creaturely wisdom. She died when he was eight, of breast cancer; he remembered asking her, shortly before her death, but before he understood the thinning away that afflicted her, why they never gave him a baby brother? 'I'm having too much fun just with you and Dad,' she said with a complicitous wink. An answer that left him in a tangle of conflicting reflections: it had never occurred to him, for one thing, that she was *having fun*, that some part of her natural and unquestioned happiness was snatched, momentary, contingent – that it could end. He remembered feeling that she had somehow joined the pair of them, father and son, for the ride; they couldn't help it, *she* could. Later, the other possibility struck him: that his father, never a natural family man, had baulked at having more children; one, indeed, may have been a source of some dispute. He wanted Howard's mother to himself. George, like his son, found it difficult to expand; the Peasbodys drew tight circles, and protected the inside fiercely. At the time, of course, both father and son had failed at that, disastrously. How quickly, after all, his mother had died.

A strange thing happened in the course of the evening. Perhaps it was inevitable, at least, foreseeable. Annie and Howard took on the mantle of parents, exchanged looks, got slowly, quietly drunk. Tomas and Francesca, after an initial stiffness, an insistence on their right to equal and adult respectability, played like kids. Tore through their presents, leaving a papery nest behind the flown eggs (which Howard, with a kind of physical pedantry, carefully collected, and stored away from the fire): a fountain pen for Frannie, gold-nibbed, with a leather diary for her freshman year; a book for Tomas, on *film noir*. This brought on a slight relapse of mawkishness. 'I'm sorry,' Frannie explained, quick to bring awkwardness into the open, 'we didn't know what you wanted. Which was hardly our fault (glance at Father): we didn't know *you*.'

'It is exactly what I like very much,' Tomas said. Annie was touched by his unsuspected human grace – began to think she 'understood'.

Later, they sat cross-legged together in front of the fire. Tomas wound and unwound a loose branch of pine from the skirts of the tree, till it snapped, and threw it on the flames. Frannie leaped back at the gritty crackle, the sparks and smoky gunshot of the needles. 'Jesus,' she said, 'watch out.' Another stiff minute. 'I'm not one of those girls who sees anything funny in *trying out* stupid little dangers.' Anne looked at Howard and smiled into her glass of red wine. Her daughter had no sense of occasion; no restraint. She always dressed up her annoyance, her fears, embarrassments, as matters of principle. Howard looked back at Anne, blankly, met her eyes. Perhaps he lifted his brow: as much as he would grant the conspiracy of their indulgence, of their *parenthood*. Then Tomas stood up, stretching, a long-armed yawn that lifted his shirt above his belly-button; and eased down a box of Monopoly from a stack of large photography books laid on their sides. Francesca sat down again, smoothing away her huff, her blouse across her glittering 'party' belt, the knees of her black jeans. 'Everyone has to play,' Tomas said, in deep Germanic frowning tones that made even Howard smile, but shake his head.

'No, I'll clear up. You kids have a game. I like to watch.'

'Everyone has to play,' Tomas repeated, louder, more childish.

Howard began stacking dishes. 'The goose', Howard said at last, to prove his good nature, his willingness to stand aside, 'was a tremendous success. Except of course for the goose.' A remark characteristic of his warmest ironies, of his best, most loving manner.

And yet when he was through – the plates rinsed and dripping in the dishwasher, roasting pan soaking in the sink – he couldn't quite bring himself at first to sit and watch. He stood above them by the fire, the print of his hands on the skirt of his apron, even that well-worn piece of cloth a slight protection against joining in. Annie had got on the floor to muck in; cards, paper bills, the jumbled hats of houses and hotels, lay all around. She was losing badly; he could tell: that angry hot strip of red ran across the tip of her nose. Nobody, in fact, seemed very happy; apart from Francesca, who sat content with her back against the fireside bricks and ordered Tomas to roll for her, shift her little Park Avenue dog across the board, collect her rents, buy, buy, buy; and Tomas, in a gentle fury Howard knew well, obeyed. Whatever couldn't be solved by bulk, by effort, by energies and enthusiasms, afflicted Tomas like a neurosis, a system failure; he developed little tics, hair tugs, nose pinches, ear scratchings, anything to alleviate his excess of useless vital forces. It usually charmed Howard to see him – turned in upon himself in that way, fretful. An object of sympathy for a man always turned upon himself, more accustomed to the stresses and strains, better balanced for them. But now he couldn't repress the slightest twinge of jealousy: they would all love him now, his funny German lover. They would all take a piece of Tomas to their hearts. The gulf between *him* standing and *them* sitting seemed impassable; he kept his apron on.

And Howard remembered what it was he hated so much about the company of friends, of equals, had hated ever since his mother died, had despised in his school mates, his college friends, his graduate colleagues: the constant skirmishing for intimacies, never being sure of your place in others' affections. Not to mention the petty, petty greed of the social instinct, always hungry for more flattery, interest, love, at the expense of everything he held dear: independence, clarity of thought, a fundamental honesty regarding what mattered in your life and what didn't. It seemed to him, you were either born into family life or you weren't. You couldn't acquire the knack. You couldn't *want* to. Annie got up, slowly after all, on old knees, to find the bathroom; Howard leaned against the mantle, observing. Tomas, having landed his lead pipe on Broadway, threw its hotel, in mock annoyance, at Francesca, who flinched with surprising violence and said, 'I don't like it, don't throw things, I don't like it'. Tomas refused to back down; he was an angry loser. Anne whispered to Howard on her way back, 'Look,' with her hand lightly on his shoulder – she remembered how little he liked to be touched – 'our family.' Her hand still somewhat wet from the bathroom sink; it took him most of his self-command not to shrug it off.

After it was all over, that spring, after it all went wrong, after Howard had managed to drive each of them away, Tomas looked back on this first night as the high point, the first best instance of their brief family life; but even then, the seeds of disunion had been sown. Howard, whether he knew it or not, was plotting a way out.

They had the usual fight that night after the Rosenblums left – said their goodnights, their merry christmases, their happy hanukkahs, put on dripping boots, cold and achy now around their hardened, fire-dried socks, stomped themselves warm or numb and out into the white world again. Their absence instantly changed the atmosphere within, damped the fire, unplugged the white noise of social good humour. The usual fight, after the last clear-up, the face washing, tooth brushing, the climbing up to bed. Lying side by side below the ceiling:

You should have joined in.

I liked watching.

You could have played along, if only for my sake.

I couldn't have, if you must know, I didn't want to.

You could have without wanting; you might have liked it.

No – this angrier now, sharper – that's not how wanting works; that's not what *could* means.

None of it needed to be said; both sides of the argument, well rehearsed, would have echoed around their separate thoughts in any case, unspoken. The usual fight; only it left them unhappier than usual, given the uplift of the occasion, the distance fallen. Tomas felt particularly desperate, far from home: and thought, if ever there was a chance, if ever there was a chance, of breaking through, it is now, it was tonight. Howard suffered only the usual, hereditary low spirits, baffled pride, habitual self-loathing.

Afterwards Howard couldn't remember exactly when he realized this was a way out, a chance. There were times of course when he considered the matter differently, but more and more as the weeks passed, the new year began with its inevitable repetitions and its added burdens, he realized something had to be done about both situations, lover and daughter, the press of people against him, the reproach implicit in their intimacy. It occurred to him, at last, that the two situations could be used to solve each other. The conviction slowly formed that he had been going about the problem, for years now, the wrong way round. Tomas had always struck him, in spite of his arguments to the contrary, as an escape from his own unhappiness, a hand-up. He had let himself be seduced by Tomas's insistent enthusiasms, easy contentment; it seemed so obvious that the answer lay in more not less of whatever stores of joy his lover possessed. But perhaps the problem was really Tomas's; Tomas couldn't accept life for what it was, the necessary valuations. All his talk of joining in was really a coded way of saying, Don't look. Let's pretend. Howard's great virtue was that he had the courage of looking. He could do without palliative habits. He could do without other people, just as he had learned to do without his mother – whose image was never far from his thoughts at the dark turning of the year.

A slight incident from that dinner party stuck in his mind. Francesca, like her mother, had a habit of lying down after a meal on hard floor. She was rather heavy-handedly making herself at home in this manner, when she suddenly let out a sharp, almost fearful cry of 'Oh, my God', in a rising cadence, which turned in the end to laughter. She had just seen Tomas's mountain bike suspended above her, from its hook in the ceiling; the bristled black tyres turning slowly above her head. Tomas followed her glance and laughed too. That bike had always irritated Howard; it seemed so aggressive, heedless; but before he could get out a sharp word, the moment had passed.

On New Year's Day the four of them went ice skating in Central Park; the thaw had set in again, and the ice puddled over – there weren't many people about. The perfect unreflecting snow had melted into browns and gleams, a dispiriting lapse from pristinity. Howard and Frannie sat out most of the time, drinking hot chocolates on the terrace above. Both felt little twitches of envy: it seemed possible to be happier than they were; the evidence was below them. The soft collapse of air in the rush of watery skates just reached them there, like a sound muffled by memory – as Tomas wheeled Annie about from hand to hand. 'So what do you think of him?' Howard asked, playing the father. 'Is it very strange for you?'

'I like him,' she smiled rather sweetly into a corner of her mouth, her mug; embarrassed, a girl telling the truth to an elder, practising confession, adulthood. 'He's so – happy and – blond. Not what I expected, no offence.' Then more quickly, 'You know what I mean. Blue-eyed, gung-ho.'

Perhaps she has a crush on him, he thought. Quite likely, girl like that, so proud and plain, allowed to play sister to a handsome boyish stranger who's out of the question. They parted at the first glow of dark in the sharpening cold; mother and daughter, lover and lover, each to their own side of the Park. That natural sinking of spirits in the set of the sun; a retreat beneath the surface. Tomas kicked a leftover hunk of ice into the road; enquired if Francesca had said anything –

about him that is. Mainly he wanted to know if Howard had asked – if Howard had been curious, considered it important, to know how the two halves of his life, old and new, were knitting.

'Yes, she did.' Howard couldn't remember the exact phrase. 'She said you were very charmingly . . . not quite what she *expected* of me. Aryan.' Now he was teasing; perhaps she *had* said something along those lines, he couldn't be sure. It's the impression she left behind: of the natural surprise a nice Jewish girl from New York City might feel at discovering an old Wasp father, his German lover. He hadn't really meant to be untruthful, or even unkind. But it shocked him how quickly Tomas went into his shell, the slapped look of his red face. 'She liked you, Tomas'; he added, making amends, 'I think she has a little crush.' But the deed was done: Tomas's embarrassment could not be soothed, lifted; he had been caught out for an offence he had nothing to do with, could do nothing about; a sin like the sin of class, accent, both too deep and ungrounded to admit expiation. It was a cold walk home; they couldn't shake off the cold of it even when they got in.

Not long after, something rather unpleasant happened at lunch. The school cafeteria separated teachers and students by a glass wall; most of the faculty didn't really dare to look on the far side of it, at the wilderness of youth. They made the most of every civil interlude. Howard had no real intimates among his fellow teachers; rather, he played the part of Eiron, or Greek commentary, on the general action, regardless of company. In short, he sat down to lunch wherever there was an empty seat; but rarely had the feeling of intruder. His conversation, he thought, was sufficiently ornamental. Mr Englander the English teacher – a tall smooth pink man, who looked genially inflatable rather than fat, and was rather a favourite among his female pupils – held forth one day about *Slaughterhouse Five*, the text being discussed by his senior elective. Howard had read the book, many years ago; never thought much of it, and began gently to bait Mr Englander in his presumption of its genius. The conversation quickly lost tone; Mr Englander had begun to puff. Much as he disliked these little vanities of the English department, Howard decided to pour oil over the waters.

'I should say now, I don't remember much of the book; of course, Mr Englander, you're in a better position to rate it. But one passage struck me in particular as very fine. It had to do with Lot's wife, praised her for turning back to look at the ruins of Gomorrah. How "human" it seemed of her to look; I believe that was the word. I remember thinking at the time: it was a neat emblem for a kind of mercy, or sympathy, necessary in any judgement about the Third Reich. For example, and there are others that occur to me, the doctors who experimented upon the incarcerated Jews. They are often held up as the bogeymen of the clinical instinct; but it has always seemed to me a very *human* ambition, rather fine and self-sacrificing in its way, to wish to experiment upon man. A natural progression of the desire to know, to look; without flinching, or pretended delicacy –'

'Goodness me,' Mr Englander interrupted, 'what a silly thing to say.' In fact, their little argument had a history behind it. Howard had taken Mr Englander to task, a few years before, over defending a colleague who had gotten himself into difficulties with one of the students. Well, Howard didn't have any compassion for the guy – the sex instinct wasn't something he sympathized with; he knew the harm it could do, especially to children; and didn't have much trouble controlling it himself. But Mr Englander was glad of the chance to cast a shot back at him from higher ground. Neither one of them ever guessed how much they had in common. Mr Englander's sleek full face suggested a gentle greed that was easily satisfied. Howard's own excesses, his pock-marked hanging cheeks, the spill of fat at his hips, seemed evidence of the fact that he'd gotten more than he wanted from the world. This, in his way, is what he had been trying to describe: the refinement of curiosity that can dispense with natural feelings or appetites.

Rachel Weintraub, the History teacher, a pretty young woman with a sickle-moon-faced shape, and a chin with a very definite point to make, added with heavy smiling civility, 'You're a sick man, Howard; a real Connecticut Nazi.'

Howard felt the blood go thin in his face; he struggled for wind. Perhaps he hadn't made himself clear; perhaps the words had somehow got in the way, as they do, proved too big and clumsy for the thought. He had offered them, foolishly, recklessly, his most intimate and delicate nature – that centre or core of being, in which alone he could judge himself with mercy. While all the rest; just look at it, just look at his life, that great expanse of cruelty, neglect, impoverished affections. A human weariness – worse, that laziness with which he excused himself to Tomas, so blighting and unforgivable, the sheer waste of it seemed wider in its way than any millions of deaths, of days. Yet in spite of all that he possessed a certain fineness, thin as a knife's edge, barely discernible to the naked eye, but vital, even noble, undulled, uncompromised, at his heart. Just this once, and briefly, he had unsheathed it; he felt as if the tip had been snapped.

'I don't like to think, Ms Weintraub,' he said, breathing slowly, carefully choosing the words, 'of your state of mind when you come to regret that remark.'

And yet he himself rather felt the sting of it; their reproof lingered with him all week and awakened a miserable sense of guilt. He hadn't for years felt so childishly rebuked, and remembered that first winter after his mother died. He used to run around with a couple of glue-sniffers from junior high, real wits, real high-rollers. His father sat him down after he found out: they'd been breaking windows, smearing a few funny words on the school walls, nothing much. Once, perhaps, a swastika; it was a statement of style, no more. 'I want you to understand that it was evil,' his father said – it or him, Howard couldn't exactly remember. 'I don't know where you pick that kind of thing up. Not from me, not from me,' he insisted, adding, 'I just thank God your mother isn't around to see this.' His father seemed more worked up about it than he was; broke into tears half-way through, and Howard left him there, listened to him from the stairs. He wanted to be able to get away if the old man came out, belt in hand. Still, Howard listened; pity comes hard to sons. Even at that age, he thought he should have the guts to listen. This is what he meant to praise in Lot's wife: the courage heartlessly to observe.

He wanted to put himself at the center of their lives – if only to feel them pulling at him, to feel his power of disappointing them. The desire seemed harmless enough, at least at first. He *was* the centre, the link; it would have been cruel to see the others get on without him. And yet – already he sensed alternative currents running between the three of them; gossip seemed to reach him at one remove, whispery with the distance travelled. He heard, from his periphery, the hum of a central life, felt its warmth. There were phone calls Tomas answered in low tones, taking the handset with him up to bed. Later, calls on the cell; unexplained. It seemed to Howard beneath his dignity to enquire. Pieces of news echoed strangely; reverberated with the little distortions of the twice-told tale. False surprises. Frannie heard from Harvard; she was in. Tomas only nodded his head. Maybe Howard was being paranoid, understandably jealous; maybe the ordinary passage of any life, closely attended to, yields these strange muffles and clanks, unexplained noises. When he said, I'm going over to the Rosenblums to celebrate, Tomas let him go. That little remark might have done its job; such embarrassments have a way of sticking. In any case, working life had begun again: everyone was busy, that quiet shadowed calm cast by Christmas and New Year had passed. Perhaps he was only disappointed at how his ordinary, unsurprising weeks revived, went on.

No; somehow everyone was conspiring to push him out from the middle of his own life; and he was conspiring with them, helplessly. The days were getting longer; he had a half-hour, an hour, after school, of walking in the Park, while night grew up around him like a rising sea. He had begun to put off coming home. Snow still littered the grass; most of the lawns were fenced off; the footpaths strewn with grit. Once a streak of colour in the gloom caught his eye, some way ahead; one of those striped scarves that reminded Howard of peppermint candy. Tomas had one; Howard could just make out the bulk of a man pushing a bicycle, turning at a bend. Howard, relenting, almost called out; then he saw the two women, slighter, emerging to the side of him as the path straightened. Howard began to run after; the shock of each step seemed to chip away at his feet, they were so cold. The beat of his breath and heart filled the air; it was impossible nobody saw him, nobody turned. He stopped to catch his wind at the top of a bridge; whoever it was had gone, but he could make out dim figures climbing the twisted path of a hill. A mock castle stood against the side of it, overlooking a lake, half frozen – dark sheets of ice floating on lighter ripples. Bands in summer played at the amphitheatre against the shore. He was sure it was them; the longer figure walked in the slow unbroken gait of a man with a bike. Howard set off again, calling out, hey, hey, hey! He only wanted to make sure, to see how far these people would go to ignore him, what they got up to behind his back. They must have seen him coming, heard him, long before. But by the time he got to the top, sweating already into the neck of his tied collar, nobody was there, and the paths split darkly away below. He wanted to say, you're nothing without me; you have no bonds. I'll tell you one thing: don't let him see you down; he won't have a clue; he thinks you're making it up; he thinks it's just a matter of will. You're welcome to him; you've got no idea. He's brutal; you've seen what they're like, of all people.

The way out eventually fell into his lap. Some Friday nights Annie assisted the cantor at her local synagogue; she asked Howard if the two of them would like to come round and hear her sing. Maybe they could get some supper afterwards – at one of those kosher Italians dotting the Upper East Side. 'Come on, Howard, play along with me.' She meant – humour me, in my dressing up, in my religion. The girl he knew wanted nothing to do with any of that . . . scene. Strange, if not worse, how these convictions had a way of thinning over time. 'I'd love to,' he said, 'but I don't think Tomas is persuadable. He never feels quite comfortable in synagogues.' True, in its way: Tomas could never sit still anywhere, and churches, mosques, temples struck him as desperately dated, out of fashion. Still, the shocked silence at the end of the line told him his remark had hit home. 'Well, suit yourself,' was all she said; an odd phrase, Howard thought later, given the circumstances.

In the end, he came alone; got drunk on red wine, one of his binges. After Frannie went to bed, the two old friends shared another bottle, sitting together on the couch. Her singing had moved him; it seemed so fine and human, free of the ugliness habitual to most gestures, accents, explanations. The delight Annie took in her outgrown tradition conveyed a warmer irony than his own. Irony, in fact, was the wrong word for it: joy itself was a kind of honesty. (These people had always understood that.) It made his detachment seem stingy, if not worse, wilful and slightly mad: the attitude of a boy with his hands over his ears, refusing to listen. Her sharp little face was as small as his mother's, as he remembered it, when she lay against the white of the hospital sheets, so thin. On good days they went for walks in the grounds; his father used to lift her in the air, with his hands on her hips, like a dancer – she was almost proud of how wonderfully light she had grown.

They sat sloping together on the orange cushions, which needed restuffing. Annie had to look up to meet his eyes. Howard, in a concessional mood, wanted to kiss her; she was such a beautiful lonely woman, so brave. He wanted to do what she wanted; it's what he thought she wanted, what he had always thought she had always wanted. He leaned and fell over and caught the corner of her lips; he wouldn't let go. For once he was grasping at life, at straws. A certain clumsiness, the sodden weight of his body, left her intentions unclear for a minute. But he persisted beyond that minute, more forcefully, his hand pressed hard between her legs with what had become the unmistakable ardour of revenge. The grunt of her breathing deepened with the first pain of sexual pleasure; until she slipped out from under him and he came down sideways on the couch. The look of untouched, *untempted*, unsurprised pity in her – 'no no please no Howard please' – instantly sobered him. He sat up and knew she thought she'd taken the measure of him again, in that awful jealous contest of human intimacies. 'This isn't what you want,' she repeated. 'This isn't what you want.'

For once, however, he refused the obvious retreat. A thin line of ache had awoken in his breast, like the first sharp pain of a healing wound after the numbness of an anaesthetic. And he offered instead, as if rehearsing the argument, 'We would never be happy together.'

She said, 'No. Of course, no.'

He said, 'We aren't the kind of people to be happy with other people.'

She hesitated, and then, almost apologetically, 'I have Frannie.'

'Yes.' He nodded; that was true; it never for a minute occurred to him that he had Tomas. What he meant was the full equality of loving. 'When you', he began, 'first – spent the night.' Her face showed its unmistakable age. In the flush of wine, every blemish of her skin had reddened; these lay like thin paint over her cheek, rough to the touch. Physically now, she inspired in him nothing but the purest, most childish revulsion. She was nodding back at him, encouraging. 'Were you willing?' He feared her answer terribly. The failure of his memory, after their first night together, had shocked him more than he realized. The fact that she had called two or three times a day; that he hadn't answered. That she had pushed letters under his door. It was as if she had walked across a field in the snow, and left no footprints. His memory stretched out white and cold in every direction. He thought, if you are capable of forgetting, you are capable of anything. All kinds of burial.

She hid her mouth between her thumb and forefinger – another characteristic gesture. She treated everything as an intellectual proposition, with honest puzzling. 'I can't remember very well any more. Afterwards it seemed so much less important than what was happening to me. I admit I was selfish. But then again, you always got so low around that time of year, so needy. You were very drunk; much drunker than me. It wasn't entirely without pity, I'll say that much in my defence. Was I willing?' she repeated, and ventured at last, smiling slightly, 'I was definitely able; I would say, probably more than you.' His old phrase for her came into his head: you always take me firmly by the hand. It seemed so comically short of the truth.

Partly what he felt was relief. He was innocent, after all, as he'd always supposed; that was the main thing. What the snow covered up was only other people's tracks. These criss-crossed him mercilessly. Everything, it turned out, had happened against his will. Every involvement. He knew that something about the whole business had angered or wounded him – violence had been done, bereavements inflicted, terrible entanglements – which he had not yet brought to the surface and might not need to now. He said to her at last, 'I don't think I want to see you any more, after all. Either one of you. You'll understand.' And then the beauty of the lie first struck him, his experiment in detachment, both lies acting in concert, and he added, 'Tomas feels very uncomfortable' – he gestured at the apartment, the mess of books, his daughter asleep behind a closed door – 'about all this.' To persuade her, he managed to confess, 'he's all I have, he's the only thing keeping me here', almost as if it were true. 'I have to . . . hunker down.'

'I don't think – I don't think Francesca will accept that, now. I don't think I can ask her to.'

He kissed her quickly on the cheek. She smelt of singing, very rich; the stench of singing gone cold, in her armpits, in the fading heat of her breasts, rising along her throat. 'We all learn to accept everything,' he said.

Tomas wasn't back when Howard got home. He showered, changed, brushed the stain of red wine from his teeth. Things hadn't gone far enough; it was time to get the whole thing over with. No doubt that drunken kiss was only a way out. You're better off on your own, advancing inward: that way you're sure of being understood. He realized, of course, that depression is also the instrument of depression: a tool that serves in digging into itself, a deepening device. He might as well use it while he had the chance.

In bed that night, under the low ceiling, he said to Tomas, 'I thought you should know, Annie and I' – it wasn't like him to want to soften the blow, but he tried – 'resumed our former intimacy.' Tomas rolled over on his elbow and looked at him. He sensed already something wrong, but couldn't tell what kind of wrong it was: something hurtful, or something untrue. Howard said, 'We got drunk.' The lie when it came seemed simpler than he'd supposed, more obvious. It had, after all, once been the truth. 'We made love.'

'I don't understand.' Howard lay on his back, looking up. Once, in the summer holidays, years before, they had borrowed a car and taken it up to Maine. Stayed at a friend's house on the shore; a two-bedroom shack a hundred yards from the rollers. The makeshift beauty of seasides. They hung their bathing towels over the curtainless rods when they wanted to sleep late, and awoke with dry sand in their faces. A rotten boarded path ran to the water; Tomas spent the afternoons fixing it up. Howard read, tried his hand at keeping a journal, began a few poems, which untangled into sketches, loving cartoons: of Tomas, of the house, of the water, ships, gulls. In the early days, when Tomas was still jealously in love and Howard could still pretend to himself that he was only letting the kid tag along. They were both unhappy to be going; and fought childishly over breakfast, over the clear-up. The sour mood persisted on the long road home, only Howard didn't seem to mind it much. He had the wheel, since Tomas couldn't drive; and whatever was said, he kept half his mind on the straight lines running away from him, splitting the asphalt; the traffic coming against him, or overtaking. Tomas's reproaches hardly touched him: you have to talk to me, you have to tell me what you feel, I can't help you if you don't tell me what you feel. Etc. Howard remembered vividly the quiet of his own detachment. It's what he liked, there was no shame in that: the indifference of control.

He said, absolutely free of passion or any semblance of subterfuge, 'What you have to understand, Tomas, is the chance I have; the chance I can't afford to miss. To be part of a family. My mother died, as you know, when I was very young – just at the age when I first knew what I had, I lost it.' He often took this tone with Tomas, patient, pedantic. It was like a scar of his profession – the habit of instruction – the brutal repetitions of gesture, of condescension, in a life spent among children. 'My father wasn't very good at – warmth. He wasn't very warm. There has always existed between us – between Annie and me – strong attractions. I've never known anything like it with another woman.' More gently, more kindly still: 'I've never known anything like it with another man. I don't want to lose this chance, again.' And then, a little sly dig at Tomas, mockingly sentimental, a wound too subtle for him to understand. 'I know, more than anyone, how *precious* family life can be. When you get older, when you realize the way *we* lead our lives, what seems so free, so easy to us, so desirable, will come to appear – very poor, very empty, almost adolescent. Annie and I talked, openly, without illusion. She isn't – she's also – rather lonely. We decided we could come to some kind of an arrangement, something that looked very much like, that wasn't far short of, loving. Something we could live with.' Tomas hadn't said a word; he was weeping, as he always did, both childishly and almost painlessly. Tears reddened his face, and left little sticky tracks across his heightened colour, which looked like blood. Howard turned towards him at last, and put his hand to the side of the young man's cheek. 'You're better off without me. You've outgrown me.' Afterwards, he dried his palm carefully on a corner of his bedsheet, so that Tomas couldn't see. He couldn't tell whether Tomas believed him or not, and didn't, after all, much care. Two birds with one stone, he thought.

The Rosenblums stopped calling. Annie, at least, following her confession, had decided to give him a little breathing space; that was something of a relief. Tomas left shortly after; it had always been Howard's apartment. They spent a silent, curiously peaceful week together, even shared a bed, as he packed up his things and found somewhere else to stay. He didn't have much; the bike descended from the ceiling, departed. There was nowhere in that long studio to hide, except the bathroom; and the night before Tomas left, Howard found him sobbing heavily there, sitting on the pot with the lid down. 'I talked to Annie,' he said at last. 'I called her; I had to talk to her. We had coffee; all three of us. She said it isn't true; she said none of it's true. You're just trying to get rid of us.' The sight of him was strangely moving; Howard reached out a hand and touched the top of his hair. 'Poor kid,' he said. 'I'll be all right.' Tomas stood up suddenly and pushed him back against the opposite wall; the top of his head cracked against the bathroom mirror, which also cracked. More violence. He felt the danger of his weight on the sink. Something was bound to give. Tomas had him pinned by the hands; his puffed red face an inch away – the sheer ugly brutish bulk of him plain as day, looming up. 'You need help,' he said at last, and let go. The marks on Howard's wrists never bled, but seemed to flake, scab none the less; these rubbed off finally only a week after Tomas had gone.

He thought of taping the mirror, but it seemed unlucky, so he threw the shards away. Then he never got round to replacing them. Whenever he stood up after washing his face, for a second he thought that the image before him was his own: those dirty black medicine shelves, mostly empty, a few pill-boxes, his blade, a bar of wrapped soap.

SPRING

A Girl as Fresh as Spring

I

Three years ago Roger Bathurst came into the English office with swollen red eyes. He squinted thickly through them; they lent an air of general discomfort to his narrow face, already scratchy with a beard. This was the old English office, before the renovations: a long broom cupboard lit at the end by a single high window, which displayed a patch of tree and sky no bigger than a dishcloth hung out to dry on a washing line and blowing in the wind. Desks lined either wall, and Stu Englander called over his shoulder, 'take a fastball inside, hey?' Stu liked to put on ordinary-Joe airs with Roger, who was an honest, intelligent, perpetually disgruntled Mets fan. 'Leave it. I'm looking for a book. I'm blind.' Roger had a student in tow, and the girl was meant to help him find it: a copy of *Astrophel and Stella* Bathurst liked to quote from, particularly the last lines of the first sonnet. Middle of third period on a late-fall Tuesday. Roger was teaching freshman English, creative writing, and concentrating, as usual, on telling them what not to do.

The leaves had turned; one or two occasionally fell brightly across the compressed view and disappeared. Stu was enjoying a pleasant dose of restless longing. He never relished the weather so much when he was out in it: he liked the pinch of confinement, the way it suggested he had vaster ambitions than these narrow walls. Roger stood with his weight on one leg like he wanted to talk. 'I was cooking, cutting chillies last night, and didn't wash my hands after. Now this, even a day later. Go figure.' The girl, standing on tiptoe, broke Stuart's line of sight picking a book from Roger's shelf; she had to stretch her longest finger to catch the top of the binding, and inch it by degrees till it tipped off the edge. Rather below the average height; curly brown hair, some of it caught inside the collar of her blouse; an oval face. Even with her lips closed in shy concentration he caught the faint full suggestion of braces. Stu leaned over to meet his colleague's eye; they were never intimate, but managed to keep up an everyday banter that seemed, to Stuart at least, a more satisfying language than that of friendship. Roger hung around in the doorway while the girl returned to class. 'Honest to God, it's like looking through dishwater.' He put his weight on his shoulder against the door jamb; they often enjoyed these respites from the pressures of the day. It surprised Stuart how happy they made him, such pauses. An easy companionable minute, of whatever kind, he often reflected, is a great pleasure in itself.

'Rather a winsome creature,' he said at last. Stu had a pink, unlived-in face, slightly puffed outwards but otherwise untouched by time (a terrifying omission). Only his steel-grey hair, combed carefully back, suggested his age. This produced a disconcerting day-for-night effect, like a painting by Magritte; a false cheeriness.

'What, Rachel? I never notice what they look like.' Obscurely satisfied, Roger turned blindly into the hall. Why it gives men pleasure to get these things commented on, Stuart thought, I'll never know. And yet, the rest of that long spring, Stu's eyes sought out her oval face when the streams of kids passed him in the hallway. He supposed she was fashionable, in a clean-cut, rather virginal way: she wore her socks high, her blouses open at the neck, and her various skirts fell just above the knee. The knee, as it happens, always struck him chiefly as a structural joint, rather overrated in the literature, and not so much titillating as suggestive of the mechanical difficulties underlying our every function. To see the bone beneath her skin unshape and shape itself again at her every step moved him to a kind of pity. Her face, above it, was invariably compressed into a frown, and she tended to walk doubled over under a backpack square with books. She struck him as a conscientious girl struggling somewhat to keep up. Perhaps there was a sexual taint to the sweetness of his sympathy for her; but even so, the sight of her always warmed him slightly, like a mug in the hand on a cold day. He told himself he would have felt the same pity looking at the boy he was forty years before – though he suspected she would taste more richly those experiences which for the most part he had failed to suffer for.

At first he didn't recognize her, when, three years later, Rachel Kranz signed up to his senior seminar on Shakespeare. The school had recently changed heads. The old guy, Hugo Bantling, also a baseball man, had been generally despised: he was not only a bully, but a drunk and a lech. His saving grace, in the opinion of men like Stu Englander, was, that in addition to all these things, he was lazy, and pretty much left his teachers to do their own work. Though it was true the females suffered under him, whether they were pretty or not, in different ways for either condition. Hugo's single preoccupation was the baseball field. It was the only part of school life he took seriously, and kept in meticulous order: that diamond green, cut out in grassy chalk and surrounded by fresh earth, sweet with loose dust almost the colour of ripe peach.

There was a second English office on the eastern end of Bertelmeyer Hall, a small room heavily carpeted and lined with books, and mockingly referred to as the Winter Palace. Teachers occasionally used the deep foam couch for a nap in an off period; or sat back in the armchair by the window – to read, or pretend to read, or to remember the days when nothing seemed sweeter to them than the combination of a book and a chair and a window. You could see the baseball field stretched out below; and, after school, the boys looping the ball along the lines gravity sketched out across the green spaces. Sometimes, you heard the gunshot of leather on wood, or the duller percussion of leather on leather; or the unmistakable public disturbance of a base hit, a stolen second, a play at the plate. During fire drills, Bantling hated to see the diamond trampled on by hundreds of no-good slouchy kids, and used to parade along the third base line to keep them off the green – while the bells rang and the traffic of students jammed against the (supposedly) burning walls. Maybe it was just as well the guy was retired, though now the grass grew ragged round the basepaths, and on warms days kids lay together wherever they liked over the patchy infield, or threw those frisbees long and slow across the pitch.

Dr Betty Holroyd, the new head, a forty-something woman with tough dyed-blond hair, had decided to overhaul the place from scratch. Radical renovations were under way, architectural and human: a number of the older teachers had been asked to consider an early retirement. Luckily, Stu Englander had a passionate following among the higher-minded kids – one of the perks of teaching poetry; and so far, at the age of fifty-nine, he'd been spared. Which didn't mean he wasn't looking over his shoulder. The thought of retirement terrified him. His wife, Mary Louise, two years older, had already gone part time at the arts foundation that she helped to administer. Stu feared that he had lost the ability, the gift of youth, to fill days on his own; and his relations with his wife no longer prompted and sustained his interest in the world. Sometimes he felt their marriage had reached a kind of intellectual dryness so pervasive it felt like burning.

Mary Louise was a very fat woman with a certain formidable elegance, the shapeliness of a filled vase: one of those Southerners who, in the course of her adult lifetime in the city, without changing her accent or manner one jot, has become a real New Yorker. They shared a one-bedroom apartment high on the Upper West Side, not far from Columbia. Mary Louise maintained an impressive unflagging interest in the lives and enthusiasms of the young. Now she spent her idle afternoons sitting in coffee shops and getting into arguments with strangers, mostly students, who, Stu was amazed to note, rarely seemed to mind. They didn't have a kitchen to speak of, and their bedroom seemed to have been bricked up around the double bed, but the sitting room stretched long and square with windows on two sides. These overlooked the traffic of Broadway on the one hand, and a few dirty trees on 117th Street. The room itself possessed what Stu liked to describe, among their rare guests, as 'a carefully distressed appearance of order'. Aside from the books lining one wall, there was the clutter of Mary Louise's sculpture collection. Mostly her own pieces – a rather disconcerting assortment of isolated limbs, heads, segments of all kinds – mixed with the work of some of her friends.

Mary Louise was a member of the Art Students League and had been for thirty years, almost since they first moved to New York together after college. She had majored in Fine Arts, and had asked around for a space to work in – they didn't have much money – and somebody had mentioned the League. Free for amateurs and professionals alike; Stu couldn't say a word against it. The studios were in a Gothic marble-faced building squeezed between high-rise office blocks south of the Park. 'Unless I paid for it,' Stu sometimes said, 'I don't think I'd get up the get up and go to make it but twice a year.' Partly exasperated; not without admiration. It was the kind of venture Stuart quickly grew out of: useless and improving at once. Something would come up, and he'd let the ease of not going persuade him that not going was what he wanted to do. But Mary Louise went every Saturday morning, 'come hell or high water': she was strict about attendance. In life, in general, she liked to say, she was strict about attendance. Attendance never struck Stu as such great shakes. He winced a little when she said it, one of his wife's less refined nuggets of wisdom; and from time to time, when they might have made other plans, he tried to unpersuade her. Sometimes they had nothing else to do and he didn't want her 'honourable busyness', which is what he acknowledged it was, to make him feel slack. Even so, on the odd sunny morning, Stuart used to wander down through Central Park to meet his wife for lunch. Both her persistence and the way she 'hung on to her artiness after college, unlike some' (as she put it) were sources of pleasure to him.

But the sculptures themselves occasionally oppressed Stu. Their careful, frozen disarray seemed a poor compensation for childlessness. They had never decided to be childless; at least, Stu hadn't. (Another instance, perhaps, in which his wife had proved stronger, more persistent, less liable to let things drift.) It seemed to have happened in spite of them, with the inevitability of time's progression. They had 'gotten' childless in the same way they had gotten old, by imperceptible degrees. As Mary Louise had often declared, in her bright unflappable drawl, 'We'll have a new baby when we have a new bedroom.' They had a life in which it was impossible to put a child.

When Rachel Kranz lifted her white and dutiful hand to signal attendance, Stu marked her 'present' without a second thought. He was particular in these matters, and carried his green-bound attendance book, tucked under one arm, to every class. He spent the first minute of instruction calling out names, sharply and clearly and without distinguishing among favourites, and lightly recording the answers on soft paper with a thin-nibbed pen. Of course, she had grown up a little; her top lip no longer swelled with the irregular pressure of steel tracks. But she still wore her hair lightly curled down to her shoulders, and she had retained that stillness, that old-fashioned prettifaction, the air of someone gently preserved, which had struck Stuart so forcibly three years before. He noted her at last at the end of class, as she filed her way unhurried to the door – not afraid to catch his eye, and ready to smile, however briefly, at him. She might have been a girl from any age, he thought; it wouldn't surprise him to unclasp a locket and see her oval face in it, dimly photographed, smiling back. To see her picture, etched in thin lines, on the wafer-thin frontispiece of a novel by Walter Scott, in some marbled and heavily bound Victorian edition. But he did not answer her look; it surprised him too quickly into melancholy.

In the seven-minute breathing space between that class and the next, he tried to puzzle out the source of it. For one thing, he suspected that her careful preservation came at a price; no doubt she laboured under the rather heavy burden of someone else's sense of her virtue. What he read as her willingness to please struck him as an unhappy gift. He'd be curious to meet her father. That reflection led him easily to the next, and he remembered his old friend Roger Bathurst. Shortly after the little incident in the English office – with the girl and the book and his swollen red eyes – Roger had failed to show up for work. It was the Tuesday following the long Easter weekend. They asked Stu to call him at home, and when he didn't answer the phone, or show up again the day after, he took it on himself to stop by Roger's flat. (Not, of course, that they had been particularly close; only no one else on the faculty seemed to know Bathurst any better.) Roger lived near the school grounds, in a two-bedroom apartment carved out of one of the neighbourhood's Victorian gabled cottages. Roger used to walk his two black labs early in the morning before school along the kerbless roads, smoking a cigar and pretending the day didn't have to happen. Occasionally, coming uphill from the subway station, Stu ran into him. They would stop and talk; Stu liked to feel the carelessness of the dogs in his hands before heading into the office.

The way to Roger's place was just unfamiliar enough that Stu had to check the road signs sticking out of the grass in the corner yards. Heavy oaks cut off most of the bright spring sunshine; nothing but dusty drifts of it fell through the fingers of the trees. Stu felt the sharpness in his stomach; he was supposed to be eating lunch. Schooldays left you vulnerable to the power of routines. He rang Roger's bell and while he waited, sat down among the leaves and twigs on his stoop, and looked out on the road. He thought, if Roger were dead, I'd be hearing the dogs now. He listened. Only the intricate movements of a spring breeze; a car turning slowly in the lane ahead. From where he sat he could just make out the broken wire fence of the school football field, a dirty square of grass on raised grounds just outside campus. Mr Arbus, the Computer teacher who doubled as the Lacrosse coach, was leading his boys through drills. Where Stu grew up in small town Ohio, nobody played lacrosse; the only thing that really mattered was football. Not that Stu played football either. It astonished him how little he had changed. His patience, his delight in outward views, in wasted minutes; in this powerful spring loneliness and flowering silence. Unless it was only perceptions, very particular, that refused to change, being too pure, while everything else aged around them. Including the people perceiving. Stu used to be such a lean and hungry youth; now he'd got fat, fat as Mr Arbus with the whistle round his neck, though not as fat as his wife. He stood up painfully to ring the bell again.

And again sat down to wait. It seemed to him then that the answer to broader questions than the whereabouts of his colleague was being deferred. It consoled him greatly that he still had recourse to these pleasant moments; he lived, as he put it to himself, more and more for the minutes offstage. He thought of De Quincey on discovering his sister's death. How he stared out their bedroom window across the broad English fields of summer, and imagined himself briefly, in the sunshine, running through it – indifferent to his present loss, the girl dead in the bed beside him. Or perhaps Stuart misremembered the passage; occasionally his own experiences entangled themselves with the books he had read, grew inextricably together. And the line 'welcome summer with thy sunne soft' ran through his thoughts. Yes, he was ready for the fullness of the year. He repeated it now, under his breath, 'welcome summer with thy sunne soft'. These echoes wakened in his thoughts throughout the day, like leaves briefly roused by the passage of wind. He had lived a very plain life, yet very rich in literary additions. Well, Roger wasn't home.

Stu stood up now and walked slowly down the neighbourhood street, in and out of shadows, letting go his loneliness bit by bit, till the clamouring schoolhouse rose before him.

By the next day, everyone knew what had happened to Roger Bathurst. He'd run off with a girl, one of his students, just turned eighteen. God, the little spice of envy in the air in the faculty lounge, how it sharpened these recriminations. The women, of course, took the matter solely as an affront; only the men harboured mixed feelings. Stuart himself said at one point, 'Well, he's gone over to the other side' – hoping, by such subtle vagaries, to say what he wanted to say about his old friend without getting caught. People nodded; yes, it was a sick thing to do, there was no turning back. Though what Stuart meant, of course, was that Roger had gone over to the side of youth – to the hungry unruly majority, who had their long wide lives before them, who swelled the hallways and the cafeteria and the baseball field and had their way everywhere but the quiet classrooms where age presided. Only the Biology teacher, Howard Peasbody, had caught his meaning, and gave him a sharp look. He'd been particularly disgusted by the affair. 'I taught the girl,' he said. 'Clumsy, too tall, not particularly bright. Always breaking Petri dishes. It required every ounce of such scholarly mercy as I possess to give her a C – for effort, as they say. I don't suppose he'll find her company enlightening.'

Stuart didn't answer at first. There'd been a time he thought they might deepen their acquaintance into friendship. His own father had taught Science in middle school; Stuart naturally admired the clinical mind. And Howard Peasbody possessed a wide frame of reference, exact tastes. Once, during a faculty seminar, Howard had quoted Ashbery at him. Dr Holroyd, the new head, wanted to say a few words to some of the older staff, on what she called the Challenge of the Younger Generation – the new crop of teachers, some of them hired fresh out of college. A source, occasionally, of envy, of irritation. 'Sure,' she said, 'they make mistakes, they learn, and it's your job to give them a hand. But don't forget they have something to teach you, too.' She was appealing to them for renewed commitment, replenished passion. 'Ask yourself,' she said, 'am I running on fumes? Do I really care any more?' This was just the kind of talk Stuart hated; he muttered, yes, and no, to himself, in answer. And Howard, sensing a kindred spirit, had leaned over and whispered: 'A look of glass stops you and you walk on shaken: was I the perceived? Did they notice me, this time, as I am, or is it postponed again?' Stuart smiled: very apt, this is just what he liked, the way art lent style to the boorishness of life. But somehow nothing came of such comradely intimations. Perhaps, he was too competitive; Stuart feared being outdone; but he heard, in his wife's voice, a kinder judgement given: Howard was a cold fish; he was a warm one. The younger man's remark on Roger's 'defection' seemed to confirm this intuition; and amidst his heavier regret, Stuart acknowledged, with an internal gesture as slight as a nod, the forfeit of their chance at friendship. His allegiance was clear; and he answered Howard coldly at last, 'We all find our enlightenment where we can.'

Stuart remembered talking to Bathurst about Dickens earlier that year, after a department meeting. The English faculty had just decided to keep *Great Expectations* on the junior syllabus, preferring it once more to the longer, heavier *David Copperfield*. Roger had collared Stuart afterwards; he wanted to unload, and he put his arm around Stu's shoulder, a rare gesture of fraternity, and led him to the Winter Palace. Roger was furious, in mid-rant; and Stu stood up to watch the end of baseball practice, leaning against the cold of the shut window. The coach was knocking flyballs back, with a runner on third waiting for the catch, and the outfield shallow preparing for the throw home. An early-spring day, a little brisk. Clouds came and went overhead, interrupting the sunshine with pearly shadows. Only the coach and the base runner had worked up a sweat and removed their warm-up tops. It always delighted Stuart to see the elaborate patience of the ball descending; the unhurried pace of gravity bringing it down, and then the instant human fury after the catch. Roger began to declaim passages from *David Copperfield*, bending the book beneath his heavy thumb. He had the gift of reading without changing tone; he simply used the stuff of his ordinary speech: his thick New York accent, his full-tongued mouth, his exasperated insistence. Stuart hardly listened; it seemed to him that Roger's indignation was only an excuse for a subtle form of boasting. They amused him, such high pedagogical passions, such vain opinions.

Well, and now Roger had disappeared. To his own surprise, Stuart felt a little lonelier because of it. At the end of the fraught, mostly wasted day (spent in hastily convened assemblies, in faculty meetings, in fruitless and emotional discussions of the affair with his several classes), Stuart repaired to the little English office, grateful to have a minute to himself. He pulled the copy of *David Copperfield* from the shelf and sat back heavily on the foam couch and began to read. Cloud cover darkened the windows – in that grey light, Stuart could see the fine grain in the old glass – and eventually gave way to rain. The first spit of water on the panes made him blink. 'You must think of me at my best, old boy,' Roger had read. 'Come! Let us make that bargain.' Stuart guessed now that Roger had been trying to tell him something; Roger had wanted to talk. Secret lives exert great outward pressure; he had wanted at least to make himself known, in some fashion, he had wanted at least to utter certain relevant sentiments. Of course, in the end Steerforth ran off with Emily; and Roger Bathurst himself eloped with one of his students. Surely, Stuart thought, we live our lives in books; though he, for his part, had been content to stop short at their pages.

A month later, he got a letter from Roger, postmarked in Santa Fe. It included a photograph. He had shaved off his beard, and, in the bright glare of red hills, almost looked the part of a prematurely balding, disreputable young hippy: in cut-off jeans shorts and high-strapped sandals, with his hairy arm around the sun-burnt shoulders of an otherwise pale, rather big young woman, trying hard not to smile too broadly. 'I tell you something,' the letter read, 'if I weren't so damn happy I'd be a miserable bastard, wouldn't I?' The girl had her palm on the head of a black dog, keeping it still. Stuart hadn't taught her himself; and over time the image of her faded in his mind, replaced by that of Rachel Kranz leaning across their line of vision to pick a book from the shelf. That was the moment, as he remembered it, when things started to go wrong.

She never said a word in class. She looked attentive, she took notes, in a rounded, flowing hand, in bright blue ink, as Stu observed, standing over her shoulder as he talked. She was unfailingly punctual, tidy, smartly turned out, gracious. When he caught her eye, she smiled back happily, exposing a clean intersection of expensive white teeth. Once, he briefly imagined the free play of her tongue across the enamel after the braces came off; and shook his head, visibly, to banish the thought. One of his students even teased him, 'You're not allowed to disagree with us, Mr Englander, when we haven't said anything.' And he didn't know what to answer; he felt quite helpless. She was an absolute cipher to him, an image of girlhood in its own carefully presented perfection. He blushed occasionally when he saw the top of her head approaching in a crowded hallway, and prepared a distant look to pass her by without having to greet her. As often as not, the brown hair belonged to someone else; and he suffered the brief collapse that follows the baffled expectation of small pleasures.

In the mornings, for the first time in years, he woke with his hand on his crotch. Mary Louise, who slept in most days, began to notice. She lay heavily somnolent beside him, breathing warmly and softly, but opened her lids a crack to see him rise. She didn't like to wake deserted, unconscious of his going. As he stood up, his penis dully lifted the front of his boxers; she smiled sleepily at him, and said, 'It's that time of year again, hon, isn't it. When the sap rises.' It shamed him, these displays; he wanted to say it had nothing to do with him, with her. And she looked strange to him in bed without her powders and paints: small-featured in spite of her fleshed-out countenance, flat. She made up heavily every day, deliberately painted on arched brows, dark lids, a full mouth; he didn't like to see her without her prepared face. He viewed her always as a large construction of her own rich full tastes; the sight of her involuntary base materials appalled him. She seemed a different person entirely, utterly helpless, babyish, in need of his kindness.

He left her to shower and came back still slightly damp to dress. 'Honey,' she said now, pushing herself a little up against the pillow, 'why don't you call in sick? Come back to bed. I miss you, sweetheart. The less I work the more I miss you, isn't that awful. I think you'd feel it the same. I hope you'd feel it the same. Except you wouldn't have to.' Wooden, he heard her say, hafta. The girlishness of that big old woman his wife filled him with distaste (a particularly terrible word to invoke given the commerce of their relations). Her accent had retained the southern stickiness of licked fingers; her syllables ticked slightly as they let go of each other. She was still dull with sleep, easily heart-broken, dreamy. 'Because you'd have me. We could take the bus down to Zabar's and pick up a picnic for the Park. It's almost warm enough to eat out, now. I'll pack a thermos. We could watch the kids playing hookey, the homeless folk, the oldies. Sit up and drink tea at the roof garden. The wind gets softer every day. Catch a matinee later downtown. I don't think there's a word in the language I like better than *matinee*. Go on – call in sick.'

She was talking into his back. He straightened his tie in the mirror, eased the tightness around his neck – an almost pleasant constriction, the way the world insisted on certain points of contact – and didn't answer. A line of Milton unbidden came into his head: 'Cyriack, whose grandsire, on the royal bench Of British Themis . . .' And he shook it away: these echoes had begun to afflict him, nothing happened any more unreverberant. He saw her reflected over his own shoulder, with the featherbed tucked under her neck; her hair spread out thin and scattershot. Only her head exposed, laid out across the white pillow. They often played word games with each other, sometimes even interrupted an argument to praise a turn of phrase; alternately, to correct an infelicity. She loved all questions of rank. 'Which view out the window do you like best?' she might ask, when a span of silence bored her, simply to break it. And they would stand together, side by side, considering each of their four sitting-room windows in turn: two views of the traffic along Broadway (all those passing lives, their 'urgent voluntary errands'); two views of the tree-lined street. Such quiet, dingy growth. 'Which do you think I like best? Let me guess what you like best.' Their marriage depended not only on shared tastes, but on their ability to guess the discrepancies. They tested their understanding of each other constantly according to such intuitions. Childlessness had kept them childish.

He said now, sitting beside her in the stink of their bed, and prompted sidelong by thoughts of Roger Bathurst, 'We could get pancakes at the coffee shop and drink coffee and read the papers. Then we could go round Ratner's and look at books. Maybe even fall asleep in the leather chairs. Have a cocktail at Henry's around three, and another bite, before heading across town to catch the 4-train up to Yankee Stadium. The crowds would carry us on from there. It's opening day.' She put her warm hand between his thighs and repeated, trying to twist some strangeness into the phrase, 'It's opening day, it's opening day.' He kissed her and stood up. 'I have to go now,' he said. 'Go now,' she echoed sadly, through colourless lips, and added, 'I like mine more, I like mine more' – before turning back to sleep, the featherbed bulking higher as she lay on her side.

He could still just about persuade himself that his interest in Rachel was largely paternal. He imagined indeed that even the thoughts of fathers strayed occasionally down the necklines of their pretty daughters. Or rather, not quite paternal, but more broadly human, more simply curious: he wanted to know what went on inside her head. He told himself that she represented to him only the puzzle of youth in general, of girls in particular – those strange creatures he had never known well even in his own boyhood. How easily, how consciously they wore their powers, especially as they leaned and gossiped together in little gangs – in the hallway between classes, in the lunchroom, on the baseball field after school, standing or lying in sunshine among their bags. Their cold sweet laughter, their sure sense of propriety; how lightly they could inflict shame.

She never raised her hand in class, except to signal her presence. She answered if spoken to, somewhat flushed and quietly, but very clear. There seemed to be a sharp outline around everything she did; her edges were crisp and defined. Most of his other students suffered from background vagueness. He was always conscious of the space that held her, when it was broached; who touched a hand against her hair, or leaned upon her shoulder. Occasionally, in class, he asked her to read. She had a fine if rather uninflected voice, and sounded, at least, as if she understood what she said. At such times he could concentrate his gaze upon her unembarrassed. It occurred to him that perhaps her beauty suffered somewhat from a certain fullness around the cheekbone, a rounded edge, liable to fattening. Though charming in youth, the breadth of her countenance might suggest coarseness with age as her skin dried out and hung a little lower on the bone. By contrast, the angle formed by the line of her nose and the curve of her brow was almost too perfect, too doll-like; too fine a structure to bear the weight of real sensuality. Perhaps she was one of those graceful children doomed to a life lived in unremitting miniature, whose beauty and fine lines had been achieved at the expense of scale.

Elaborately casual, he asked around about her in the lunch-room. 'Got a girl in my class', he said touching a napkin to his mouth, 'won't talk. Well-mannered, punctual. Can't get her to say a thing.' A few teachers offered suggestions. This or that strategy had worked for them, etc. But he broke in with, 'It's a senior seminar for Pete's sake. By this point they should know how to speak their minds. Rachel Kranz's her name' – he felt he had taken his heart in his hands to utter it aloud – 'Anybody have her?' Yes; and Stu realized as they answered, that he hoped she spoke up in their classes, he hoped her silence had some particular cause centred in him. Her father, someone said, was sickeningly rich, a partner in a big mid-town firm; not very well just now, as it happens: cancer? heart? Her parents divorced. Rachel lived with her mother, a piece of work by all accounts. One of those jobless New York ex-wives whose antecedents you can read about in Jane Austen, in Dickens: nervy, hectoring, sentimentally tubercular, idle and ill done by. Part of the great tradition of well-to-do women prisoned in their own restlessness, their own narrow views. Not particularly bright, poor girl; not that she needs to be, given her inheritance. Tries, bless her. Here Miss Weintraub, the history teacher, cut in rather sharply. 'I don't know about that. The boys are terrified of her, you can see. Won't touch her. And for a pretty little picture like Rachel, that takes some doing. She's no fool.'

He read her first essay, on *Hamlet*, without realizing who had written it. (A fact, which, for various reasons, he later managed to forget.) She had printed the text of it, and signed her name simply Kranz, a word that conjured up in Stuart's mind the image of an old industrialist. By the first page he had realized that the essay would arouse in him that generosity of response which is the finest pleasure of his profession:

The play is called Hamlet and not Ophelia because Ophelia really does go mad. Hamlet's father has been killed and Ophelia's father has been killed. So the lovers have a lot in common. But the play isn't about the problem of action – if you look at him clearly Hamlet does a lot of acting from the beginning – but the problem of going mad. Going mad is the only honourable thing to do in those circumstances: that is, if your mother divorces your father and kills him. That's why Hamlet insists 'I have that within which passeth shew', which is a pun on the word show, which can mean either something displayed on the outside or something demonstrated, something reasoned and proved. Hamlet really wants to say that he's unreasonable, that he's got what it takes to go mad. Really, he's agreeing with Claudius, who says that it isn't reasonable to grieve over what's inevitable, 'that father lost a father' etc.; and Hamlet basically agrees, but he hopes to prove that he isn't reasonable, that he's capable of going mad over the things in life that you should go mad over, like the death of your father. But the trouble is, it's not in your control if you go mad or not; it's like falling in love. And he comes up short. That's why he's suspicious of Ophelia, because she goes mad, she's capable of losing her reason, of escaping from it. And in the end, Hamlet can't even kill himself; that's the real tragedy of the play, that he doesn't manage to commit suicide whereas Ophelia does. Ophelia isn't really a tragic figure because she feels what she should feel and escapes reason; but Hamlet can't escape reason and can't kill himself. That's why he has the play named after him. There is no tragedy if you feel what you should feel. Tragedy happens when you don't . . . .

Of course, there were problems with the essay, and Stuart's fine eye spotted them each in turn. Careless repetitions, run on sentences, unsupported statements; in general, a certain looseness, imprecision, a tendency to rest the argument on grand rather than particular supports. It wasn't clear, for example, exactly what was meant by 'reason'; and Gertrude had neither divorced Hamlet's father nor caused him to be killed. And the thesis – concerning the incompatibility of madness in a hero – demanded at least some reference to Lear; fair enough, the old king was next on their reading list. But there was also a pervasive problem with the tone, which was too insistent and personal; though whoever wrote it proved herself capable of a more clinical line. That bit about the punning 'shew' was very good. Of course, it was written by a girl, their Ophelia-fixations were easy to spot (though this one seemed more occupied by the filial than the romantic); and that reflection tallied suddenly with the name under the title and he realized that Rachel herself was the author.

He puffed up almost visibly at his desk, went pink. 'I have a paper here,' he declared to no one in particular, speaking loudly to let out air and rubbing his fingers back along the grain of his hair, 'I have a paper here I could not have written myself. A paper that reminds me of exactly those considerations that led me to become a teacher in the first place; that led me to give up on my own work and devote myself to guiding younger hands.' Nobody turned from their books, their papers; but he saw the little public confessions of a smile, here and there, as his colleagues continued reading. Of course, they were smiling at him, at his windy tone; but also, he thought, with some pleasure at the simple acknowledgement of that truth he had uttered. It only struck him after he said it that he meant it, that it might be true. Moments like this were his reward for giving up on his own ambitions.

Stu remembered chiefly about his own boyhood its pervasive hunger. He'd been a lean bony awkward kid, an only child, too tall, with badly cut hair and the bedroom pallor of loneliness. But never unhappy; or rarely unhappy, among his books. He dressed in chinos, sneakers, plaid shirts, regardless of the weather: sweated in summer sweats, froze his thin legs in the hurrying, windy Ohio cold. And never kissed a girl till he got to Penn, though he was certain even before then that wide stores of experience would be made available to him in life. His intellectual pleasures were only a foretaste of the real thing. And he had large ambitions, unembarrassed appetites: he wanted to see the world and he guessed even then that the best way to see it, in all its human particularity, was through sex. Nightly desires had begun to oppress him; he dreamt unpleasant things and did not shirk from facing up to them. It was clear, whatever else was true, that he had stumbled upon a great source of power. He decided, rather seriously, to give in to it; nonetheless thrilled by the fact that he had reached that stage in life when such conscious interior adjustments could bear large and enduring consequences.

When he arrived in Philadelphia, he was only slightly surprised to find that his over-earnest manner and heavy touch proved attractions in themselves to a certain class of girl. He seemed like a nice boy, tall if not good-looking, spare in the face, sharp-boned, clever, parochial, rather intense; the kind of kid a sweet girl might take pleasure in drawing out. Of course, he fell too heavily in love; he overbalanced. It didn't really matter in the end who the girl was: all that was needed was someone patient and social and sufficiently disaffected with her own class and kind – for the time at least, those heady first years of college – to take interest in an obvious outsider. Molly Hancock could trace her family line to the Revolution. She wore her black hair straight down her back, stood very still with her feet tucked together, and conducted herself in a manner Stuart later characterized as 'the false demure'. In other words, she knew exactly what she wanted, and had discovered that the soft sexual air of vagueness and pliability she exuded was a good way of getting it. She had thought, once, of becoming a poet, but quickly decided her talents were far too conventional to justify such a career. She seduced Stuart just before she had reached this conclusion (though not, incidentally, before *he* had), and dropped him the summer after.

That summer was the most painful, the most passionate, the loneliest of Stuart's life. He returned home to Ohio after his freshman year and waited for the fall. In the meantime, he made a few bucks mowing lawns; put off continually his determination to 'get back in touch' with a number of high-school friends whose uncertainty obscured their scarcity; read Rilke's *Letters to a Young Poet* slowly in the original German and wrote long letters to Molly Hancock. He felt as if his skull had been slightly expanded, such spaces opened up within it, surprising him with sudden views, outward and in. For the first time in his life he had the sense of his brain as a chamber in which he could roam freely. Only he couldn't get out; he could hardly speak.

The family dinners became his sole source of human contact: roast chicken on Sunday and either mash potatoes or tater tots; followed by chicken soup on Monday and cold chicken sandwiches for lunch. Pizza once a week. His grandmother's meatloaf on Friday nights. His father Edward (whom Stuart would resemble more and more) quit his job at the middle school when his son was born to make money. He sold new Toyotas. He did it honourably and well, managed his own lot, but felt the shame of the salesman in most relations other than the professional; secretly, he liked his job, the conversations among men. His private passion was Native American history; but he had a great appetite for information of all kinds. Read indiscriminately, fiction, non-fiction, whatever he picked up from the cardboard boxes of neighbourhood yard sales. Also, television; he had a wonderful memory for detective plots. Asked to comment on what he'd read or seen, he tended to recount the story in broad detail. He complained sometimes to his son of having no opinions, no small talk, no refinement of taste. As he grew older, Stuart admired more and more his father's large silent appetite for news of the world. He took in all he could from his position on the couch; the hair over his ears standing on end, but his bald head very clean, his cheeks clean-shaven, his countenance ageless and well kept, the wrinkles fattened away.

Stuart's obvious unhappiness, his silence, his unhealthy

summer complexion (spotty, flaccid, slightly swollen) was a great source of worry to his father. Stu was putting on weight. His lean features thickened somewhat without suggesting satisfaction: rather, physical complacence, indulged idleness. The new distance between self and son oppressed Edward. He didn't understand what the boy was reading, a shameful admission. He said it himself, he lacked taste; a line of apology he often adopted that summer after pressing Stuart to explain those books he holed up in his room to pore over. 'I tell you what it is, son,' he interrupted, 'I'll read anything, I don't care. I suppose most of it's bad for me but I don't know better. But this, this, I can't make head or tail of.' Edward realized of course what the kid was suffering from, but couldn't bring himself to say it didn't matter. All that worry about sex would soon go away; nobody could persuade you when you were young how little sex counted for in the running of the world, in keeping happy. It was useless trying. Instead, Edward talked about the work to be done on the reservations; there was a lot to be said, he said, for living in the open air.

During this time, Stuart's sexual memories of Molly became exceedingly painful. He believed it had to do with the powers of scent and touch, senses that offered only a vague approximation of scale, and which, consequently, were impossible to keep in proportion. Nothing could compensate him for Molly's smell or feel. He recalled once discovering a pair of her underpants at the foot of his bed; a white excrescence crusted them. So she was unclean. He had always been an unusually finicky eater. But the insistence of her physical nature, impossible to dam or staunch, only aroused him now. The pallor of her belly was wonderful, suggestive, the colour of moonlight on concrete. Rachel, he reflected now, going over these memories, no doubt possessed the same white underbelly. It would give way to his face easily, depress under his chin, and slowly, as he lifted up, resume its former fullness.

Such thoughts occupied him more and more – as he rode

the subway downtown after work, or caught the school bus uphill in the morning. On the john, during his lunchbreak. One day he got a letter from Roger, delivered to the school. He opened it after a morning class, sitting at his desk in the emptied room. 'At last I've taken Sidney's advice; I've been meaning to write for a while.' Roger was working towards a Ph.D. and commuting twice a week to Albuquerque ('so late in life', he wrote, 'renewed ambitions!'); his wife had finished high school, and was closing out her sophomore year at St John's. She had taken a year out to have the baby, now almost three: little Emily. He enclosed another photo, this time a city scene: baked sidewalks, dusty trees, a square one-storey house in town, the family lined up on the front stoop. (Closer inspection revealed it was a pizza parlour, a day out.) Roger had grown out his beard again; he looked unchanged, fretful, happy, as he always had. Mrs Bathurst had put on weight, wore glasses, tied her blond hair behind. Nevertheless, her skin had grown wonderfully brown, the colour of summer; she wore a tie-dyed T-shirt, a corduroy skirt. Her heavy long thighs sloped outwards like a Henry Moore, suggestive of warmth, fertility, and pressed the skirt wide and tight before her thin calves cut back straight to the ground. Emily, with braided hair, stood exceptionally small and primly. Stuart began to weep, silently, red in the face; his tears left a tacky film on his cheeks which cooled like sweat; he touched the salt to his fingertips, to his lips. If you reduced him, he thought curiously, what was left was this mineral bitterness.

He skipped lunch and walked off campus into the neighbourhood. Calmer already, he enjoyed the shadowy preserved richness of the mansion houses, the quiet of the broad asphalt, the grassy neglected yards in which children play – their deflated plastic balls, their rusting tricycles. The weather had turned for the last time, entered the home stretch towards summer. Blue and white skies passed rapidly overhead, exchanging place. Floaters of pollen, of seed, hung in the sunshine in the air. He sweated lightly into his collar as he walked now and loosened the tie around his neck; the touch of his own moisture in his chest hairs on his fingertips aroused him slightly. He remembered his wife's words: his sap was rising, his sap was rising. He sat on the stoop of Roger Bathurst's old house, trusting that no one would come to disturb him. 'Come out and see us,' Roger had written. 'My wife's friends are twenty; mine for the most part aren't much older, twenty-five, thirty. Trust me; there's a difference. I get tired of telling them they'll learn.' Later he repeated his request. 'We're happy but lonely.'

Stuart, with his chin on his arms on his knees, could smell his own warmth; his body still had reserves of animal ardours. His face, he thought, always pink, must look properly mottled now; his hair, run back from his forehead in strong grey lines, glistened no doubt. That girl wouldn't stay unpregnant long; Roger's beard always suggested the fertility of the goat to Stuart. He had a strong, versatile nature, equally passionate about disparate things; and never acknowledged the conflicts from which Stuart suffered. Spring in Santa Fe could run into the nineties; you hardly needed sheets as you lay in bed; you hardly needed clothes.

Strange, he mused, how his thoughts of children, of childlessness, blened with his sexual longings. He had slept with only two women in his life, Molly Hancock and Mary Louise. Two women in those first two years away from home and never another again. For all his appetites – and he was an ambitious, hungry man – he had discovered, to his relief and regret both, that he was also very easily, very lightly satisfied. His desires grew, readily prompted, while another insistent voice urged: enough, enough. Always enough. This was the central contradiction in his character. The fat on his bones swelling his clothes like a light wind, filling his cheeks, testified to the gentle ascendance of contentment in his life. A squat middle-aged woman, probably Chinese, probably a housekeeper, walked by, towing a small dog, pushing a shopping trolley. Briefly he imagined his knee between her thighs; and shook his head again to dismiss the thought. This time there were no students near to upbraid him.

His relations with his wife had hardly been sexual in years, she had got so fat and winded easily. Even in college, when she was only plump and opinionated, rich in tastes and arguments, she never ran high in sexual fevers. What bound them instead were strong intellectual affinities. It had thrilled him at first – after the heartbreak of Molly Hancock, after the exhaustion of his emotional and sexual forces – to spend his afternoons with a girl as clever, as curious, as he. Privately, even in the heat of passion, he had never thought highly of Molly's intellect or originality; she offered other, more immediate compensations, satisfied simpler appetites. He could not honestly claim to be surprised, however, that his marriage had yielded no child; there was something dry about his friendship with Mary Louise. It showed a wanton disregard for certain natural virtues to let yourself get so heavy: to confine your physical interest in the world to questions of taste, the pleasures of the connoisseur: to restaurants, theatres, galleries, views of all kinds.

The maid had turned into a side street and faded in and out between trees; she kept up a steady, unhappy pace. He remembered that Molly had never come except under his hand, under his knee. They had always promised themselves a day spent entirely in bed; but somehow he grew bored or restless after the first bout, and she sensed it and gave up. Appetites, even such appetites, were never as simple as they appeared; they were themselves an expression of another kind of desire. He wanted to want more from the world. She spent that summer with a cousin in Paris; never answered his letters. Such letters! He lay at home in Ohio, in his stinking room on his unmade bed and wrote, in a small hand on large sheets of yellow paper. Every day he sent another one off. She told him later, that fall, after she'd broken off from him, at their first reunion – almost tender with the aftermath of spent sentiments – how much they terrified her. They arrived unevenly, in clumps and bursts, sometimes three in a day; she couldn't get through them. She thought they had nothing to do with her. He described his empty days, his house, his father, carefully went over certain memories of their spring together. How they slept side by side in a narrow dorm-room bed for a week before he summoned the nerve to kiss her; that slow wonderful build-up of frustration. His growing sense that something would happen, the inevitability of it, which persuaded him at last that the world would not pass him by without event. Until he acted on that faith and they kissed; his lips and eyes were red in the morning, sore as sunburn.

Later, as Molly's silence grew more ominous, he experimented with certain thoughts, especially towards the end of longer letters. He wrote, 'Sometimes I'm not sure I even like you. I don't think we have much in common. You have too many unimportant ideas.' He blushed now to think of it, forty years on, as he sat on the stoop of Roger Bathurst's old house. 'You have too many unimportant ideas.' What an awful young man he must have been; and he thought of Rachel, her wonderful essay, how generously he warmed to her. Yes, perhaps he had changed for the better. And he laid his face gently against the thought of her stomach. She shivered slightly, cold with fear and expectation; he daren't undress her yet. But she put her small hands in his hair, around his ears. My child, he thought, my daughter. She was almost eighteen; he thought, she can't help but live through more than I have. It's like having money, being young and pretty; you can buy life with it.

That fall, when they got back to Philadelphia, Molly told him how much his remarks had upset her. She wept at the recollection, as they sat on her sophomore dorm bed side by side untouching; but then she always wept lightly. He asked her if she would return his letters to him; they might prove useful to him, later. (In fact, he never wrote as much again, composed so passionately.) That summer ambition had hardened within him. She had sent him an answer at last, late in

August. He took the envelope unopened up to his bedroom, weighed it carefully in his hand, noted the French postmark. Outside his window, the suburban street curved thick with Midwestern summer, those unmowed lawns. Cars stood parked in the moving shade, their windows rolled down to slow the build-up of heat. His heart raced; in spite of himself, he was conscious of a kind of excitement. Something was about to happen in his life, break the monotony of those quiet days. Decisions had been struck regarding his fate. She wrote that she had fallen in love with a Frenchman and was very unhappy at the thought of leaving Paris. 'Can we talk when we come back in September?' she said. 'Can we say goodbye properly?' He was heartbroken but instantly dismissive. It was clear to him what difficult life lay ahead: he would be a writer.

II

He showed the essay to his wife. Mary Louise sat over their finished dinner and took out her glasses; black-rimmed with wide sharp lines, glamorous and exaggerated. She dressed always like a much prettier woman, unrepentant; Stu occasionally admired her large shamelessness, occasionally grew embarrassed by it. She looked over the paper with a narrowing eye, drew in her lips. 'I'll tell you something for nothing,' she said at last. 'That child's got unhappiness at home.'

'That's too easy an answer. I admit she gets in a tangle over the question of divorce; a suggestive misreading. But all these kids have divorce on the brain. It's the word they're taught to use for tragedy.'

They often argued, obliquely, over such matters. Stuart liked to think that people's lives could have nothing to do with their work, that something was left over, private. Though the privacy he treasured lay rather in the head than in the home: he hoped the mind could move free of the sordid dissatisfactions of the life. Brains can play games. Mary Louise believed that in the end everything came back to biography. Her father had been a failed writer and a not much better lawyer in Savannah. From an old Georgia family, a generation removed from being rich. As she liked to say, not without affection, 'He drank like a writer; unfortunately, he wrote like a drinker.' And never finished anything. Only fragments of novels, first and last lines, character sketches, situations, occasional snatches of dialogue. Not without interest to a sympathetic eye, patient enough to piece together their several dimensions, but he lacked the talent for connecting threads. 'There are two kinds of things that happen in the world, the things you can't do anything about and the things you can. The first writers call description; the second, plot. According to my sense of life, there ain't much plot,' he once told Stuart, a young man then. What that means, Mary Louise commented afterwards, is that he can't get his own act together. And yet for thirty years on Saturday afternoons, all she sculpted of people were their parts: their hands around bottles, their knees on bathroom tiles.

He asked to see Rachel after class. This was also an act of some slight courage on his part; the syllables of her name were too heavy; to utter them in an ordinary tone taxed his strenuous tongue. Another teacher had the room next period, so he led her, gesturing loosely with his arm around her shoulder, untouching, towards the Winter Palace. It occurred to him as they walked, silently – his chin above the top of her head – that he might never know who she was. There is always a danger in these relations of projection. She would simply play the part of his own insinuations and desires; he might never scratch her surface, scratch her surface. He did not see her concentrated face as she skipped a little to keep up at his elbow.

The room, thank God, was empty. Half the kids were at lunch, he could see some of them lying on the baseball field with their heads on their backpacks. He thought, youth looks very happy from a distance; nothing could repay him, not even such moments, for the forfeit of his own. He should have spent it better; at each stage in his life he promised himself to live more fully, more widely, outside his own head, his books; and yet, almost without exception, when experiences, of one kind or another, presented themselves to him, he turned them down. Of course, there was Molly Hancock. Not that he didn't resist her, as well, at first. Sometimes he thought that he had never recovered from the initial shock of her sexual power over him; the way she overrode his reluctance. He felt helpless in front of her, beneath the insistence of her wide experience; there was another word for what she did to him.

'I wanted to talk to you,' he said, 'about your essay.'

She sat with her hands pressed into her plaid skirt, between her knees. She wore high white socks and leaned forward slightly. 'I'm sorry, Mr Englander,' she began, 'I know –'

'But first I wanted to talk to you about your manner in class. I've waited a month for you to say a word. It isn't just a question of the grade, though there is that, too.' It amused him how easily he could adopt such a tone. He saw, between her skirt and her socks, a few folded lines of her knees. 'One of the great pleasures in teaching literature, I've discovered over the years, is that it is one of the few subjects pursued at the high-school level in which I, the teacher, have a real chance of learning from you, my students. I like to make the most of that chance.'

'I know. It isn't that I'm shy, really. Only I never know what to say on the spot. I like to make –'

'Everyone's shy. There's no shame in that. Once you get started you'll find it much easier, I promise.' Her face, perhaps, had taken on a slightly heightened colour; she was always pink and brown, but now her pink faintly predominated. She opened her blue eyes very wide – he recognized the gesture, designed to show willingness, attention – but pressed her lips together, involuntarily, the sign of someone refusing to be bullied into talking. Her top lip was overheavy, and hung down in the middle across her lower lip. It's true, the closer you looked at her countenance, the more you saw the slight excesses to which it inclined, that breadth of cheek.

'No, the real shame', he continued, 'only struck me when I read your essay. And I found what a brilliant' – he almost said 'little girl' but stopped himself in time – 'writer you are. This by a long chalk is the best paper I've come across this year, the wisest, the sharpest. I won't say it doesn't need work, because it does.' She was all pink now, the blood rushing to her face in swift concentrations. It touched him wonderfully to see the power he had of giving pleasure. 'I won't say it doesn't need work,' he repeated, 'but, what's rarer still, it deserves more work, and I'm more than happy to help you with that. There's a senior essay competition I have in mind. But, more importantly, I want to tell you such thoughts are too good to keep to yourself, young lady, and I only wondered –'

'I read. All the time.' She broke in at last, defensively. 'I read on the schoolbus. I read myself to sleep. None of the other girls –'

'I only wondered how I could persuade you to talk up in class. What it would take.'

She sat *stumm* now; her hands had moved on top of her knees and clasped them, sweating slightly. It occurred to him, with sudden insight (such insight, which, even though it may serve vanity, has stepped clear of it at last), that this was a moment of great significance to her; *she had been recognized*. The uncertain wealth of her inner world had been laid out for him to see, and rated, highly at that.

He remembered the first time he showed Mary Louise a story. They had fallen in together, naturally, after arguing violently in a seminar on the Italian novel. He had a strong corrective habit, and she had baulked against his insistent pedantries. Secretly, she liked being 'called out', as she put it. Roused by the heat of debate, he finally mustered the courage to ask this big-chested, voluble Southern creature to coffee. Look!, he thought wryly, I have come through! In the last heats of fall, they walked; acorns pulled down leaves after them, clicked underfoot. She was wearing, rather remarkably, a kind of cape. When she sat down at the coffee shop the hem of it caught under the leg of her chair and gathered dust. But the shadow of Molly Hancock had been lifted; he felt he could breathe again. He didn't have to stoop in any way to talk to this kid, she was larger, louder than he, more widely read. For months, and he blushed to think of it now, he referred to her only as de Staël, and she played along.

Well, he had turned one of his letters into a kind of story, and decided at last to show it to Mary Louise. For a week, whenever he saw her, he wondered if she had read it. She never mentioned it either way; then, one night after the library closed, she asked him up to her room. The heating vented dirty jets of steam; she kept the room hot, the windows shut. Condensation speckled the dark green ficus in the corner by the door. The wiring was shot, she explained, all the lamp could take was a thirty-watt bulb, and under its dim sunset they talked. He had never noted before how poor light can rob the world of colour, of life. The only place to sit was her bed; he took off his jacket and saw pages of his handwriting lightly scattered on the floor. She wore a spaghetti-stringed satin top that exposed the fleshy sides around her armpit; he could just trace the first swelling of her heavy breasts. He smelt her, very sweet and warm, thicker than air. Molly never wore scent.

His story was about a young man who falls in love with a beautiful woman; nevertheless, he suspects her intelligence, even her virtue. Her chief attraction for him is sexual; though her wide experience also repels him. He writes her long and ornate love letters, believing that this is what she expects from him; after all, he isn't good-looking or charming. The best he can hope for is to play the part of the shy poet. To test her, he encodes in these letters an account of how much he dislikes her, how little he respects her. If she understands him, it proves she is worthy of his higher nature; if she doesn't, she isn't. The problem with such a proceeding is obvious even to him: she will only reward his epistles with loving warmth if she is too stupid to see his hidden meaning. Any attempt to test her character will also, if she passes it, expose his doubts to her. The story ends, however, much more simply; she thanks him sweetly for his letters, but explains that she has fallen in love with someone else. His subtlety has been entirely lost on her, wasted.

Mary Louise knew and disliked Molly Hancock; she thought the girl was a 'cold fish posing as a warm one'. That was her line. She read Stu's story the night he gave it to her; it hurt her deeply. A boy who could have written *that* wouldn't give her a second look. She had come up before against the problem of suitable young men who think they deserve better than intellectual companionship in their loves; who think they deserve beauty. She had wondered all week what to say to him, and decided, at last, that her only honest response would be to say how much she disliked it. Of course, her feelings were more complicated than that; but it was true, the character in the story did not reflect Stuart's best nature. It exposed his narrow sexual greed, his high-minded arrogance. And she had had enough of the writer's pettiness in her father, his enduring disappointments, his persistent sniping. 'I think', she said, putting her strong hand on his thigh, 'you're better at correcting than creating.'

Of course he was disappointed, almost heartbroken. But even she had not guessed it would leave him so open to her charms, so desperate for warmth. She comforted him against her broad breasts; he proved more experienced in bed, more sure of himself, than she'd expected.

'Well,' Stuart said at last, after Rachel did not answer. 'Maybe we should talk about what you need to work on.' He discussed at length now the problems of tone; her need for stricter textual supports; her occasional grammatical infelicities; the lack of structure. He sat beside her now, her papers spread loose across his knee. The foam couch sank somewhat beneath his heavy weight, pressing his hip against hers. She shifted slightly over; he could smell the soap in her hair. Whenever he praised her she blushed, and he remembered the power that giving pleasure accorded. This reflection awoke other, unhappier memories. After a week of nothing but kisses, Molly had begun to get bored of his innocence; they slept tightly bound in a single bed, and she let her hand stray between his thighs. His sense of pleasure was wonderfully acute, he felt helpless before it. He said, no, no, not yet.

A minute passed; he noted that his hand was on her knee, on one of the pages on her knee. 'I suppose you'd better get to lunch,' he said at last. 'We can go over this later.' She looked up at him, and sniffed slightly; the face of a girl willing to make a decision, conscious that such decisions were becoming possible to her, even necessary. Unwilling to put off any longer the next stage of her life they would usher in. 'Even if I don't speak,' she said finally, standing in the doorway and bent slightly under her bag, 'I want you to know that I read. I read everything we're supposed to read. My mother will tell you. She says the same thing, she says you have to talk if you want them to count it, otherwise it doesn't count. But it counts anyway, doesn't it? I read all the time.'

After she left, he didn't stir for a minute, recounting slowly the movement of Molly's hand. For whatever reason, this, his first sexual act, had never lost the power to arouse him. He had been an unwilling participant; the force of his own pleasure, his own capacity for pleasure, left him trembling. She, on the other hand, had scarcely allowed herself a sigh; he lay very still, saying, please, not yet, please, while she let his body's involuntary answer provide a sufficient yes. She had gathered herself at the foot of the bed and taken his boxers in hand and drawn them slowly down his legs. He felt his penis gathering weight as he sat in the office; he didn't have to touch it. Then she kissed it, wearing only a white undershirt; he could see the hanging slope of her breasts through the low neck. Still, he didn't move. After a minute, she crawled along the length of his body till her face stuck wetly in the soft skin under his chin. She reached her hand back, and with a mechanical fumbling that surprised him, pulled his penis into her. He felt the scratch of her hair; her tightness. Only then did she open her mouth, expelling air. He came quickly, gently; even now he had to hold back the thought of its sweetness, the press of his trousers against him was proving almost irresistible. For weeks he worried she was pregnant, he was syphilitic; at the same time, he felt helplessly dependent on her. Angry, too; she had no right any more to withdraw such possibilities of pleasure.

'You're very distant,' Mary Louise said to him one night. They were reading in bed side by side, propped up on squashed pillows against the wall; she held her book at arm's length below her breasts against the heap of her belly. Now she took off her glasses to consider him. 'I feel you get up in the night and sit in the dark. For a while I thought you might be entertaining yourself on that damn computer.' She laughed. 'This morning I checked the machine; but there was nothing on it. I want you to know I wouldn't mind.'

'I have been going over old memories,' he said, staring ahead. It amazed him sometimes how openly they talked; he knew he had her courage to thank for the fact. And was grateful for it, too. She never shrank from unpleasant reflections, or allowed any personal soreness to deflect their probing. She was very sure of him. He looked down at his book and widened his eyes suddenly, as if it had surprised him. 'I can't take in any words. I try but I can't.'

He felt it was necessary to preserve some corner of himself from the gaze of her large understanding. So he added, 'I got another letter from Roger Bathurst, do you remember him. He said why don't we come down to see him this summer; they have a little house out in Santa Fe. A child, too, Emily, just turned three; he sent a picture, a very proper little girl. I thought we could use some real sun.'

It was a subtle subterfuge, because it also put her in the way of his real reflections. But he hoped that the account of Emily would catch her eye. Some years ago, Mary Louise had fainted coming up the narrow stairs to their apartment. He had supported her slow weight the rest of the way and put her to bed with a glass of water. One of those New York summers; the air-conditioners dripping on to the street and sucking in only hot air rising off the asphalt. But she admitted at last it wasn't the first time; she'd been getting flashes for months. The news unexpectedly left him in despair. He refused to touch her; her new infertility appalled him, her decaying mass. He realized that something about her wide human warmth, her large-heartedness, had deceived him from the first; she was sterile, dry. Her broad cool air of understanding masked the absence of deeper passions; she suffered greatly from a dearth of blood-lust, she had grown fat from the absence not the excess of real appetites. She knew, of course she knew, how greatly Stuart had wanted children; it was the one dispute on which she kept mum because she realized that in time it would resolve itself in her favour. Her own family had left her with no desire to reproduce its passionate mistakes. Stuart, she knew, was fonder of his father, felt guiltier about him. But she was quite happy to let the world get on without them after their deaths.

He hoped his reference to Emily would lead her thoughts down these reflections. But she said at last, 'I've been thinking about that girl's essay. I wanted you to know that I don't mind if you have strange thoughts sometimes. It's natural; I don't think a man can think anything that isn't natural.'

Over the next few months Rachel Kranz began to send him unmistakable signals. She caught his eye at the beginning of class and would not let it go; her blue gaze, wide as innocence, followed him everywhere. Much as it roused him he found he lacked the courage to meet it. Two or three times a week she came by the English office, or looked for him in the Winter Palace – where he sometimes graded papers during a free period, sometimes picked an old book from the shelf and read for pleasure. She nudged her head shyly round the door; whenever it opened, his heart began to race. 'Mr Englander, Mr Englander,' she said, in her faint clear voice. She wanted to talk to him about her next essay. She was going to write on *Lear*, how the play was really about greed, the greed of inheritors, and that Cordelia was the greediest of them all. Only Cordelia realized that money was a symbol for love, and that love mattered more than money: a simple truth, but her sisters got mixed up the other way around, and wanted to use love to get money.

'One of the things my father once told me', she said, 'is that when you fight about money, you're never fighting about money.' Her voice adapted slightly to her father's tongue; she sounded older, larger; like many pretty girls, Stu thought, pliable to influence. He could make something of her, this girl. She wanted to argue that the play was really about the cunning of Cordelia, her triumph: the way she got her father to herself. 'That's why she says,' Rachel spent a minute growing redder, looking for her page, 'she says, *Sure I shall never marry like my sisters, To love my father all.* Read the line straight, without sarcasm, and that's what happens.' The pair had to die because they couldn't make love, she was his daughter, after all; death brought them as close to sexual ecstasy as they could go. It amounted to the same thing. Stuart could see such revelations were dear to her; she exposed herself widely when she read aloud.

But she could also keep silent, sit primly on the foam couch and let him speak – occasionally displaying a slight discomfort by scratching her pink knee or shifting in her seat to hitch her skirt up. It amazed him always, how easily he could talk to her; how easily he could adopt a professorial manner. Most of what she said was rather obvious, but he granted her, there might be a seed of an idea there, worth planting. And she would frown, with heavy consternation, nodding her head at each slow word, 'I know I need to improve my tone.' She had begun to touch him; she touched his elbow when he looked over her work; she licked her finger and rubbed a stain from his tie. It amazed him how small and sharp her tongue appeared between her teeth. Once Amy Bostick, the new Biology teacher, said to him at lunch, 'I think you've got an admirer, Stu. Better be careful.' A skinny creature who had seemed rather miserable at the beginning of the year; he used, expressly, to sit down to lunch with her. Amy would heap her plate with cold broccoli, cottage cheese, sliced carrots – with good intentions – and pick at them and never finish anything except a chocolate doughnut. She'd had the tearful, earnest pallor of a girl looking for, as Howard Peasbody put it, 'her next object of gratitude'. Now Amy's thinness seemed rather a sign of self-possession. It's awful, Stu remembered thinking, how experience makes everyone the same; all salted meat tastes alike. 'I've seen,' she added, 'personally, what father-fixations can do.' Well, perhaps she had the measure of him too, now; he blushed so heavily he had to cough.

But as the term continued, Rachel's working habits only got worse. She was still punctual in person, tidy, neatly turned out. Her homework and in-class essays were written in a girlish impeccable hand, flowing, rounded lines: *order* it seemed spooled forth from her on an endless thread. It is what she produced. But she still refused to speak in class, and had begun to miss assignments. Even what she turned in on time was hopelessly abbreviated, perfunctory; she seemed to be daring him to chastise her. Once he caught her kissing by the bins behind the cafeteria; a stocky, smooth-faced boy, not especially bright, though rather apologetic and polite. Her face was mottled from his lips and the outside heat, particularly glaring over the concrete footway; the width of her cheeks had become very suggestive. She flushed quickly red; he saw the moistness around her neck, and imagined himself, to his guilty amusement, drying it off with toilet paper. 'Mr Englander, Mr Englander,' she called, running after him. When he stopped and turned she almost ran into his waist. 'I'm so ashamed, I'm so unhappy.' He was certain she had timed her performance especially to arouse him. He said, in the heat of the moment, 'I don't think I'd like my daughter spending her schooldays necking, do you?'

Still, he couldn't get the image of her sweet disorder out of his head. The rest of Herrick's line ran on in his thoughts. Yes, wantonness is exactly the word. And he finally allowed himself to undress her that afternoon, after school, when he had the office to himself. The first heavy day of the year; a foretaste of the summer. When he ran his hand back along his hair he felt the slickness left over from a long afternoon. His armpits stank; he was rich in sexual heat. A fly flew loosely around the room, missing the opened window, again and again. His nerves had been stripped down to the fresh wood; nothing in the office, in the outside world, could move or sound without inflicting a corresponding shift in him. He imagined her lying naked on a white sheet, lying in the grass perhaps, or on the floor at his feet. The fly buzzed to a stop at last, composing its restless legs on her scratchy unripe pudenda. Gently, in his mind, he brushed it off; it interrupted his contemplations. But he found his thoughts had already strayed. There was of course the famous verse by Donne; which he'd often taught, always careful in seminar, for obvious reasons, to keep the tone strictly analytical. There was a danger in these times in permitting any free discussion from experience. And Tennyson's wonderful pendant cooling the pink depression between his wife's breasts. Rachel's, he supposed, were rather less developed; paler, possessing an almost green coolness, thinly veined. He doubted she'd ever exposed them to the sun. Larkin, too, did something clever with Donne's flea, transformed it into a city, Oxford, which Stu himself had visited one summer many years ago in what he liked to call his 'far different youth'. These thoughts provided him with necessary nourishment; they left him highly agitated, almost eager – an upset very much like hopefulness.

That night he refused to come to bed. Mary Louise had guessed his overheated state. The air had softened in the growing dark; she wore black silk and waited for him with the duvet at her feet. But he did not want to translate these fresh sensations into an old dead language. He did not want to accept her comfort, give in to her solace, which extended to his sexual frustrations. He sat up watching television. She woke briefly when he snuck in and said, 'I don't mind who you think of, darling. I want you to be happy.' He pretended not to have heard: these were difficult admissions, he wasn't sure how much explanation their marriage could stand. He lacked her faith.

More and more it struck him as cowardly not to act on these longings. They had begun to overgrow the background of his thoughts, like seeding grasses, gaining weight and colour in neglect. 'Sooner murder an infant in its cradle,' he remembered his Blake, 'than nurse unacted desires'; an unhappy image, strange how everything led him back to his books, his childlessness. He began to obsess about Rachel's period; he looked at her legs, her cheeks, to see if they bore the weight of her waters. Once, she asked to 'use the bathroom' next door; while she was gone, no more than a minute, he couldn't keep his mind on their set text, *Much Ado About Nothing*. He called on one of his students to read aloud. He imagined he heard the cool trickle of her pee, not the more silent searching adjustment of a tampon. Her fertility itself infected him with desire.

Besides her backpack, she carried a small candy-cane-striped handbag to class. She left it on her desk one day. He saw it and picked it up, felt the loose assortment inside, a comb, a tube of lipstick, through the fine leather in his hands. Some change. Quietly, with trembling fingers, he unzipped the top; and pressed the opening wide. A cool small plug in white wrapping lay inside; as he was probing Rachel came back in the class. She said, 'I forgot my purse' – stopping short, and blushing.

Molly Hancock, as it happens, had had an affair in high school with her English teacher, a much older man – married, too; his wife taught in the same school. At the time it rather titillated Stu; he kept asking her, how did he summon up the nerve? What did he say? 'Oh,' she said, 'I knew what was going on, believe me. I had the situation very much in hand. One day he simply let me know, he said, I want you to know this, Molly, if you ever want to sleep with me I can make arrangements. I want you to know that offer stands. I don't care when you feel like you need it; believe me, at my age we're much less unsure of what we want. We can afford to wait.'

The memory was suddenly strong and Molly was getting dressed at the time, putting on dirty underwear after a night in his room, already late for class. He was playing hooky, lying up in bed in his boxers, still skinny, still young. He hadn't done the reading anyway. He almost said to Rachel, 'If you ever want to sleep with me I can make arrangements.' He said, 'I wanted to see whose purse it was. Is it yours?' He held it out, still open; his fingers were sweating, and when she took it from him, she touched his hands.

The rest of the day he heard laughter. Whenever he saw Rachel, she was standing in a group of girls; they were laughing, leaning together, carelessly in contact. The shame was unbearable. I can't go on any longer this way, he thought. I have to do something.

He kept thinking of Molly's offhand remark, 'believe me, I had the situation very much in hand.' He knew, of course, that Rachel could see through him; part of her attraction lay in that fact, in how large and obvious he must appear to her, how crudely exposed. 'I still don't see how you started up with him,' Stu had answered, feeling green, prudish, Midwestern, young. 'Oh, that wasn't hard.' Molly was dressed now, and he had tried to restrain her, pulling her back towards his bed by her hands, pushing his cheek to her breasts. 'Stop it, stop it, stop it,' she repeated half-heartedly; the fact was, she wanted to tell the end of the story. She could see his boxers slowly tenting outwards, and laid her palm against his belly. 'I sat in his office and burst into tears; it's true, by the way, I was unhappy. One of my boys had been cheating on me; I took it personally. It's no hardship to a girl like me, by the way, crying, that is; I always have enough reasons. I've never thought of myself as a happy person; mostly,

I just keep up appearances. Anyway, he closed the door. That's the first thing he did, I remember thinking it was very calculated, very mature; and came over to comfort me. He put his arm around me; I could smell his excitement and my face was already wet; it slipped a little against his beard till I found his lips. Once that was over, he could take the initiative; all he needed was a go-ahead. It was quite a relief to me, after those high-school boys. Anyway, we worked together on the literary magazine; he drove me home one night and we stopped off at a motel. I'd been thinking about it for days, but it didn't take long. I cried afterwards, he was brusque. But by the time summer came I was ready for it to end; after a while everything I did made him unhappy. He was totally dependent.' She left him then, running late for class. Stuart spent the rest of the day in bed, surprisingly low-spirited, sympathetic. Feeling utterly helpless in the face of her cool assurance, his strong desires.

Rachel's work went from perfunctory to non-existent. The only thing she did was show up. He had another look at her *Hamlet* essay; really, he was almost surprised at himself, there was nothing but mistakes. And she had done little to correct them. He remembered Mary Louise's sly comment: that kid has unhappiness at home. Yes, it was probably true; her instinct about such matters was surer than his own. Occasionally her certainty oppressed him; it seemed rather cold always to be right in these small ways. But he also found great comfort in her judgement; nothing could happen to him, he could do nothing, outside the scope of her large sympathies.

He called Rachel to his office. 'I'm worried about you,' he said. 'Your grades are slipping; I won't be able to pass you. You won't graduate.'

'Yes,' she answered, frowning sweetly, 'I'm worried about me, too.' But her turn-out never faltered; she wore her prettiness like it was cut in stone. The next time he called her in, she changed the subject. 'You know Mr Englander, I think I should warn you, somebody's stalking you. One of the girls. They know where you live. They know what you buy from the pharmacy.'

He remembered her laughter in the hallways. It sounded like a threat, a sly revenge for his own inquisitiveness. Unless she only 'had the situation very much in hand'. The thought that her experience in such matters might already be far wider, far greater than his own, appalled him. What have you done with your life, he thought. These kids. He suspected that if she gave him the least hint he would fall at her feet. He would be unable to resist her command. This quickly turned into another source of worry. He began to imagine detailed scenarios, her various attempts at seduction; his own responses. More often than not he failed such tests; but they gave him tremendous pleasure, compressed and intensified by the force of their secrecy, their guilt. He hardly ate any more; he had begun to lose weight. He often thought about Roger Bathurst, the months leading up to that Easter week-end. What powerful, remembered days; a source of great nourishment to him, of self-renewal, in moments of dejection. While he sat on that man's sunny stoop, Roger was changing his life.

It was clear to him that he had long ceased thinking clearly. Nothing in the world bore its own natural weight any more. Wherever he looked he found grotesque additions and omissions; a kind of cancer, working both ways, growing and retracting carelessly everywhere and out of all proportion. And yet he hadn't felt so vividly at the mercy of things since the summer after his freshman year. It was true; madness was the only appropriate response. The world was enormous, it couldn't be measured by such slight scales as human sentiments. The idea was ridiculous. At the root of it all was the problem of sex (the blood-lust, the making of children); he never minded any of this so much when he stuck to the cool of his thoughts.

The Friday the senior essays were due, Rachel didn't show up for class. End of April; he opened a row of heavy windows as the kids settled. Outside, the view sloped down towards the warehouses on either bank of the Harlem River. He could make out their grey roofs and stacks over the sketchy green tops of spring trees. Hot rain fell in strong lines. Also, the heaters ran full and couldn't be shut off, and he felt the contrast in warm air as he stood in the windows: the pregnant outside blow, the stale wet heat rising dully from the radiators. He ordered a kid to put a bin in front of the door; it kept breathing open then drawing the rain in on the back gust, and slamming. 'Still,' he said, 'I think the fresh hot air is better than the stale hot air.'

The other students sat at the seminar table arranging their papers; someone had a stapler, passed it round. Occasionally one heard the heavy percussion and release of a hand banging down on the head of it. Stuart always liked due dates; the kids were restless but interested, still carried the weight of their enthusiasms. Curiosity, Stuart liked to say, picks up momentum; ideas, especially one's own, become addictive. On such days, he let the kids blow off steam, talk about their papers, the problems they ran into. They all wanted to talk. It touched him to see the unashamed delight they took in self-expression, what wide possibilities of meaning they read into their slightest thoughts. Their little wagers on the dark horses of wisdom. He remembered it well from his own youth; the way he hoped words, their suggestiveness, their inaccuracy, would trick him into profundities beyond his meagre intentions. That someone else would make sense of what he wrote but did not yet understand himself.

'Has anyone seen Rachel?' he asked at one point. He sat on the sill and felt the wind at his back, the wet. 'Is she in school today?'

'I – think I saw her,' a girl said, looking round. 'I'm not sure. She – I think she's having a hard time at home.'

After class he returned, surprised at himself, how heavy

and slack he felt, to the second English office, for a little quiet. She was waiting for him on the couch, patiently. Neatly turned out: a white blouse, especially white against her skin. In the rainy half-light, she looked as dark as stained wood, her face, her neck, her arms bare from the shoulder. A hair band drew the hair up from her eyes, left blank her forehead.

'Well, what am I supposed to do about this?' he said, almost angrily. 'I give up on you. I give up.'

'Don't say that, Mr Englander.' Softly reproachful. It touched him greatly, the tone she took: as if she knew the forgiveness he was capable of, the mercy. As if she needed from him only what she knew he could give her. But he hardened his heart.

'I don't have a choice. I've given you every chance, every encouragement. It isn't up to me; there are rules I can't bend. This isn't the kind of behaviour I can let pass.'

'I tried to write. You have no idea. I've given up on everything else. But I wanted to write for you.' She began to cry, soft gasps broken now and then by a babyish clucking, like the swish of a loose bicycle wheel against the fender, followed by the clank of the chain. She didn't lift her hands to her face, but leant forward slightly; her countenance was extraordinarily clear. Sharply defined, the line of her cheek, her chin, a little too wide and full perhaps, but still fresh, smooth. The pink of her colouring warming and rising to her wide blue eyes. Her tears left a shine of wrapping on her skin. He was right from the first, she suffered somewhat from the indignity of scale, the delicacy of miniature. But even where he sat he could smell her, on that hot thick day, the strong animal odour of her grief.

He moved to sit beside her, and she rather quickly turned her face against his armpit. 'Hey, hey, hey,' he said. 'Rachel.' He felt very tender speaking her name. He had never held a girl so slight before, so easily shifted. The pressure of her breast against his ribs roused him a little; he pulled his arm tighter across her shoulders. His blood began to thicken, and he leaned and kissed the top of her head, the tight, smoothed hair: an act of gentleness both sexual and fatherly. Molly had said, 'Believe me, I had the situation very much in hand.' The thought that Rachel knew what she was doing to him almost overwhelmed him; he wanted to expose himself to her, and let her youth, her experience in these matters, guide him. 'All he needed was a go-ahead.' He could put a chair in front of the door; and come back to her. If only he'd shaved. His lips were too large for hers; he felt the roughness of his face against her throat, against her belly, and winced. *Whenas the rye reach to the chin* ran through his head like a nursery rhyme. He could carry her with his right arm between her legs supporting her back and his left holding her neck, her shoulder – carry her like a baby, she was so light, and kiss her stomach.

When Molly let him into her room, that long-ago fall, for what she called a proper goodbye, he asked to kiss her. She looked at him unhappily, sideways along the bed where they sat, and put her hand behind his head and kissed him gently, leaning forward. He pushed back the other way and spread her on to the bed beneath him; her sexual touch was too strong for him, left him helpless. She said, no, no, please not, as he put his hand between her legs and began to press the butt of his palm against her. The thought of what she once offered to him blinded him briefly; what a world it was to take pleasure in. What she had withdrawn. Also, he was touched by a soberer anger, and felt like saying: now you know what it feels like, lady. Now you know what it feels like. But there was something human, something *just* about that thought that held him back. (This almost in spite of himself was the note he gave when struck, the fine faint vibration of his character.) He lay breathing heavily and sobbing with his face against her sheets for a moment; she couldn't stir beneath his weight and waited. And he let her go at last.

Rachel at last stopped crying and looked up, her face no more than a foot away from his own. She could not feel the thickening of his penis where she sat; but he wanted very much to reveal it to her. If he shifted a little and turned on his hip she would feel it and press against it; if he pulled her towards his lap she would feel it too. Roger Bathurst had had the courage to risk such shame. Stuart knew it was sinful, corrupt; sin however seemed necessary to him. He remembered the uncleanness of Molly Hancock's undergarments; these were fertile stains. And Roger looked happy, had a girl, a young wife. It seemed to him a real possibility that if he kissed Rachel now and locked the door and let come what may come, in five or ten years' time, if all went well, he might be happier than he was today. If all went well. A real possibility.

Rachel said, 'Mr Englander, please. Mr Englander, please.'

He almost bent down then, to open his mouth into hers and taste her lips, her tongue, soft no doubt and sweet with youth, and small. 'Mr Englander, please,' she repeated, more urgently; when it occurred to him that he was only pressing too hard, that this was the first time she guessed at the part she played in his thoughts. She looked terribly scared; sobered from grief, swiftly adjusting; he could see her pupils shrink into the blue, her breath slow consciously. He thought of wiping her wet blubbered mouth with his shirt sleeve. Perhaps a minute had passed since she began crying into his armpit. The fact that she might have recognized him for what he was helped him also to see her more clearly. A girl, seventeen, rather pretty, polite, and rich; not particularly clever. Terrified now and unsure of herself, unhappy. No, he couldn't hide it from himself any more: not particularly clever. The whole business suddenly wearied him enormously; the sexual restlessness, the waste of head space. All that necessary intellectual condescension; what a way to spend the rest of your life.

He got up and went to the door; opened it briefly. A janitor walked slowly ahead of his spread mop along the empty corridor, shiny with tiles. Stu looked down the length of the hallway, regular and institutional, interrupted to right and left by a series of classroom doors. A window at the end of the long hall gave a faint grey light. He hooked the door back against the wall and returned to his desk.

'It's better,' he said, 'for various reasons, we leave that open. Some of them legal, I'm afraid; such are the times we live in. Our powers of comforting are greatly circumscribed. Tell me what's wrong.'

She didn't answer, and sat very still, leaning forward. He realized now this was a defensive posture: it shrank the space exposed between her head and her crotch. Her tears had dried and left dirty tracks across her cheeks. He thought of Prior, dear Chloe, how blubbered is that pretty face. Yes, he knew the word had come to mind from somewhere. Rain fell in heavy blows against the window behind him, as though some resistance had slackened, letting their full weight through. He wondered if he would feed later on that touch of her shoulder, her strong smell. 'I hear you're having troubles at home,' he said at last.

'I'm fine, thank you.' In spite of everything she sat quiet, waiting to be dismissed; a very proper child. Her prettiness, her careful order, even a little tarnished now, concealed great interior adjustments. He saw what subterfuge she was capable of; why, she was almost frozen with distrust. The tragedy struck him from her point of view: the end of a brief thaw. Though he doubted now his ability to read her at all. These kids led lives he could never begin to fathom.

He felt tired and shabby. The blood eased off in him, seemed to let go. 'I can give you another week, that's all. Of course, I have to mark you down for it. I don't know what's happened; I had great hopes for you. I can't say how much you've disappointed me.'

She took a folder from the back of her heavy bag. 'I tried to write; I couldn't. There was too much I wanted to say; I couldn't stop or start.' She gave him what she had, a few pages of notes. Then shouldering her heavy pack, made her way to the door. 'I'm sorry, Mr Englander,' she said, slowly, carefully. 'I know you tried with me.'

Still, he didn't want to let her go. 'My father-in-law once gave me a piece of advice; at least I think it was advice.' Just to keep her in his view a minute longer; her knees held the weight of her wonderfully. He could almost feel the tension, like a pulled kite string, in her calves. 'A rich character, my father-in-law. A Georgia gentleman, a drunk. He grew fat as he grew sober. He said, I always thought I wanted to be a writer, because I liked books. I carried one with me everywhere, in my back pocket. I dipped in it every quiet moment. In line at the A&P. Waiting for buses, doctors. Between innings. Very comforting, but it also drove me wild. They made me want to see the world, try everything. Now I've realized it wasn't ever true, he said. I had misread my ambition from the first. What I wanted all along was to be a reader.'

After she left, he looked over her notes. Rather incoherent; but if you made sense of them, you found she had nothing unusual to say. No wonder she stopped short; as soon as she explained herself in plain terms, she turned into a very ordinary young woman. To clear his head he opened the window and leaned out. The warm rain fell against his face, so he closed his eyes to it. It tasted sour as leaves, as water from a tin cup.

Fridays he and his wife dined out, mostly at Pablo's, a cheap Mexican restaurant across the road. Abstemious as a rule, Stuart was nevertheless partial to margaritas. He said to Mary Louise, 'The school is doing another round of early retirements. Cutting away the dead wood. I've been thinking: I might take them up on it this time.' She couldn't help herself, she clapped her hands and held them against her lips, a rather extravagant gesture for such a large woman, very girlish. 'Well,' he said, a little drunk, wanting to withhold pleasure, 'it's only something I've been thinking about.' Regardless, Mary Louise began making plans; they hadn't travelled in years. They only took a couple of rooms on Fire

Island in August to get out of the city heat; but now she had her summers free as well, there was nothing to keep them from going further afield, spending some real time together. She had a cousin in England. At one point he interrupted her. 'That girl I mentioned to you. I showed you her work; I think you were right. An unhappy home. She came to my office today: she's completely gone to pieces. There's only so much I can do. She began crying; I had to open the door. I even said to her, my powers of comforting are strictly circumscribed. It's a ridiculous position.'

Mary Louise seemed to ignore him. She was trying to get the attention of the woman at the next-door table: a heavy-faced dark-skinned lady, who had seen too much sun in her day. Excuse me, she said, excuse me. She often talked to people dining alone; she had no respect for solitude, or, more to the point perhaps, no respect for what Stuart thought of as the 'caste difference' of people eating out on their own. More than once, he'd complained to her, 'These aren't people you want to know. They're on their own for a reason.' And his wife had said, 'It wouldn't be so hard for me to be one of them. Or you for that matter. If we weren't so lucky.' Lucky, he sighed, echoing her – his father's habit, repeating words. It meant disagreement, but sometimes Stuart applied it in curious affirmation: yes, we should be so lucky. Now Mary Louise wanted to know where the woman had picked up the string of cornelian folded in the lines of her neck. Mexico, was the answer. 'We never go anywhere,' Mary Louise explained. 'Mostly my fault. When you're big like me I'll tell you, an afternoon in an airplane seat is the last thing you need. But that's no excuse for Mexico, is it? We could drive there, if we had a car. But who has a car in New York, right? I'd like to go on a cruise.'

But afterwards, over coffee, she said to Stuart, 'I know you've had things on your mind. I've been very unhappy for you. But there was nothing I could do. There are some regrets you can't talk your way out of.'

He realized that she'd answered a question he hadn't asked, but he accepted the fact. As usual: he lacked the persistence to bluff against her. 'No,' was all he said, 'I see that.'

After supper they took a turn round the block, arm in arm. The rain had cleared and taken the sweats with it; it was a fine night, rather cold than otherwise. Restaurants had begun to spill out on to Broadway, setting their tables and chairs on the pavement. The candles kept blowing out; and the smokers lit them again with their cigarette lighters. Couples held hands to keep them warm across the tables before their food arrived. 'Life here is very rich in other people,' Mary Louise remarked. Stuart said, 'When I think of how far I've come from the kid I was. Without having to change too much. That's the main thing.' He was unusually drunk. 'I've stayed true to myself.' Later, as they mounted the narrow stairs of their apartment, he said to her, 'You have great power over me. You should know that.'

That night he dreamed of Rachel for the first time. They were in class, busy with a test. She raised her hand, and he followed the curve of the seminar table to the corner where she sat. It was clear from her demeanour that she had seen through him, his excitement. He could barely contain himself; and she had accepted that fact and taken pity. When he reached her she touched her small hand to his crotch and began to press. His shame was terrible, burning; he felt himself go red. All of the other students looked up in silence. Rachel continued to hold him in her palm, patiently; he was very close to coming, his pleasure had spread to his hands, his feet, his heart. He couldn't tear himself away from her. He was completely exposed; and imagined what would happen if she didn't let go that minute, that second, but she did, in time. Not that it mattered any more, he had nothing left to hide. He felt himself waking unsatisfied, and began to push desperately against her neck, her hair, her face as she turned, then her chair, when she ducked to evade him. At last he lay on his belly on the table, blind at least to the children surrounding him now, highly amused, waiting for him to finish. But it was useless, the moment had passed. His heart was racing when he opened his eyes, the broken light of spring dawn fell in straight lines through the window blinds across their comforter – grey and white slats of light shifted in the wind. Birdsong, irregular, expectant, entered the room from the dirty city trees outside; it was almost summer.

His shame was terrible, but gratitude filled him when he woke to the solitude of his bed, his head – his secret intact. His innocence preserved; his whole life he had done nothing to be ashamed of, that was something. There were only his thoughts. Who knows, if he'd had a daughter, what his temptations might have been. Something else to be grateful for: the gentle protection of uneventfulness. He turned on his side to kiss the neck of his wife. He wanted to take in her smell, some proof of her body, warm and sweet with the creams she applied before sleep. She stirred a little, waking. 'What's this, what's this,' she said and looked at him. 'I've been very unhappy for you,' she murmured again. She felt his frustration against her leg and smiled, blindly, through thick lips. 'You've been dreaming, haven't you?' It is true, he thought, her sympathies are large, consoling. She reached a warm hand under the bedclothes and began to relieve him.

SUMMER

Inheritance

I

Rachel's mother took her down Madison Avenue on Saturday afternoon. Mild milky February weather, weeks after the latest snowfall. Only the grit remained. This is what Tasha loved best, the bright clothes and elegant shoppers, the costliness of everything, the fellow feeling among the rich. She often said, holding a garment by the hook at arm's length, observing the hang of it, 'I couldn't carry it off any more. But you, so petite. It isn't right the way the clothes make love to you. Me, any old sack will do.' It wasn't true of course and Rachel said so. In fact Tasha made herself up with a high hand. After her hair went grey she dyed it blond, wore it short in a bob, to show off her long neck, only a little mottled. Her wide swollen cheeks remained sensual, even at fifty, though her chin had begun to work free of the face, stand out. She had worrying eyes. Rachel could see the pale film on them and imagined lifting one by the finger from a corner of her whites. They were flat, too, like an insect's, bright and large and vivid, but shallow behind. Tasha knew this herself and wore wide shades. Her lips were heavier, richer, the top drooped over the bottom; she had a lazy mouth. Rachel had seen photographs of her mother in her youth: long-legged with long thin arms, hanging awkwardly, touching her thighs. Excessively beautiful; she had the sleepy nervy look of a satisfied addiction.

She'd been working, more off than on, as a model when she met Reuben, Rachel's father. An older man, a lawyer. One of his clients was Grace Kupchak, the designer. Occasionally, he came along to an after-show party, and the girls, set free by his age, his propriety, made a fuss over him. They found him attentive, bemused, uninterested. Tasha was part of that crowd; really she tagged along with a cousin, hoping to get snapped up. She was twenty-six, twenty-seven, already past the age when anything seemed possible, getting tougher. And then the lawyer, a small-boned man, a little dry in his humour, nevertheless strong and sweet in manly odour with his top button undone beneath the loose tie, teased her for her accent. Tasha's family were German, French, Canadian, Polish, Jewish. These influences still clung to her breast; raised in America, she suffered her ancestry palpably; she lived among long shadows. A beautiful daughter often bears these burdens, heavy racial memories. She grew up well preserved, untouched, perhaps over-loyal to the family love, its lavish attentions. No doubt there was also a taint of affectation. Reuben discovered she came from his home town: Port Jervis, a land-locked stopover on the way to Syracuse in upstate New York. She felt younger in his company, more naive, richer in illusions.

Mother and daughter had a late lunch at Pimento's on 62nd Street. A shuttered kosher Italian with overgrowing window boxes whose green hair fell over the glass of the shopfront below. A leather-goods store; Rachel could smell it, like a man's hand in her face, as she stepped up the narrow stairs. They sat in the window looking up and down Madison, eating breadsticks and drinking Pelegrino. 'Why don't you have a glass of wine with me?' Tasha said. 'They're very European here. They'd understand.' Rachel said no. Tasha got a bottle in any case, though she never finished it. She had less appetite for decadence now than for the show of it. Still, after one glass, she began to question Rachel about her father. 'I bet the food rots in the fridge. That man lets nothing go to waste. Do you know while he was staying we couldn't get rid of the mice? Him with his doggy-bags, his leftovers.' 'While he was staying' meant before the divorce. 'For one thing, he can't control the help. You have to keep after them. All he does is watch and pay the bills. He thinks he can pay his way out of anything; but I told him, you have to take real human interest in life, or else everything goes to pot.' This choice of word surprised Rachel; her mother was beginning to delight in common touches. They always came out wrong. 'Is the maid in his bed by the way? You don't have to answer. I know.' In fact, as far as Rachel knew, Tasha was the one who had had affairs. Perhaps it pleased her perversely to think he was still active in these matters. This made the affront of their quiet sex life more personal, direct, a subject for blame rather than commiseration; and Tasha's life was short on personal implications. She said to Rachel, not for the first time, 'He never wanted me, he wanted you.'

The girl never knew what to answer. She understood quite well what was meant, and secretly thought it likely; perhaps she hoped it was. Even so, Rachel protested, in condescending pedantry that also shamed her, 'don't be silly. I didn't even exist. You were a beautiful young woman, a model. He was almost an old man.'

'If you think I was after his money, you're not as smart as you think. I had plenty other offers. I wanted a life.'

No, no, that's not what she meant. She felt the pressures on her mother's heart strongly; these were painful sympathies she'd rather shirk.

After lunch they walked uptown again and bought what they'd been considering: a pearl-buttoned shirt with a floppy collar; a high-necked red dress, demure across the bosoms, and short below the hips; blue jeans with small square pockets at the top of her thighs, too tight to warm anything but fingers. Her mother usually bought two sets of everything for her, one for each house. This Rachel hated, it spooked her. For once Tasha almost forgot, and Rachel teased her, 'Just one?', instantly regretting it. Of course, her mother insisted. 'You're as bad as your father. It's only money; it isn't anything. The only way to live with it is waste it. And I won't have you choosing, here or there. I know I'd lose.' Rachel said nothing. It scared her slightly, these alternate, almost identical lives laid out for her.

They dropped one set of purchases at the doorman on Park and 82nd Street. Then he waved down a cab to take them five blocks east. It was always a production fitting the glossy rectangular and pleated bags in the cramped backseat. Tasha liked to have her hand around all the string handles at once, and they bunched up in awkward array in the middle. She wouldn't let go; Rachel squeezed to one side. The cab pulled in just short of East End Avenue by the fire hydrant. It was easy to spot their house, with the red front door, painted thickly; you could see the finger-like marks of the broad brush. It looked still wet. And Rachel always imagined flecks of red on her palm on her clothes when she held the door open for her mother. Her menstrual blood, when it stained, reminded her of this brightness. The parlour was dark and narrow, flagged in black and white tiles that clicked under heel. The fact was, Tasha was the untidy one; a box of clothes for charity lay open in the hall, and her mother had been rooting through it to find something she didn't want to throw out. She had pushed, on her own, in an unhappy fury, the exercise machine into the corner, scratching the checkered tiles. Provoking one of her rare moments of humour. 'The only exercise I get from that *verkackte* machine is lugging it here and there out of the way. Look at how fat your mother has got.' And she pinched her hip under the gold cashmere; her skin, in spite of the sun bed installed in the guest room, paled as she held it in her fist. Rachel for once didn't correct her; stood rather on tiptoes to kiss her cheek.

At this, Tasha began to weep; she had seemed overwrought, humid, under great pressure all day. And now this animal reaction to a kind touch. As if her eyes had been lanced and these salt humours released. She didn't have to screw herself up to it, or suffer for it. 'Don't worry, don't worry, don't worry,' she said. 'It's only my pills. This is what they do to me.' Tasha had had a breast-cancer scare the year before; at the time she hoped it might bring Reuben back to her. She was never shy of speaking her mind. 'What do you think, if it was the other way around? How long could I keep away from his bedside? If he called to me. A minute? Fifteen seconds before I broke down the doors?' Rachel frequently suffered for such displays: what could a daughter do? Tasha sighed thickly and touched her eyes and upper lip with a handkerchief. Later, she went to the bathroom to blow her nose privately on toilet paper. 'Are you staying with your father tonight?' she called up the stairs. Rachel had begun to take her bags up. She stopped on the steps and turned round. 'If you'll be all right,' the girl said.

'I am what I am,' Tasha answered. Adding, 'I think your father has something to tell you.'

Perhaps he's marrying again, Rachel thought, unsure of her possible jealousies, probing inward, attentive to self.

The rest of the afternoon passed quietly; the place was heavy with time idly spent. Rachel once calculated: just for the three of them, counting her mother's home, her father's apartment, they had two kitchens, three sitting rooms, a dining room, five bathrooms, seven bedrooms. But she loved, almost in spite of herself, her mother's house. (Really, her loyalties lay with her father, her father's life.) Tasha had expensive but disorderly tastes. Among other things she collected painting and sculpture, even when the space to put them in ran out. She had invitations to every Armory show, and for a night, in her pearls, in her Vivienne Westwood gown, felt the love of salesmen, rather refined. They touched her elbow, her hands. They kissed her cheeks three times. A week later the goodies arrived, and sat in the front hall till she found a place for them. A narrow wooden dining room ran along the parlour and looked out over 82nd Street: the peeling fire hydrant; a silver birch, planted among ornamental cabbages; the gleam of parked cars in the deep neighbourhood shade, broken only at noon by vertical sunshine. At Sunday lunch in winter, for company, the maid lit a fire on the bricks of the fireplace; its glow was much richer than the daylight reflected in. On the far side, a kitchen opened through wide sliding doors on to the garden. They had an apple tree dropping green leaves and rotten fruit into a pond. In February, its bare lines were reproduced clearly in the still black water. No grass, but flagstones, uneven, dirty in the cracks; puddles sprang up like broad grey flowers at the slightest rainfall. A rotting wooden bench, sticky in fall with wasted fruit, was only very wet the rest of the year.

Rachel's bedroom was the tidiest room in the house and looked over the garden. (She once said to her father, 'I think I'm going to write a book. About my life. I am going to call it: *Unfurnished*.' He answered, '*Unfinished*. Clutter will come. You'll see.' But he appreciated this sort of conversation; it satisfied his sense of style. She said, 'Look at the way you live. There isn't anything.') A single high window framed the still life below. Sunshine fell plentifully in, and dappled on its way through the old glass; it cast irregular lines like rain shadows on her wall. An alcove set into the wooden panelling held her books. She had an armchair pushed up against the window, and a small kelim laid out over the floorboards. Her bed she made as soon as she woke up; laced pillows, a quilt in which colours, red and pale blue squares, proved the exception rather than the rule. Trying to sleep, she rubbed the wrought-iron poles of the headboard between finger and thumb. Now the paint flaked, and dull grey shone through. On the wall beside her she tacked postcards and photographs, scattered unevenly from a central concentration: Jimmy Stewart, Keaton, Corot. Her tastes were old-fashioned; she disliked contemporary passions, they seemed short-sighted. The rest of the room was bare. Her clothes were kept neatly in a walk-in cupboard, where she had also squeezed a chest of drawers to store what she referred to, conscious of quaint flirtation, as her *delicates*. She hung up her mother's gifts, and imagined herself performing the same task at her father's apartment that night.

The rest of the house bore the mark of her mother's accumulating habits, her wide tastes, her loneliness. Televisions in every room; Tasha spent a great deal of time at home and couldn't bear quiet; it made her talk to herself. Conversations, real and imagined, their attendant emotions, often specific, painful, came into her head – simply to fill space. She positioned large expensive sets, guarded by black speakers, on every floor. Rachel often heard several shows going at once all over the house; and in bare feet or thin socks she could sometimes feel the threadbare staccato of the bass line running along the old floorboards. Tasha's appetite for art was catholic; she admired, among other qualities, scale, but mounted her purchases indiscriminately. Modern and monotone oil-paintings, heavily framed, leaned creaking off the panelled walls. Beside them, she blue tacked posters picked up on her holidays. She couldn't pass a thrift shop without going in: cancer charities, MS societies, Christian aid, all benefited from her curiosity, her idleness. She liked spending money, she liked grandeur of all kinds, but she also had an appetite for variety, for cheap thrills. She bought a print of Salisbury Cathedral framed in brown plastic because she had the right change in her pocket and a gap on the wall to hang it in. Rachel's father said to her once, 'We didn't get divorced, we ran out of room.' But Rachel understood him: he wanted to live in greater modesty, more elegantly.

Then there were Tasha's plants; creepers hung from baskets off hooks in the ceiling. Spiders lived in them, flies drank from the rich soil: patience and restlessness at war. Thick-leaved ficuses sprouted between the windows, outgrew their pots, leaned and twisted to the light. You could smell them everywhere, wet, dark, flourishing, inhuman, the smell of a greenhouse on a cold day. But she had an equal passion for mechanical oddities: a hairdresser's helmet sat on a Fifties mannequin, her legs crossed, her nails red, in the sitting-room window, on a barbershop chair. Once a week it still caught Rachel by surprise; she thought she saw her mother naked, youthful. Rugs lay unevenly across the boards, overlapping.

Tasha bought several new ones a year with nowhere to put them. One of the bedrooms had been turned into storage, and Tasha spent much of her time inside, perched at awkward angles, going over old purchases, looking for something.

Rachel, too, found it oddly comforting there. Chairs and tables stacked upside down, cracked vases nested in each other; loose canvases rolled into one, the frames in pieces and kept in a box like firewood. Also, family papers, school reports, old *Vogue*s. Dusty tasselled lampshades, mustard yellow. A leather armchair losing its stuffing. A sculpture, picked up from an art-school sale: fat clay fingers nursing a real shot glass, which rested uncertainly on the pinkie. The layered slates of a billiard table, heavy and lustrous, unbudgeable. Somewhere, in a wooden box, the balls. Family photographs; black-and-white studio portraits in card frames. More recent holiday snaps, their reds and greens particularly rich and deep, unnatural; everything else fading to tan.

Southern light fell through the uncurtained window. It caught the cheap gleam of a small plastic trophy Rachel had won in seventh grade for spelling and dictation; her name was misspelt on the marbled base: Miss Krank. Sunshine emphasized the woodstain of her first tennis racket, in its antique press; the glint of gilt lettering from what was left of her grandfather's library. When her grandfather was a young man, he began buying books, whole collections. The complete works of Sir Walter Scott. Rachel suspected he never read them; it was a show of learning, a neglected ambition: 'If I had time I would read deeply into the world.' They lay in damp cardboard boxes and many of the spines had flaked off; they fell apart in her hands, stained her fingers brown with rotten leather. When Rachel dipped into them she looked for any marks he might have left.

His business was in produce and canned goods; he came over from Hungary to work at his uncle's grocery store. Together they expanded. For a while, the names Kranz and

Myerson were well known between Port Jervis and Schenectady: brought back friendly, indifferent recollections among strangers. 'Kranz, Kranz, I know you. My mother sometimes bought milk and eggs from Kranz & Myerson's on Sunday mornings for making pancakes.' But other thoughts followed, inevitably, the usual lamentations: even convenience stores may serve as symbols of lost youth. 'Kranz and Myerson's, I remember. On the corner of State and Orange, opposite Liebman's pharmacy, where we sat up drinking ice-cream floats. Now it's a Safeways; my corner shop's run by Koreans.' The company sold out some time in the Sixties; by this point, however, Rachel's father was already a rich man, a lawyer, though he liked to talk about his youth in retail, how he stacked crates in the summer, his blistered hands. The humid stink outside the service door, the fruit-flies, the rats, a real *Kindheit*. From which he had preserved Rachel.

Towards the end of her parents' marriage, she liked to sit in the armchair with her legs kicked out, looking through everything. She could hear her mother's raised voice. 'When you don't answer I like you least. When you stand there *stumm* with your hands in your pockets as if your silence were of a very superior quality. As if nobody kept their mouth shut before. Go on, talk, say something. Surprise me. I'd rather be accused than pestered like this.' Tasha, her father once explained, could never let anything go, anyone. Wherever she gave pleasure, she felt too strongly the duty of giving it. Another way of saying she had a sweet tooth for flattery. It meant too much to her, but then she was lonely, idle. Tasha had great appetites, wanted a full life to match her full heart. And really he offered only . . .

Rachel read into this what was intended. Before the divorce, Jimmy, Tasha's 'cousin' from Port Jervis (really only the nephew of an aunt by a second marriage) had come to stay – lived with them several months, sat on their pot, washed his hair in Tasha's bathwater, ate their takeaway left-overs at lunch. A photographer, he said, freelance. Reuben said this meant out of work. He had a long face, a pimple on his chin he scratched with dirty nails; nicotined fingers; long thin pale legs he showed off when he could, when the sun was out in cold weather. Other friends followed, knocked on the door, stayed late, got drunk. Tasha turned no one away. Reuben retired early to bed and left them to it. He never mentioned these things. Perhaps he found them too painful; or he guessed his indifference would appal her. Instead, they argued about money, her collecting habits. Rachel heard them at it, while going over old photographs in a shoebox: their honeymoon in the Maldives, her father in white linen, her mother holding a sandy towel against her pale breasts and laughing.

'This counting of money is a very bad sin. Thank God I know how to spend. For someone who grew up with little enough I can throw it around. Something to be grateful for. I couldn't bear to be tight-fisted.'

'Oh, you, come off with that. You'll make me angry. What is there I don't give you? That isn't the point.'

'For heaven's sake why should you grow angry? It's not your marriage too. Of course, none of this applies to you. Why should you lose your rag?'

'I come home I can't open the door. The house looks like a pawnshop. What are we selling? And in the mornings I can't take a leak without watching James shaving, one hand on the blade, another holding up his towel. Rachel preparing for school. Every day I clean out his hairs from the sink. You know how precious these minutes are. There isn't room for me here. I want you to throw something out. One thing. As a gesture of love.'

'No.'

'One thing. As a gesture of love.'

'Not one thing. Nothing. No.'

Also, her cleanliness; it was erratic and mostly directed at Reuben, her strictures. She had ambitions to entertain largely, glittering receptions, but no gifts as a hostess and no wide acquaintance. Really, something low class let her down. When she threw parties, she relied on Reuben's connections to fill out the occasion. The thought of their judgements oppressed her all week. He said, 'Call the whole thing off, I don't care, I never wanted it in the first place.' On top of everything, such proof of how little he understood her made her miserable. Couldn't he see what it was like to live in your own head, to spend so much time imagining life? Occasionally, you needed to act on these ideas. She thought she could bear anything so long as she had his understanding, his sympathy. For his part, he passed over these reflections quickly; of course, he guessed her point of view, but it didn't seem weighty to him, significant. What she required wasn't sympathy, but to learn to treat her own needs more lightly. If he commiserated, she only suffered more. So she found ways of making him suffer back. Before the guests came, she wanted him in the parlour to greet them. He couldn't so much as pee in the loo lest he stain it. So when they arrive, he says first thing, 'Go on, have a look at the toilet. I'm not allowed to use it till you see it pristine.'

Nobody moves.

'Will you do me a favour,' he repeats, 'and look at the porcelain. My bladder's killing me over here.'

Tasha blushes heavily; but something sisterly, combative, in her marriage forces her hand. She loses her cool. 'You could sit down.'

'I'm not going to sit down to take a leak.'

'We've got a bathroom upstairs.'

'I'm not going upstairs in my own home. At my age. With the waterworks under repair, no sir.'

Their parties were rarely a success; and after a while, Tasha gave up on them. Still, they argued – Tasha never gave up on arguing. But with the door shut and locked, it didn't seem relevant to Rachel. Her inheritance struck her rather as a subject for curiosity than regret. Everything passed eventually, and left these jumbles behind: the only things that survived were what you spent money on. Tasha herself once said as much to Reuben, the only days she remembered were the days she bought something. That's why she refused to throw anything out.

Rachel spent the afternoon in her room, reading; lately she had acquired a passion for books. Not that she was friendless, rather the reverse. Her recent preference for solitude surprised her, too. Partly, company tongue-tied her; she didn't like to express any common opinions, and since she found her thoughts no more remarkable than the general she kept them to herself. The prospect of college oppressed her: all those people. Wesleyan had accepted her for the fall; she dreaded leaving her father, the city. 'Your father has something to tell you.' What could that mean, she wondered; Tasha and Reuben hardly spoke. Also, the growing pressure of foolish adult expectations: that she would fall in love, break out on her own, etc. She had nothing to rebel against, no one to fall in love with.

Even Reuben, who should know better, worried about drugs, sex, booze. 'Daddy,' she said, in what he called her voice of patient petulance, 'I haven't changed just because I turned seventeen. You don't have to look for condoms in the wastepaper basket. I'm the girl I always was. People don't change just because the clock ticks.' Tasha, for her part, pestered her with very different worries. Why doesn't she ask anyone over? When she was her age she couldn't get enough of boys, just their smell, leather jackets, cigarettes, beer. Kisses like warm bread in the mouth. 'Nothing is happening to me,' Rachel cried more than once. 'Everyone expects something to be happening to me but nothing is.'

'Well, you're very quiet.' Both her mother, father complained of this. Tasha said, 'Why don't you bring that nice boy round?' What boy, Rachel answered, though she knew quite well who. 'I don't remember his name, quite pink, face like a lollipop.' They all have faces like lollipops, Rachel said.

'Without a name, there isn't a boy.' Reuben never mentioned him, but offered to take her old friend Frannie to the theatre. Frannie was a girl from Hebrew school; they were bar mitzvahed on the same day, Tasha threw one of her more successful parties for the pair of them. This was before the divorce. Francesca's mother, *Ms* Annie Rosenblum (Tasha pursed her mouth as she said it), had many friends. 'Very literary people,' Tasha said afterwards, 'never short of something to say. Hungry and thirsty, too. Like locusts they ate and drank.'

It was a shame Ms Rosenblum didn't get along better with Tasha – who, at that time, could be condescending to single women. 'Her pants barely reached the top of her socks,' Tasha complained, giggling. 'Like an old woman she stood there in flat shoes. I wanted to stoop at her feet and pull down the hems.'

'Sweet like Jewish wine,' Anne Rosenblum remarked to her daughter afterwards, making a face.

A pity that Frannie herself rubbed Tasha the wrong way. 'Frannie likes to talk,' Tasha explained. It was a line more or less everyone connected to the girl, including Frannie herself, used to describe her. But Rachel enjoyed the opportunities for silence Frannie offered her; she, for her part, liked to listen, and keep her real thoughts to herself. Though lately Rachel's sweet looks had become a subject of reproach. Once, taking the subway uptown after a party, Frannie complained of the way Rachel drew everyone's stares. She pointed at each of the men in the carriage in turn. 'Do you want her? Do you want her?' she asked. 'Do you want her?' They lowered their eyes. Frannie was conscious, among other things, of being at least an agent in their titillation. Yes, it roused them a little, such humiliation. Later, she apologized, after a fashion. 'Believe me,' Frannie said, 'if I had a *tusch* like you I'd wear jeans like that, too. How much did they set your mother back?' There was also, always, the question of money.

The boy was Brian Bobek. He came new to the school from Pittsburgh in the ninth grade, a short round kid whose shape seemed a testament to his good nature. He took a week to settle in, quietly looking about, then declared to anyone he met that he was in love with Rachel Kranz, 'the crown of Riverdale'. Apropos of nothing, he offered his heart. Such words he used. He said he'd made careful observations of the entire student body, and now he hoped to do the same to her. This was his kind of schtick, corny, unashamed. Quickly, he made a name for himself; many friends. Brian had a fine line in self-mockery, though not entirely without its optimistic undertones. 'Five eight and still growing,' he said, 'in case you're asking.' His colouring was pink and lent a peculiar vividness to the skin, which seemed an unusually accurate reflection of inner qualities: bloody health. He confided in Rachel from the first; she answered him with quiet affection; it took some such bullying to make its way into her heart. Frannie attended a school in Manhattan, but ran into Brian on weekends. She decided he was a boy she could talk to – that was her phrase; his confident effusions matched her own. Rachel occasionally felt jealous of her brash friend. It occurred to her, for some reason, that Frannie was capable of falling in love with him, while Rachel couldn't.

In the next three years, Brian became, as he put it, a *metal* head. He spent every afternoon after school in the weight room, and caught the late bus home to his father in the Bronx – a divorcee, a sales rep for a computer company. Brian was a scholarship kid. At first Rachel teased him for his efforts, touched his arm under his shirt, cooing. Little Brian Bobek, she said, is growing bigger. The blush was hidden by his high colour. She felt a delicate sense of her own power, such contact was a gift to bestow, she was very conscious of her hands. But Brian had in fact begun to change shape; he was remaking himself from the raw materials. His round face sharpened into strong lines; his bent nose stood out against the hook of his cheekbones. The Polish inheritance pushed through; before he looked like a full-fed American. His shoulders took on a relaxed gravity; when he lifted his arm you felt his self-restraint. It involved you in physical sympathies with him, these withheld forces. It amazed her, his power of influence over the stubborn stuff of the self.

The day before, he'd asked her to watch him work out at the gym. Friday afternoon; if she stayed after school, he'd treat her to a bite, a movie. This took some chutzpah, Rachel supposed; what he offered was himself on display, a vain abasement of love. But Brian seemed unabashed. She perched on the hard seat of an exercise bike – a cocked hat – and resolved to wash her skirt when she got home. Such a *masculine* landscape, she thought, stacked iron, warped mirrors, worn matting, very depressing: windowless, repetitive, bare. But heavy rhythms of music quickened her heart; as did the odours, perfectly fresh, emitted from the surface of the skin, these fine instant scents, among staler, more familiar smells. Looking around, she deliberately entertained sexual thoughts. But just as she began to taste his salt on her lips, she drew up short. Conscious of imperfect privacy. Even in her thoughts, her father was watching her, not without a certain satisfaction. In any case, Brian's sweaty crotch aroused only a girlish and mannered disgust. These superficial feelings lay deep in her – often, from internal coverts, she startled another one into the light.

Brian's attention, screwed inward, seemed to require great patience with himself. He lay on his back and pressed the dumb-bells upward in sharp strokes, grunting softly, one, two, three. Almost sexual exhalations, painful, releasing, it seemed, trapped gases, old frustrations. Rachel in fact saw the bar bend under the rings of weight on either side; she feared for him, but also disliked such animal powers. He carefully wrapped a towel around his neck before taking on weight and descending to his knees; his face sweated heavily and burned redder, but offered no other change of expression. Even she could discern the care he took over precise small movements; others, often larger boys, hoisted more wildly. Brian confined himself to very small variations. To trust in their effect over time seemed to her to require extraordinary faith.

Afterwards, he bought her a slice of pizza from the hole in the wall under the elevated tracks. Brian ate nothing – never hungry after a workout – drank a Diet Coke and smoked one cigarette. Rachel made a show of disapproval. He sweated lightly, in spite of a cold shower, and pressed his palm to his forehead. Apart from the smoke his other smells were perfectly clean. She wanted to touch his arm again but didn't dare. Maybe he had fallen out of love; maybe it was only a joke from the first. In fact, he thought how fresh she seemed; her scent was girlish, unspoilt. Most sexual thoughts oppressed him by their uncleanliness; but he could imagine her naked with her legs wide and odourless, the inside of her thighs cool and pale, no different from the skin on her cheek, her neck. They caught the train downtown, and she leant against his shoulder, very still, sleepless, with her eyes closed; they had run out of talk. It was Rachel who insisted Frannie come out to the movies with them. Standing under the awning after, on 86th Street, Frannie bummed a smoke off him; she stooped and he lit it with the smoulder of his own cigarette. Rachel wanted to scream. So much was forbidden her; and she had such poor desires. She walked home early and left them to it.

Lately, books had been her consolation. She had discovered a passion for reading; and wondered if it, like Brian's weightlifting, could effect a change in mass, in personal gravity. For the first time in her life she felt she had inward alleys to explore. Her teacher, Mr Englander – a tall sloping man with a pinned-back countenance, full in the cheeks, somewhat pink, also humorous, reserved – had a habit of catching her eye. She realized that her answering look satisfied him; and like her mother, she couldn't resist giving pleasure. But she lacked the nerve to speak her mind; whatever she said sounded so much tawdrier than what she thought. Mr Englander was famous, especially among the girls, for kindly pedantry; they sometimes teased him by provoking his corrective habit. Rachel rather feared it; she disliked being caught out in imperfections.

Inevitably, of course, sex talk came up in class; but his manner was cool and proper. Rachel rather admired him for it, and envied the attainment of an age, a position in life, when such thoughts lacked heat, and could be clearly, fully discussed. She remembered her own insistence: 'I'm the girl I always was.' Well, nobody expected her to be; they wouldn't let her alone. Whatever she said or did was burdened by heavy interpretations; people had such dirty minds. These seemed almost a literary requirement: her classmates found sex at the bottom of every metaphor. Mr Englander, to be fair, usually discouraged them. They had been discussing Shakespeare's influences. He had assigned them a packet of contemporary verse: a black-ringed binder with thick uneven paper that took in the sweat of your thumb. That afternoon she lay in bed, the bars of her bed against her back, and read, quietly unsticking her lips at each line:

> When as the rye reach to the chin,
> And chopcherry, chopcherry ripe within,
> Strawberries swimming in the cream,
> And school-boys playing in the stream;
> Then O, then O, then O my true love said,
> Till that time come again,
> She could not live a maid.

But her ear baulked at the word *chopcherry*, though it pleased her, and she couldn't connect the thoughts: whose *chin*, what *time*, why *maid*? Was a girl or a boy speaking? She had a very particular brain, like her father's, a stubborn streak. He praised her for it once, saying her best intellectual gift was the refusal to understand. She would have to read it over again later.

Around eight, she walked to her father's for supper. Tasha was napping; Rachel looked in on the sitting room and found her on the carpet in front of the television, her mouth open, lengthening her face. The television left on, its pixilated talking heads almost as large as her mother's sleeping one. Beside her, a space heater blew thick vents of air; Tasha chilled easily, and loved the almost human touch of warmth of any kind. Rachel tiptoed to turn it off, conscious, quietly guilty, that she didn't want to wake her mother for selfish reasons.

The cloud cover kept the heat of the city, such as it was, in for the evening, low to the ground; one of those cool nights you sweat into your woollens. 'Your father has something to tell you.' Yes, Rachel had been uneasy for months; Reuben had been working Saturdays since Christmas, which is why she spent her weekend afternoons with Tasha, shopping. He looked hassled, out of sorts. At seventy-five, seventy-six, it seemed undignified to keep up such a pace. Sometimes her mother was right: never to waste time is sinful, immodest. 'Who are we we have to do so much? The world will turn. Leave it be.' For a time, Rachel thought he worked only to keep away from an unhappy home. And, in fact, after he moved out two years before, those first weekends, months, he was very solicitous, dependent on his daughter. Greatly softened; too much almost, she didn't like to see such sweetness in him, like the juice of an old apple, a sign of rottenness. 'Come here, let me put my hands to your face. I need a *menschliche* touch.' His lips, when they pressed her forehead, wet, uncertain. Later, his manner was more correct; perhaps he had found another woman. This was his announcement; no wonder Tasha's tears lay so close to the surface. At his stage of life, there seemed something wonderfully ambitious, wilfully blind, in these fresh starts. As if he said, 'I begin again as often as I want. Don't tell me there isn't time to see things through.' He had been losing hair.

She crossed the quiet two-way traffic of York Avenue, the corner deli, the laundrette. She had enough to think about: Brian Bobek, standing on the street with Frannie, considering options, sharing a smoke. Rachel sensed their shyness as she 'left them to it': her own phrase, quietly repeated, suggestive rather than conclusive. These cigarettes: her father had a morbid horror of them. Occasionally, Tasha bought a pack and smoked it out in the course of a month or two; just for the feel of it in her hand, she said. When she was a girl young men used to fall over themselves to reach her with a match. Another source of argument. As Reuben once declared, 'One thing I'm thankful for, we'll never run out of arguments.'

'Me, I don't want to live for ever,' was Tasha's line. 'I'd use up all of my love and couldn't bear it. But your father gets along very well without. He can keep going for years.'

Rachel regretted dragging Frannie along. Saw her stoop to the cigarette in Brian's lips. Their dirty intimacy demanded a reluctant respectfulness; shared sins were binding. Rachel's innocence, carefully preserved, left her lonely, but she wasn't willing to spoil it simply for company's sake. Recently, around the pair of them, she'd become conscious of her diminishing rights. Brian had always protested his love for Rachel openly and cheerfully, but people's high opinions of you also made certain claims. The opinions changed if you didn't satisfy them. Rachel wasn't sure her inside materials could ever live up to anyone's expectations; apart from her own, possibly her father's. Even so, such food for reflection offered a kind of nourishment; she was in no hurry. And the way was familiar, the six-block journey west from Tasha to Reuben: out of the rich quiet neighbourhood by Gracie Mansions, and through the dirtier blocks around Second Avenue, where the Rosenblums lived.

On the side streets, she passed dingy apartment lobbies, the brown-tinted fronts of cobblers', tailors' shops. Repetition of trees at even intervals, black heaps of garbage sacks, thrown-out ovens, yellow fridges. She wore a cream skirt, loosely pleated, printed with a few red roses, each on its cut inch of green stem. A pale green top heavily flounced at the neck, and a long brown woolly cardigan, knit large, with a single button just below her breasts. Slate-grey tights, little blue shoes. Her father always praised her turn-out, and she liked to please him. Tasha used to satisfy his sensibility; he had a fine eye for womanly qualities, and Rachel guessed that in this respect at least she had supplanted her mother. Tasha's style, in any case, ran to excess as she grew older; she hoped to hide behind vividness. Rachel was conscious of the subtler interior regulations demanded by her attention to appearances; she stepped prettily along the pavement, waited with still feet at the traffic lights. And enjoyed, in spite of her worries, the sense of a well-ordered personality, arranged in the best of taste.

Townhouses began to appear between Second and Third and then the apartment blocks grew taller, grander, after Lexington. She glanced down the long central section of Park Avenue towards the heart of midtown where her father worked. The lines of planted daffodils, in the mild February weather, had just begun to lift their heads, suggesting both method and profusion. Yellow cabs rivalled the flowers, clustering at the lights. A stately, humourless avenue, *sans* shopfronts and pavement stalls. The doorman, a wide-hipped Italian, stepped on his cigarette under the awning, and offered to take her shopping up in the lift. Mr Toretti. One of the buttons above his belt had come undone; he shyly occupied a corner in the elevator, leaving room for her, conscious of grossness. She smelt the grey smell of his Marlboros, his lived-in uniform. Two years ago, he might have pushed along a conversation with Miss Kranz. But she had grown in that time and begun to occupy her surrounding spaces, in which men fell silent. She felt the static uneasy pleasure produced by her presence, and looked at her shoes. Thinking of Mr Englander. Once she saw him with a hand in his pocket, adjusting.

The lift opened into her father's sitting room, and the doorman left her there, among her bags. 'Daddy,' she called out, 'Daddy'; she always called her mother Tasha. Her father had done little to furnish his apartment since moving in; its high ceilings, wide halls, still echoed slightly, offered clear perspectives. Tall windows looked over the Avenue and the rows of daffodils, taxis. There was a long deep couch in the sitting room, bright red, with square arm rests and a low back. A coffee table constructed of glass and steel. On the mantle, above the fireplace, a picture of Rachel at her grandfather's funeral, in a short black dress of wispy chiffon. Her colouring pink, eager, concentrated, her eyes wet with dutiful tears – producing a vivid effect not unlike joy. A woven rug, of braided blues and reds, hung against one wall. Other than that, only a poster under clear glass broke the white expanses: an architectural design of the Pont Neuf from an exhibition at the Met. Pencilled elms along the pavement had been wrapped in heavy white cloth and bound tightly: a picture in which the muffling also suggested flame, brought out the torch-like quality in the procession of still trees. One of Christo's jokes. In a high-backed wooden armchair her father sat, reading the newspaper; only he had fallen asleep, and a corner of newsprint lay dipped in the cup of cold coffee at his feet. Rachel had a sudden image of her mother, the television murmuring to her dreams, her open mouth. She stood quietly a minute, pitying herself for her ageing parents, before she removed cup and paper and set them on the coffee table; touched his elbow, and woke him by a kiss on the cheek.

Reuben Kranz was a delicate-boned man with a handsome narrow face; his countenance sharp, small-eyed, brown, finely wrinkled. It suggested the prolonged action of vinegar upon it, sour humour, cleanliness, preservation. He wore thin corduroy, a grey wool jumper, open at the neck, a tweed jacket; silver cufflinks in the shape of golfballs, a lonely eccentricity. The clothes bulked larger than the man as he got older, but he needed to keep warm. His hair was usually cut short, a grizzled grey; but as he lost it he let it grow. Thin strands waved in the air like weeds under water, and upset Rachel: she remembered him always as carefully groomed. Tasha was taller than he; they had made an odd couple at the best of times. Rachel recalled a photo from one of the shoeboxes in the storage room. The pair of them posed on the black and white squares of the tiled parlour: Tasha glittering in sepia, her low-necked dress and the slant each way of her breasts suggesting an open heart, recklessness; Reuben, elegant in evening wear, his hand at her full hip, steadying her. About to go out to a party. He widened his eyes at his daughter, very grey. 'Oh god Rachel you shouldn't have waked me. I didn't sleep well in the night.' Then he composed himself. 'I'm glad you're here: I have something to tell you. Let's get a bite to eat.' His mild displeasure, chastening habits were seductive. 'I'm sorry,' she said, consoling herself with the thought that his authority remained intact.

She dropped her bags in the bedroom; undecorated, aside from a white pot of lilies in the fireplace, blooming against the bricks – the housekeeper's kindness, Mrs Fuentes's – and a gilt mirror over the mantle. Rachel looked steadily at her reflection: she wanted to see if she was happy. Stray hairs along her temples, very fine, suggested worry, disorder. Perhaps he intended to talk to her about sex; nobody could believe that she hadn't changed. An old argument she was growing tired of hashing out in her thoughts, so she gave up on it. The way his clothes bulked around his shoulders, his neck, dismayed her; Brian, in his youth, enlarged himself, acquired mass, but her father was shrinking. Her window looked over a courtyard, a fountain among low trees, stuffed garbage bins lined up against a wall. When she laid her cheek against Brian's shoulder on the subway downtown, she felt him stiffen and begin to regulate his breathing. A little nervous, but perfectly controlled. Afterwards, combing out her hair before bed, she smelt his cigarettes.

Reuben waited for her in the hall, umbrella in hand. She said it wasn't raining, it's the kind of low cloud that never rains. He shook his head, a peevish gesture, and called up the elevator. 'How's your mother?' he asked.

'Asleep when I left. She took me shopping.'

'So I see.' They stepped into the lift, brightly lit; the mirrors, however, had been covered with brown pads.

'She thinks you're having an affair with Mrs Fuentes.'

'No she doesn't,' he answered very final, sure. He propped himself with two hands on the umbrella; a whimsical posture, Rachel imagined him breaking into dance, he must be light on his feet, so thin, his puffed-out clothes seemed to hold him in the air.

'She said you had something to tell me. Are you getting married?'

He gave her a sharp look, a close-lipped smile. 'Yes,' he said. 'To Marilyn Monroe.'

'Marilyn Monroe is dead.'

'Exactly.' As they stepped out into the marbled lobby, he said to her, between the knocks of his umbrella at his heel, 'When I said I wanted to talk to you, I didn't mean I wanted to listen.' But this was always his manner with Rachel; that he suffered her grudgingly, that he didn't adore her.

They walked a block west to Gertrude's; Rachel held her pace back. Reuben liked to look in windows; he had never outgrown the habit from his first visit to the city, when he was only a working man's son, a Jewish bumpkin with high ambitions. He liked to imagine himself in the lives of the rich. Sometimes he said, 'You can't get rich in a generation; the best you can hope for is to see your kids well off, to the manor born.' Rachel understood well what was expected of her; and she had graceful inclinations, she liked to please in all movements, without calling undue attention. But always, the word 'kids' struck her as odd. They saw a man at his desk behind the French doors of a first-floor balcony; he read with one shoe off and his bare foot on the desk. The newspaper twice doubled over in his fist so it opened like a book. Then the phone rang. 'Yes,' he said, through the opened doors. 'Yes, I see.' At the corner of Madison her father hesitated. 'I never remember which way.' She led him left after crossing the street.

At dinner, waiting for the food to come, he put his hand to

the back of his head, as if to stretch his neck; this had become a characteristic gesture. 'I'll tell you a story,' he said. 'A couple months ago I was playing squash with Bert Conway over at the Yale Club. Build-up to Christmas, midtown very busy. I was in a sweat just walking down from 57th Street. A close match; he's no slouch. At one point, after a tough rally, I notice I can't find the ball. Then I'm looking round for Bert Conway. So he puts his head in the door, already wet from the shower. He says, OK, I give, you win. If it gets you off the court. You coming or not? I lie to him, I say I'm stretching out.'

A waiter, Slavic, with honey hair, arrives in a sidelong flourish, holding a tray high with upright elbow. Wherever they eat, her father orders steak and fries and a bottle of house red. 'You eat like a fat man,' Tasha used to say. 'A poor man having a night on the town.' He was proud of his appetites, his spare figure. 'Do you remember the little mole on my nose they cut out a year ago?' He cuts into the meat which bleeds richly on to the potatoes. Rachel has fish; she lifts the delicate skeleton between knife and fork. Her father's manner with food is still rough; he talks through a full mouth. It pleases her to see this forceful appetite. 'Very unpleasant, a real eyesore. After the operation, you met me; I had to lean on your shoulder. We walked to the movies against a few flakes of snow. Coming out, we saw all the heavy work had been done; such a bright afternoon.' He paused to consider it and drank, still swallowing his beef. 'Last week I forgot to get out of bed. When I remembered, I couldn't. I called the only number I could think of, yours, but you were at school. Tasha had to bring me in.'

Rachel laid her knife and fork side by side on her plate. Weeping, she drank from her glass of iced water, appreciating the cold. 'What are you saying? What's wrong?' A piece of ice was thick in her throat.

'I suppose we're all dying. Me, I'm only in a little more hurry.' His stuffed clothes seemed a necessary prop; they held him up. 'Come, come, my dear. I've always appreciated your quick sympathies; but it hurts me too. I don't want you to feel so much for me.' She remembered her mother's easy tears: Tasha knew. 'How long could I keep away from his bedside? If he called to me. A minute? Fifteen seconds before I broke down the doors?' Perhaps it meant they would make another go of their marriage, if only to see it out till the end. Rachel couldn't tell, in such conditions, if this was desirable to her or not; she prepared her heart against jealousy. 'I have been diagnosed with a secondary metastasis. Multiple lesions in both cerebral hemispheres and in the cerebellum.' Such specific language offered him some consolation; he always enjoyed technical detail. In the weeks to come, however, he would lose his grasp on precision. 'I have seen X-rays; my brain looks like mouldy bread. There's no point in operating. They don't like to say *how long*, and then they say, set your affairs in order, take a holiday. (Me? A holiday?) What they mean is two months. One two three months.'

She felt barred from the significance of what she heard; her weeping answered only the first and simplest understanding of this news. It was like eating without appetite, merely for taste. Shut in a dry light skull, almost soundless, she considered his death; if she ever managed to break out of her own head she would scream. But inside, the weight of it could not reach her. The garlic in her fish seemed distasteful, much too rich in flavour; she would have preferred simply lemon, perhaps a little butter, nothing heavy. The oil made its way straight to the skin of her face; she was sensible of a faint mottling. Her complexion was generally clear, it is true; but now if she touched her hands to her cheeks a residue of her meal thickened her sweat; she rubbed together the tips of her fingers.

She said, 'I don't want you to die. I'd rather Tasha had to die.'

'She's a young woman still, don't worry. You won't be left alone.'

'Please don't leave me alone with her. You don't remember

what it's like. You couldn't bear it.'

His head seemed too small against the tall back of the chair. He was always fine featured, long necked. He wore a silk crimson shawl wrapped round and tucked into the front of his open shirt. Well bundled, he looked filled out with straw. Even so, much of the meal, he'd complained of the cold. 'I've given this a great deal of thought,' he said. 'You'll be provided for; you won't depend on anybody.'

'I don't want your money. I want you. I won't touch your money. Give it to Tasha. Let her spend it.'

The waiter, a heavy-lipped young man with smooth wide cheeks, refreshed her glass with cold water from a sweating copper jug. She said, 'Thank you', soft-voiced over her shoulder. (Manners were bred deep into her pedigree; sometimes she thought her truest voice was polite confusion.) When he reached towards the bottle of red wine on the table, Reuben gestured toward it with his hand. 'I can pour my own drink,' he said, knocking the bottle over. 'Oh, look. Such mess.' His distaste, heavily expressed in the raised corners of his lips, squeezed eyes, was real, impatient; unaffected, it seemed to Rachel, by age or circumstance. The wine left a widening track along the white table cloth, which soaked up very little – 'A cheap material,' Reuben later remarked – and ran over the edge of the table on to the floor. Rachel blushed; she was painfully embarrassed. 'I'm not a drunk,' Reuben said, 'I'm not a drunk.' For the first time, his daughter noticed a certain thickening in his speech. 'We're trying to talk. He won't leave us alone.' Two other waiters appeared. The wine, half finished, had spent itself; Rachel always remembered the way its red flow died out at the level of the bottleneck. The broad flourish of the stain, poised at its own edges like a filled cup, seemed to express the larger disaster: blood was being spilt, nothing could clean it. With quiet grace, they removed plates, glasses, cutlery, candle and replaced the cloth. Only the purple darkening wetness at her feet remained. Reuben had lifted his elegant hands open-palmed in the air as if to say feh to this, feh to all this.

'I've given it a great deal of thought,' he repeated. 'The money is yours; do as you please with it. This is what I can give you, what I've worked for. Now you don't understand the difference it makes, but you will. My life has been too narrow; I confined myself to very specific ambitions.'

'What you want is', Rachel interrupted, 'I should end up like Tasha.'

'You could do worse. Your mother has generous sympathies, they give her great pain.'

'So you walked out on her.'

'I couldn't compete,' he cried, pulling at the silk at his neck. 'I couldn't compete, for space, for air!'

Her fish lay in thickening oils. Dark folds of skin among the fine bones at the side of the plate yellowed as they dried. Reuben continued to eat. 'Even so,' he said eventually, 'I understand you.' Eyes in the head of the fish looked up from the broken neck. Rachel imagined her dead father as he ate in front of her. 'I don't believe you,' she declared, folding her napkin. 'I don't believe the doctors.'

'It's true she is difficult to live with – we suffer with her. No, you should be free of these restraints. I think, Rachel, you've been too caught up in the battle of your parents. You keep fighting it out. You want me to win this time, I know, I'm flattered. Well, come fall you'll be rid of us both.'

'I don't believe it.'

'Well, listen to me, keep your mouth shut. I understand that this isn't something you can answer with any real feeling, any grace. Not now, but later, I want you to consider what I've said. What I've worked for all my life offers you real freedoms; do what you want with them, that's all I ask. Don't confine yourself for form's sake.'

'Sometimes Tasha is right. The way you talk about money is a real sin. Please, let's go. I don't want to be looked at any more.'

He left money on the table, his wallet was thick with bills, he disliked banks. Standing up, he reached out for his daughter. She caught him by the hand and then the elbow; he was very unsteady, also light, easily supported. 'I'll tell you what they're looking at,' he said loudly. 'They think I'm an old drunk taking out some piece of skirt.'

'Hush.'

'Some old drunk.'

He picked up his umbrella at the door, and let go of her, shifting his weight. Into the cool night air; spring was coming to the city, its concrete and iron. You could hear it in the taxis, the grit in their tyres loosened, the hot hum of the running motors; smell it in the air coming down 82nd Street from Central Park. Rachel remembered the photograph of her at her grandfather's funeral: such pretty grief, her pricey black dress, worn once. Now she felt ugly and dry. She didn't know what to look like; she couldn't feel anything. 'I've said my piece. You have a large inheritance. I want you to live like it.' Rachel, with her hands over her ears, 'I don't want to talk about money. I don't want to talk about money.'

He couldn't remember the way home. His anger at this fact was very real, very like his old manner.

Later, Rachel's tidy habits offered her some consolation. She flossed in front of the bathroom mirror on cold feet. A white mosaic of small hexagonal tiles; she felt the grouting in her toes and dug in. Her face contorted oddly in her hands, as she pulled the waxed string between empurpled fingers; her gums bled lightly. She rinsed, tasting her own salt, and spat. She rinsed and spat again to clear her mouth. Cupped fresh tapwater in her humbled hands and drank; it tasted of pipes and porcelain. She spread her wet palms across her cheeks, rubbed behind her ears, at the back of her neck, vigorously, ungrieving. Before bed, she lifted her recent purchases out of their bags, their tinsel paper, and hung them in the dressing cupboard, her blouse, her dress, and folded her new jeans over a hanger. Tasha, at first, hadn't thought to buy two pairs, till Rachel prompted her. It must have seemed a waste to her mother at the time; the arrangement wouldn't last much longer.

II

It seemed to Rachel at first, that her knowing was in fact the cause of his rapid decline. After the announcement at dinner, in the days following, she began to spot the inconsistencies in his manner, his sudden imbalances. Sometimes he seemed his old self, kindly, sharp; and even took a cab to the office. When she got home from school, she found his apartment empty, the sports page stolen from the paper on the coffee table. This is what he liked to read on the way downtown. Tasha told her to move in with him. 'I won't have him living alone now, and he doesn't want me.' By living, of course, what she meant was the other thing; Reuben had always chastised her for euphemism. But in this instance, Tasha's generosity surprised Rachel; she had guessed her mother would be jealous of his dying, another one of Reuben's characteristic retreats into silence. She herself chided her father prettily when he got home, grey in the face, worried-looking. (Rachel, amazed, that such grave concerns still took the shape of worries in his features, his thoughts.) 'What do you want?' he said. 'I should watch myself die. No sir, I'd rather make other people watch. This is what money can do at this stage in life.' Rachel offered to stay home from school, if that is what he wanted.

She watched him too closely; this is what he complained of. Indeed, Rachel felt complicitous; the least stumble in his manner she attributed to dark causes. As if she herself had come to collect death's debts. In fact, she didn't believe he was dying; a lack of faith that also made her miserable, since she had already spent so much mourning on him. As if, in spite of her disbelief, she wanted the grand event. Often she wondered how she might greet sudden good news. It's all off, an improbable mistake. Clearly, relief would take some of the wind out of her sails; she was conscious of living richly, in high weather. (Her mother's great flaw, as it happens; Tasha's passion for dramatic occasions.) And, for once, she had her father to herself, idle, dependent; she had the nursing of him, these were tender relations, unequalled. And soon enough, his condition took away her doubts – he was deeply wounded, fast fading – and left her the peace of mind to concentrate on the task at hand. She came home from school, sweating lightly in her armpits, her shoulders, along the line of her bra straps, her backpack, in the dirt of the subway and growing heats of spring; after washing her hands and face, she found Reuben in bed, fully dressed, unsleeping, slowly going mad.

The things he said to her! He had an itch in his head, under his hair, which was both growing longer and falling out in patches. (The doctors tried what they could with chemotherapy; these were difficult questions in arithmetic, equations of life and pain.) Rachel scratched his dry scalp with her manicured fingers. She found the build-up of his skin under her nails very distressing, and at night, before bed, washed herself thoroughly in the heavy shower, applying a bristle brush to her fingers' ends till they grew pink and raw. Even so, his suffering was much deeper, on the brain. He was convinced he could feel the lesioning. She couldn't touch him there, or unpersuade him. All his life, in spite of his careful and conservative habits, Reuben had wide curiosities and an unchecked tongue. Tasha often hushed him embarrassed – the things he said! Now he indulged it freely.

He said, 'I read today that in certain creatures, the anus and mouth are indistinguishable in gestation.' The papers lay on his bed, a happy mess in other circumstances, say a long Saturday morning. Rachel had come home from school, sat beside him with her hands open on her lap. He kept the heating on and the windows shut; she sweated lightly, her palms were plump and red. 'One of Annie Rosenblum's pieces, your friend's mother. A highly suggestive fact. I thought, all our itches are very deep, internal. We get at them anyway we can, through the body's holes: mouth, anus, even the ears, the eyes, the navel. The penis, naturally. It doesn't matter which; everything inside desires a human touch. Of course, for the most part, out of our reach. For this reason, perhaps, women take greater pleasure in sex. I must say I've always found the homosexual act abhorrent, but this fact gives me certain sympathies. If, as she writes, the mouth and anus are interchangeable.'

Rachel didn't know what to answer. 'Oh, look at you,' he said. 'So prim. At your age. Believe me, I know what your thoughts are like.'

She blushed brightly and moved to open a window.

Often, however, he addressed more personal memories. The first time he met Tasha, at a party in Grace Kupchak's sitting room. Her high windows framed by little palm trees, hot-smelling as summer grass, the views overlooking Fifth Avenue and the Park: what luxury, the limousines sleekly moving among the one-way traffic. God, what a young man he was still, at fifty! A partner in his firm, Reuben had spent less of his life unworking than those pretty kids. Such appetites they had for company, for making talk; these, he noted, often required secondary passions to serve as points of contact. Fashion, of course, and gossip, but even higher matters were entertained simply as food for conversation: art galleries, films, politics. He preferred to spend his enthusiasm on what concerned him personally. Not that the news was unimportant, far from it, but he disliked the airs of the younger generation, the way they couldn't so much as kiss without the sanction of some higher cause. Any sense of what was private and mattered privately, and what wasn't and didn't, had gone out the window.

OK, he was a lonely old man, and didn't mind the way these young women touched him by the elbow and displayed the hand's breadth of fine skin between their breasts and throat. But he couldn't talk to them as a man; and they seemed to take his silence for disinterest. It cost them nothing to hover around Grace's dry-witted, overdressed lawyer, making nice. Grace always said, 'Oh Reuben, we'll find you something; it's just a question of seeing what fits for a rich man.' Grace was no great beauty herself any more, fat in the hips and cheeks, with thinning hair; her bright clothes did no justice to these features. Still, her ugliness had its sexual undertones, the pucker of her lips like squashed cigars. And young men she had no shortage of; though Reuben suspected their real interests lay elsewhere. Perhaps Grace herself longed for quieter company. In any case, all her girls thought he was harmless; it shamed him.

But this kid from Port Jervis was a different matter, her vivid high spirits, easy to tease, admire. She offered plentiful material for conversation. Her accent, for one thing; a little sour-mouthed in the vowels and sharp in the endings, her clipped 't's exposed just the tip of tongue-flesh on the edge of her teeth. It seemed to him an affectation, very charming; and then they talked about neighbourhoods, families. These subjects he was comfortable with; they involved natural sincerity. Also, Tasha herself wasn't so young any more, twenty-six, twenty-seven. Already she had an eye for the value of kindness and courtesy; qualities she could rely on when her looks went off. Reuben's attentions were flattering. He took her out to an opera at the Met. His uncle had served as cantor for the synagogue in Port Jervis. The Kranzes all had rich voices. Large unhappy music moved them easily to tears, their tongues, their lungs twitched in sympathy, the back of their throats ached, they wanted to sing. When he moved to Manhattan, Reuben decided to become expert in this one field. Among other things, he took pleasure in growing knowledgeable about something high class, difficult, expensive. Reuben, in bed, wrapped in his summer overcoat from Barney's, propped on pillows, sang *Qu'ai-je vu? O ciel, quel trouble!* to his daughter, who tried to quieten him with tea.

In fact, Tasha was already in some difficulties. A month

after the opera she met him for shabbas dinner red-faced with tears. She carried herself haughtily; when she had unpleasant news, she grew angry in the telling, especially when she was herself to blame. A characteristic fault; later, this always enraged Reuben. As he said to Rachel now, 'This way I suffered coming and going. I couldn't win.' That night he took the seat in the window at Vespa's, a Kosher Italian on Second. He himself liked looking at the traffic stopping and moving on, but this way, no one but the waiter could see what a state Tasha was in. He ordered a bottle of house white, which Tasha preferred, and meatball spaghetti for two; something humourous in the eating he hoped might cheer her up. As it happened, she barely touched her food; only from time to time dipping her bread in the tomato sauce. Reuben complained of all the food left over. Well, your trouble is you never listen, she said; I told you to get what you liked I wasn't hungry.

'You said no such thing.' Even after all this time, Reuben was insistent. 'So she says *with me you have to read between the lines.*' Drinking heavily from her glass of wine she confesses: I've been heaving my guts up all day. I'm pregnant.

'Well,' Reuben said, his handsome head active, the lines on his face shifting, persuading, in spite of the still body tucked in like a lump beneath his sheets, 'you could tell she had worked herself up into a real fury. Of course, the kid wasn't mine.' He wriggled his hands out to gesture more widely; he took Rachel's wrist in his fingers, they were sweatless, cold. 'Belonged to some fellow she'd been going with before, a photographer. The reason, I suppose, she wasn't having supper with him, he had no money. And she was tired of living off other people's lifestyle. She was too old. Besides you couldn't do it with a baby.' He didn't want Rachel to turn away; this was part of her inheritance.

Rachel briefly imagined he wasn't her father; she could shrug off the grief of his death. The suffering she had in front of her involved something else, a change in perspective, new relations. Reuben let go of her. 'I couldn't abandon her, this Jervis girl. You should have seen her high colour: flaming. Boy could she fight for her rights. Drank half a bottle that night and dared me to say a word. Looking back, I see she played her cards right; I couldn't let go a chance for correcting her. For stepping in. Of course, I insisted on an abortion. At the time, she was grateful for these arrangements, for my practical talents.' (Rachel remembered her mother's words. 'He thinks he can pay his way out of anything; but I told him, you have to take real human interest in life or everything goes to pot.') 'I had the pleasure of comforting a big beautiful girl. Walking home, she leaned her head on my shoulder, her hair fell down my back. By great efforts and careful words, I could put to sleep her conscience. I'm sure she guessed how tempting I found these tasks. But afterwards, she suffered real horrors; the way she moaned in her dreams, when she slept in my bed, was terrible. I almost imagined the blood on my hands, between her legs. There was nothing I could do. I was lost in admiration for her, deeply in love. Such high passions she had, what a talent for suffering. I tell you it put me to shame. In fifty years I had hardly suffered at all; but boy did it start when I took up with your mother. These were thrilling times, very miserable. So I sat up in bed and watched with my palm on her hair. If I woke her she reproached me bitterly, but I couldn't bear for long to hear her sleep-whimpering. Like someone in her dreams was beating her with a stick.'

Rachel had never felt so cold towards him, this at the height of her grief. But she guessed something of what he meant: 'These were thrilling times, very miserable.' She had inherited such sympathies: an appetite for great emotions, no patience with small ones. Father and daughter both relied on other people to supply them with the usual human furniture, anger, love. A woman like Tasha made deep appeals to Reuben. As he used to say of her in happier times, 'She has plenty of weather, your mother.' By contrast, their climates were dry, steady. Yes, in some ways, her parents were perfectly matched. Reuben had worn himself out and asked for something to drink. She filled his glass in the bathroom and watched his Adam's apple make space for the water going down. He finished it with wet lips and asked for another, which he drank half of, and set the remainder on his bedside table. He said, 'So we married. Most people rush into these things when the lady gets knocked up. We had the opposite problem. Having got rid of the brat, we felt like we had to get hitched. Only decent; otherwise, what was the whole thing for? I thought at the time it's bad luck to get started on a shared sin. And it was years before she consented to have another child. You were a difficult birth. There had been complications. And after you, nothing.'

She ordered in Chinese and he made a great show of getting up to eat, washing his face, his hands. They sat in the kitchen and ate with their forks from the boxes bending in the heat of the food. Later in life, these scenes were often replayed in her thoughts. One thing that struck her as significant: that he took positive pleasure in explanation, in spite of everything.

At school, she wondered whom to tell. The pressure of this secret was great; also, as her father said, thrilling. Her private concerns for once were utterly absorbing; she needn't envy the busy lives outside her. Still, she felt called on to explain herself, she wanted to give some kind of account. It occurred to her that the news might pull Brian towards her again. Tragedy bestowed a kind of weight, gravitational force; it drew some people to its centre, very attractive. For this reason, she kept quiet. She suspected that he and Frannie had been making out, after school, on weekends, without telling her, sharing cigarettes and kissing, till their throats, lips felt rough, sore. It seemed undignified, for many reasons, to stoop to confessions in order to win back his attention.

They were reading *Hamlet* in her Shakespeare class. The school had invested in cherry-wood seminar tables and high-backed chairs. No expense spared. The chairs alone ran each to several thousand dollars. Their effect was elegant, wasteful. Even modest lines and a matt finish can intimate money thrown around. Rachel could almost feel the fresh wood dust fine as chalk in the palm of her hand. Mr Englander opened the windows. Someone complained of the cold draft, already pregnant with spring suggestions of growth. Full gusts shifted papers, open books rattled like fan belts. So he shut the windows again, one by one, looking unhappy. 'I don't know,' he said, 'to be stuck inside. On days like this. At your age. The fact that you don't seem to mind makes it almost worse.'

'Oh, we mind,' someone said. Laughter. Mr Englander wore a red bow-tie, knotted at a slant, and a knitted cardigan to hide the spread of his belly. His healthy colouring was a little uneven, as if he'd pressed his fingers to his face, leaving bloodless spots. His hair, steel grey and black, ran back from his forehead in flat lines, suggesting a wet comb. His head had sharply defined edges; you could sketch them with a single stroke of a pencil. Rachel found him a comfortable presence, large, unhurried. An air as if much of the sadness in the world was owing to simple grammatical and correctable errors. 'I want to talk about Claudius today,' he began, still looking out a window down the hill. 'That much maligned old man. Rachel,' he said, turning round and looking at her with his unevenly shaped brown eyes, 'will you read?' Instantly, her hands began to sweat, leaving their marks on the cherry-wood grain. He leaned over her shoulder to point out the passage; she smelt the must of wet wool.

''Tis sweet and commendable in your nature, Hamlet,' she began, 'To give these mourning duties to her father.' Her voice frail. She read blindly, red-faced, conscious of the attention fixed on her. Later, when she settled into the rhythm, the lines moved in her only the ordinary fret inspired by schoolwork. She crossed her brows and concentrated; she had been directed to understand this difficult thing, and usually did as she was told. 'But you must know, your father lost a father.'

She squeaked sometimes, trying to give depth to the words; this after all, was meant to be an old man's voice, his kingly tones. By the general quiet she guessed a certain rigid discomfort; nobody shifted or sneezed. They couldn't hear her: how she despised her mousy accents! And then she thought, perhaps they knew. She had suddenly understood what she was reading. Perhaps they were embarrassed for her because they knew. Her father was dying. Only Mr Englander, restless on his feet, seemed indifferent to her. Oh god. No doubt they all expected her to burst into tears. Whatever she did she mustn't burst into tears. 'Fie! 'tis a fault to heaven, A fault against the dead, a fault to nature, To reason most absurd, whose common theme Is death of fathers . . .' So shaming, to be exposed in this way; to feel their embarrassed sympathies. Afterwards, she couldn't remember getting through it. Someone else took over for the Queen.

It was only later she realized how much to the point these reflections were. And part of her had enjoyed the quiet attentions of the class – her mother's daughter after all. Later, she reread the passage, on the school bus home, moving her lips, the top lip hanging slightly below the bottom, pushed out in whispers. Its personal application astonished her. Her private feelings, in this context, seemed only a means to an end: a way of better understanding the world.

Afterwards, she decided to talk to Frannie. They met at Gracie Mews, a wide-windowed diner on First at the foot of an apartment block. Frannie ordered pancakes, then changed her mind to French toast, then settled sighing for the fruit and cottage-cheese plate, and finally persuaded Rachel to split the pancakes with her. So they sat picking at them while the syrup cooled, its skin wrinkling. Almost eleven o'clock on a Thursday night; the street lights reflected very white on the plastic tabletop. Rachel, for once, was spending the night at Tasha's and she didn't want to go home.

'My father is dying,' she said. She had a vanilla milkshake

and drank thickly through the straw. The sugar had gone to her head; she was almost happy.

'What do you mean, he's dying. We're all dying.' Frannie wore a wide burgundy shawl around her shoulders, picked up from the Met – a print patterned off one of their tapestries. It hung across the top of her shoulders; her gestures involved it in complicated folds and stretches. She could not reach across to sip from her friend's straw without a certain constricting flourish.

'That's what he said, how he broke the news to me. I can see why you two get on. He's always asking after you. *Why don't you bring your friend Frannie round? I like her. I'm no company for you like this. It's very depressing for a young girl.* That's what he said. *For an old man it's also depressing, to suffer with you.* I said, you're the one who's dying.' She sat now with her hands on her lap. 'Brain cancer,' she said, feeling the weight of these two words tenderly. A dramatic revelation: both true and important. She sensed the pleasure in this, and entered briefly into the medical details.

Frannie's tears were instant. Her full nose inhaled roughly, with a catch, and she waved her fingers rapidly at her eyes. 'I'm sorry, I'm sorry, I'm sorry,' she said. 'Only, I feel everything so strongly. My mother's always complaining, why do you have to suffer for everything so much? Who are you to suffer so much? Only I'm very tender-hearted. You wouldn't think it to look at me but I'm very tender-hearted. Oh Rachel.'

She leaned over to put her hand to Rachel's cheek, but her shawl was in danger of dragging in the leftovers on the pancake plate, and in the end, she stood up and moved over to Rachel's side of the booth. 'Scooch over, girl,' she said. 'Scooch.' And embraced her awkwardly with one arm. This isn't what Rachel wanted; she felt almost as if Frannie's sympathies made larger claims than her own first-hand grief. It was awful, this fighting in her heart, to be heard loudest. Quite unlike her. You couldn't blame Frannie, really; she was used, in their friendship, to taking centre stage. Why should she change now? 'Today in school,' Rachel began again, her manner demure, childish, 'my English teacher made me read out a passage about dying fathers. It was awful. I was suddenly convinced that everybody guessed, they were all so embarrassed, they didn't know where to look. I blushed to my roots, my voice began to squeak. Eek – eek, like a mouse. The worst of it was, by the end, I felt so – excited. I wanted to scream, this is about me. Listen, this is about me. Me. Me.'

'Stop it,' Frannie said, 'you're breaking my heart.'

'I'm worried my parents are going to get back together.'

'Why?' From this side of the table, Frannie picked at what was left of the pancakes with Rachel's fork. She couldn't help herself, often complained of feeling bored; she needed several operations going at the same time, as she expressed it. Rachel wanted to put her hand on her wrist and pin it. You fat girl, she thought; the pancakes are cold; leave them. Butter-smears stuck in the hard syrup. You have no sense of . . . of disgust. To keep eating like this.

'I don't think it would be right. Just because he's dying. They knew what they were doing before; he was very unhappy. To give in, like this, just because it's almost over, doesn't seem right.'

Frannie considered this. True, Rachel thought, forgiving, she isn't a bad listener, in spite of all her bluster. She liked to work out her various opinions. This required a certain attention to facts. It amazed Rachel sometimes to hear the things Frannie comfortably asked, said. She had a frog-like mouth, protruding upper teeth that pushed the thin line of her top lip out. A pursed mouth, as if she sucked on the tip of her tongue, not unattractive in itself. 'I don't know; it isn't only *your* death.'

Rachel bridled at this rebuke. Of course it is, she thought; it's mine, it's mine, it's ours. But some time later remembered it with grudging admiration: the girl would speak her mind.

'I never told you what happened with my father.'

'Yes, you told me.' Rachel determined to cut this short. For once, she had her own news to discuss. Also, Frannie's last remark still stung. She thought when she found out Reuben was dying she wouldn't care any more what anyone thought. This solid fact couldn't be changed: he was dying. All her other worries were unimportant. It didn't matter what people said. He was dying. She could use it as a point of comparison; nothing would seem significant in its light. If she concentrated hard upon his image – in his bed, propped against white pillows, the physical creature diminished by bulky protective covering, the featherbed, his light summer overcoat – the rest of the world would go away. Her father was dying. Frannie had always bullied her with her greater suffering, her worldly experience; Rachel was sick of it. 'You live in a bubble,' Frannie once complained. 'So pretty and petite, you want everything pretty around you. If something's ugly, you turn your head, you don't want to look.' Rachel turned her head at the time, full of pity: that her friend could confess so openly, shamelessly, pleadingly, how ugly she was. But now she too wanted to claim this prerogative: look at me, how vain I am in grief, jealous, loving, what an ugly heart I have. Shut up, you, I demand full attention. I take what I want.

'No, I mean, what happened afterwards. We don't see him any more,' Frannie continued. Outside, a little rain fell on the slant, struck the window, desisted. Flower baskets hanging off the lamp-posts swung in the wind. From where they sat they could see its wide orchestration: when a wet gust came, a woman, carrying shopping bags in each hand, ducked her head into her neck, retracting. A young man walking his dog stopped, holding the flaps of a trench-coat against his breast; continued. 'That's the phrase we decided on, Annie and me. WE DON'T SEE HIM ANY MORE. The truth is, he won't see us. He took one look at us and said, no thank you. Afterwards we went for coffee with his boy lover, this German kid. My father broke it off with him, too. The lies he had to tell to get rid of us, you wouldn't believe.'

'Let's sit here a little longer. I don't want to go back out. I'm staying at Tasha's tonight.' Rachel called the waitress over: a Greek woman with a heavily lined face, dyed hair, a kind of sexual gruffness. She brought her a cup on a grainy white plate; hot water and lemon, the tea-bag on the side. Rachel unhooked the bag from its wrapping and dangled it in; slowly brown stains seeped billowing forth. She pressed the slice of lemon between thumb and forefinger, and cleaned them afterwards in her mouth. 'I can't wait for summer.' A casual thought; as she said it she realized her father would be dead.

Frannie had ordered black coffee, and began snapping a sugar-satchel against her palm. Once twice. She tore open its contents; the granules gathered on the dark surface, soaking in colour before descending.

Rachel looked at her face bending in the teaspoon. 'My eyes are red. I think I'm coming down with something.'

'So my mother says, I pushed him away again, I always push them away. This by the way is true. Meanwhile, I'm sitting in Rohr's with wet feet. All of us at the counter, staring at the road. The German is crying. Annie is comforting him. Nobody's drinking coffee. A real scene. Suddenly I know how my father feels: count me out. People looking in at the window; they probably think he's my boyfriend. My mother puts her arm around his shoulder; too weird. I keep shaking my head, as if to say: it's got nothing to do with me. I'm an innocent bystander here. I hardly even know the guy.'

Frannie was raising her voice, as always protesting too much. It came from the back of her throat, harshly. Rachel resisted putting her fingers to her ears. She quickly claimed an interval of silence. 'I don't want to give it to my father,' she said. 'That's the last thing he needs. A cold.'

'God knows what goes on in their lives, these people.' Frannie was unabashed. 'Well, the daughter of a single woman has certain responsibilities, as you know. Afterwards, all I said to her was, easy come easy go. To comfort her. To let her know I'm all right. She was practically in tears. So I said, let's go out to the movies, what do we need with these men.'

She took a sip of her coffee: still too hot. Rachel observed the way her friend's thin upper lip protruded over the rim of the mug. She kept it there, blowing, and tried again in a few seconds, a childish impatience. Still too hot. 'My mother said to me, I don't want you to think that way. I'm unhappy you should think that way. I thought, you can't win, can you?' Now she drank, holding the sip on her tongue before swallowing. 'I won't be able to sleep.'

'Easy come easy go,' Rachel repeated.

Frannie exchanged with her a frank look, sympathetic – widening her eyes and taking her bottom lip between her teeth. It confessed that once more she had said the wrong thing, and begged Rachel not to judge harshly. 'Look at us with our fathers,' Frannie said. Rachel was suddenly conscious of unusually strong fellow feeling. She knew what Frannie meant: at their age, having these difficulties. In spite of it all their lives would continue interesting. The Greek woman came by, saying, 'Hot water hot water', with a tin pot in her hand. Rachel put her hand over the teacup; she could feel the steam in her eyes rising from the narrow spout, a soothing heat. She realized how cold her hands were. The rain, never steady, had gone away altogether, leaving only a low white sky behind. Street lamps sent their yellow light upwards; the levels of the apartment block across the road – pale bricks, curtained windows, balconies protected by brown glass – repeated themselves with only slight variations. Plants over the kitchen sink. A bicycle left out. The irregularity of the lights left on and off, suggesting a complex mathematical function. Rachel wondered how many people living there had more reason to be unhappy than she did. By no means a straightforward question, but not impossible to answer. Some yes, some no.

'Have you told Brian?' Frannie said, putting money on the table.

Rachel, sliding and rising out of the booth, shook her head. 'Only you. I wanted to tell you.' She dipped her arms into her white coat, rumpled irregular wool, bunched up at the sleeves and collar. 'I thought it might mean something different telling a boy.' Rachel took out her purse from her handbag, her face narrowing in calculation.

'Look at you, so pretty. Such a pretty suffering thing. Embrace me.' Frannie had to stoop somewhat, her chin held up by the top of Rachel's head. Rachel submitted to this, counting the seconds, one two three. Her hands ended up at Frannie's full hips under her shirt, warmed themselves on her damp heat, grateful for that at least. In fact, there was some comfort in her old friend's body. She let go.

'When did you start smoking?' she said.

'I don't smoke!' Exasperated, emphasizing each word in turn. Undeniably pleased, too, obscurely flattered. 'You're as bad as my mother. Sometimes I have a cigarette, that's all.'

Oh, Rachel thought, applying the whip internally, I am a tight, prissy little girl. But these pains offered some consolation. She suffered in more ways than one though the sufferings also alleviated each other. Vanity and grief offered balms fraternally. But still deeper hungers demanded satisfaction. They parted at the corner of 82nd and First; Rachel then turning happily enough towards the richer quieter side streets to the east.

Dying, he did in fact pick up her flu bug; the very human, very lively suffering contrasted strangely with his other grander affliction. A fuzzy head, the shakes, a runny nose, made him childish, loving. Kissing her goodnight, he asked her for an extra blanket over his feet. Laid on top, not tucked in: at his age, to find yourself fighting in bed on your own! No good. He fought enough with her mother; he didn't need to have it out with the sheets.

When she came back, rug in hand, a green army blanket from her grandfather, he said, 'I've been thinking, I want you to know. Don't blame me. Don't blame Tasha.' Her name sounded very tender in his mouth, a word with vintage. 'Rest assured, whatever your suspicions, what happened between us happened *between us*. There were no third parties that mattered. OK, that photographer, an insignificant man.' Rachel asked if she could get him anything else. He said Alka Seltzer, but made a face at his first sip and gave it back to her. As if to say, what does it matter? I'm through with these medicines. She moved to bring it back to the kitchen, but he wanted to talk.

'I thought, let her be happy if she can.' Rachel was standing in the bedroom door; he never let her go. 'But soon as I left, your mother put him out on his ear. *Reuben didn't mind enough* was all she cared about. I was worried about *her*, not these *dudes*. Tasha has a suspicious taste in dudes. Look out for it. Long hair, leather jackets, zoot suits, the works. I didn't suffer much for my own sake. These were small men, peanuts. Couldn't buy a girl a cup of coffee. Real nothings; two weeks with him was enough. *What did I care, I had you.* But living with your mother was something else, I tell you, something else. Who am I talking to, *you* know. She was very depressive, very difficult. Eager, unhappy, both. But things had been done to her, partly in my name. That affair with Jimmy never got to run its course. These relations have a way of coming round. OK, I take responsibility.'

The next night, at the height of his fever, he couldn't feel his feet. He complained miserably of the cold. 'It's like the grave in here,' he said. 'Touch my hand.' Rachel knew he was teasing her with these remarks; dying had given him great funds of humour. The kind of joke he always liked: uncomfortable rather than amusing. But it was worse when his humours passed. 'They're trying to freeze me out,' he said. 'I won't let them. I'll kick.' The way he said 'kick', Rachel had never seen such mean spirits, such pettiness. All the while the vents made a constant rumbling like a washing-machine. Hot humid air dripped from the inside off tall windows. She sweated and smelt strongly of her sex, even in spaghetti strings and softball shorts. Her blood swelled just below her skin, the softer blonder hairs on her arms, her legs, her upper lip waved lightly standing on end. A real animal, that's what she felt like in all that heat, a real caged animal.

As she kissed him goodnight, he whispered, 'I'm very cold I can't feel my feet why don't you come in to bed with me? Rachel. Rachel.' Such tenderness, she couldn't resist it. She took off her shoes and climbed in, turning her back. He held her shoulder in his arm and pressed against her from behind. The bed stank of unhealthy sleep. She held her breath, counting, one two three, and breathing out. Inhaled carefully through her nose till her cheeks plumped up – such a child, at seventeen; acting like a girl, on her first trip down the subway, among dirty men – and began her count again, one two. His hands felt like a sack of frozen peas. He disgusted her; she disgusted herself. 'I've never had a woman in this bed. I want you to tell Tasha that. I've never had a woman in two years.' She became sensible of certain involuntary reactions; human nature at its simplest responds to the feel of things and makes mistakes. 'Go now, go now,' he said, sobered. 'It isn't right, a beautiful girl like you.'

Oh god she would go mad; she would go mad. How could anyone bear to live in these circumstances? But surely, this kind of thing was always going on. She wasn't in the least unusual. Reuben used to say, years ago, at the house on East End Avenue, when they were all together, when Tasha asked him to help with this or that, around the house, in the garden; when one of their few friends was having people round, he used to complain, just keeping the lid on his voice, 'I'm under intolerable pressure.' At work, sometimes he added: at work. If he lost his temper, if he didn't eat, if he couldn't bear company, that was his excuse. Rachel never liked the phrase; the pedant in her baulked. A grown-up phrase: dramatic, untrue, unlike him. Of course, he *tolerated* it, he didn't go under. But she remembered it now, sympathetic: that feeling of coming to boil. She kissed him goodnight and stepped straight in the shower before bed.

In the morning, a Saturday morning, he said, 'You need a day off. I want you to buy yourself something, something for your mother. Spend a little. Feel free.' A windy sun blew litter down Park Avenue. Spring was coming in a hurry. Rachel could smell it; she wanted to get out, out. Sunshine the colour of apple juice fell in the kitchen window.

She said, 'What should I get for Tasha?'

'You know me. I never had any taste. Your mother was always very superior; I never dared pick out anything for her. The way she turned up her nose. I couldn't keep up with the fashions. Real *Port Jervis*, she used to say. I mean look at this place, just empty. I don't even try any more. But you, you're a beautiful girl. You'll know.'

Later, before she went out, he said, 'It's a wonderful thing to give pleasure to your mother. She's very susceptible to it.' A repeated sentiment; still, he had not uttered it in years. It drew fresh blood. 'Very generous,' he added, considering. She kissed his brow. In the end, she bought her pearls from Bendel's. Tasha had once said to her, 'When all else fails, there's always pearls.' The way Tasha skipped to the long mirror in her bedroom, her touched-up vanity – like a little kick of sugar in her tea – Rachel thought these things would appal her. Instead she had to fight back tears; she had stepped into the shadows, merely a go-between.

She began to play a game in her head with Mr Englander, simply to pass the time in class. She sat mostly in a far corner of the room, where she could look out, across the table and the assembled heads, through three tall windows to the outside air. A chestnut spread its branches high enough they sometimes knocked their knuckles on the panes. She heard the wind in it, plangent, gusty, wet exhalations. Its leaves had grown full, large in the palm, with fat fingers. Through them, uneven clouds shifted rapidly. At odd angles, light broke through, sharpened by these obstructions, strongly radiating from a central point. The blue skies of growing spring were urgently, repeatedly interrupted. Between the leaves, downhill, the landscape fell away towards the Harlem River and Manhattan. She pretended that Mr Englander was sneaking sly looks at her, and kept her eyes fixed on him, ready to respond.

Of course, Rachel suspected what lay behind this . . . recreation.

Her father was dying; his old assertive manner weakened by bedrest and wide regrets. His insistent recollections exposed a patchwork life. She had never guessed before he was unhappy, no, not unhappy – unsatisfied. Not that either; rather, what he longed for surprised her. Sure, he'd had great personal success; the kid from Port Jervis had come up in the world. A rich lawyer, a big man, his daughter educated at great expense, in the best traditions. But what should he do with his memories of sandlot baseball? Every day after school till the sun dropped, and later some summer nights, when the lights from the Walgreen's car park glimmered on. There was Bobby Spandau, now a claims adjuster in Syracuse. The Polkawitz boys, who all three went into their father's shoe-store chain, and expanded into Middletown. And Erwin Manno, later a basketball coach, fired for passing out bribes, diddling exams. (There had been a tearful confession of guilt, broadcast live on local news. Reuben's sympathies had been painfully refreshed, yes, he wanted to suffer with Manno, make equal expiation: we have all come a great way from what we were.) Important figures now with no part in his life; these, once, had been to him all in all. And little enough he had to show for their replacement: a failed marriage; alimony payments; two kitchens, three sitting rooms, a dining room, five bathrooms, seven bedrooms, maintained on his nickel; sure, a beautiful daughter. OK, he had achieved a certain personal dignity; but it helped him little enough with his hair falling out in her hands. His appetites diminishing, his thin frame, always a source of pride, now ridiculously exaggerated: as if he claimed kinship with other survivors, mocking them. What Rachel wanted, he knew, was that this final process should be presided over by his own firm will; she couldn't bear to see him in this matter as helpless as she. So he was disappointing her, too.

Rachel knew that her playful interest in Mr Englander was only a kind of transference. His big-boned filled-out frame made certain assertions: I'm not going anywhere, you can rely on me. Sometimes she imagined climbing up him like a small girl, making a ledge of his kneecaps, grasping his elbow, his hip, rising to arch her arms around his neck, clinging. His accent, in spite of thirty years in the city, was pure Midwestern: patient, clear in the vowels. It suggested plain-dealing, a practical intelligence applied, in his case, to questions of some subtlety: grammar, literary reference. Reuben always admired Midwesterners. He disliked Manhattan childhoods, he often said as much – fond of his own anonymous, up-state American youth. Sand lots, high-school bands, kids going nowhere in life: at least, nowhere far.

So she dutifully followed him with blue glances. And when Mr Englander turned her way, she looked wide-eyed encouragement: as if to say, keep talking, you're doing well. If only he would take notice. She imagined certain unavoidable confrontations in great detail. The class hour seemed long, there was plenty of time to give to such dreams. Meanwhile she kept her eyes on his clean, pink face.

There was a general storage room at the end of the corridor, one floor below, by the stairwell. An L-shaped closet with doors on both walls of the corner. Part of the unrenovated school plant: a thirty-watt bulb hung low off white cord, forcing a tall man to duck beneath it. Dimly, it lit the bending shelves, stacked with notepads, blue-backed exam books, boxes of staples, red pens. Vanilla and dust smells of breathing paper. A crate of white-out jars, mostly crusted at the lid. White-out was banned because the kids sniffed at it, but the staff still borrowed a pot from time to time – their fresh lemon and old milk odours very strong. To see in the corners you had to swing the bulb, or hold it by the hot cord. The light, egg yellow, cast long and short shadows against the stippled-card ceiling tiles, the ceramic floor. A spot of rare peace in the school crowds, its solitude concentrated by the clamour outside. Or, when the halls were quiet, the consciousness of being hidden. Teachers sometimes sent their students to fetch something from the *cupboard,* as it was called. This usually involved a laborious hand-over of keys, a clattering drawn-out search for the right one. Sometimes, to save time, they went themselves. Rachel, quiet but dutiful, often volunteered, fisting the singled-out key in her dented palm, letting the rest dangle.

Sitting in class, she imagined carefully what would happen if she came in one door and Mr Englander, opening the other, surprised her there. 'Rachel!' She heard him say it, the tone shifting. 'Rachel.' Her name, spoken aloud, revealing private meanings. The fact of the two doors was significant. He didn't trap her exactly, but approached in sudden view, from the entry by the stairs. To come deeper in, he would have to stoop below the bulb towards her face. The way she pictured it she didn't flinch.

When Mr Englander caught her eye, he turned away first.

In class his manner was dilatory, collegiate. He said, 'Sometimes you get into a business out of one kind of interest, one set of concerns. Single-minded: this is what you want to do; this is why you want to do it. Then you find, to your surprise, the compensation of . . . other pleasures.' He called for a volunteer and opened the classroom door. 'We need a king.' One of the boys, a fat, rough-shaped kid with messy yellow hair, shoulder-length, much-loved, stepped out. 'Kneel on the floor in the hallway, as if you're praying. Back towards us. Not far from the doorway: so we can see.' Rubbing a blond clump between his fingers, the kid let it fall in the wet edge of his mouth and trail out. 'Gross,' someone called under his breath. Mr Englander raised a flat palm, then lowered it dramatically, pointing. 'You, Hamlet,' he said. 'So superior. Step up.' Smattering of applause among the girls. (Rachel did not join in.) Hamlet lifted himself on his elbows, swinging from the table. 'Stand in the door with your hand in your pockets, looking at Claudius.' He gave them each an open copy of the play.

Later, Rachel remembered the layout clearly. The boy in the hall, with bent head: a closet thespian, letting his hair hang loose across his face, arms spread wide on the dirty floor. The lounger in jeans shifting on his feet, irritable, glad to be looked at. Mr Englander, gesturing, enacting – these rehearsed thoughts. How often must he have said this bit before? And discovered, amid the necessary repetitions, a way of working out deeper feelings. Her father clearly had fallen short in this. 'In some ways, this is the most important scene, the moment that turns Hamlet into a modern tragedy. *Now might I do it pat*. Remember the tradition of the revenge play: the hero raves, the heroine cries, all stab, and everybody dies.' Mr Englander moved to the window ledge; the pane rattled loosely at his back. His was restless bulk. 'Hamlet has his chance here. Consider what would follow if he makes the simpler cut. Would he become king? Marry Ophelia? Fight a civil war with Fortinbras? The play would take on wider political questions. By doing *nothing*, he drives the action inside, where it belongs, in the head and heart.'

The boys began. Claudius, with his back turned, loudly, bravely: 'Now my offence is rank.' The words rang rudely in the hallway. It suggested a strange freedom, which all of them enjoyed, to hear his unembarrassed echoes along the corridor. His tone unexpectedly patrician. The manner of a boy used to loneliness, long words, private dramatics. 'Help, angels!' – his voice rising grandly, before it broke into a squeak at the back of his throat – 'make assay; Bow stubborn knees; and heart with strings of steel Be soft as sinews of the new-born babe. All may be well.' At that, he pressed his head between his knees; his hair spread across the floor tiles. Rachel imagined giving it a good scrub between soapy hands.

Later, the words 'all may be well' offered her some comfort. Brian Bobek repeated them to her when she fell quiet; but many other things had come between them by then. 'OK, Hamlet,' Mr Englander broke in. 'Take your hand out of your pocket. Before any protest: I know I *said*.' Claudius had won a few laughs, and this good-looking kid felt put out by them. It seemed suddenly beneath him to give it feeling.

> Now might I do it pat, now he is praying;
> And now I'll do't: and so he goes to heaven;
> And so am I reveng'd. That would be scann'd . . .

Afterwards, Claudius rose grandly to his feet, and turned into the doorway. He had to hold the hair out of his face; his book propped open by the thumb of his other hand.

> My words fly up, my thoughts remain below:
> Words without thoughts never to heaven go.

Rough applause. Claudius bowed widely, sweating, puffed up, out of breath – just once, his gifts acknowledged. Hamlet had already sat down and crossed his legs.

'Perhaps,' Mr Englander remarked, 'Shakespeare should have called the play *Claudius, King of Denmark*. A more passionate protagonist.' Such licence with the name made an impression on Rachel; it never occurred to her books could be called anything but what they were. That choices had been made, inside, outside the text. When the door closed behind him, she caught his eye. He sighed through his nose: these kids. A complicitous frown.

He began to discuss in detail both speeches, 'answering soliloquies'. This short scene – his tone quiet, pervasive – lies at the heart of the play, its literal centre. (What an old ham he was, really, Rachel thought, perching at the window in his bow-tie.) This is what happens when you fail to act. Among other failures, the failure to communicate. Hamlet could have killed Claudius on the spot, his prayer had fallen short of God. (Rachel imagined balloons flagging and sinking as the helium leaked.) Each soliloquy involved a significant refusal: Claudius would not give up his wife or throne, and so condemned himself knowingly to hell. There is also, of course, God's rejection of the prayer to be considered. And Hamlet refuses – to fulfil the purpose of the story, his father's revenge. And why? Because the language of *doing* is very inexact. As soon as you *do anything*, mistakes get made. So he wants to think about it. He wants to work out the whole thing in his head. The modern experience, Mr Englander said, standing now, pressing his hands together flat before him, is defined by this: if you refuse to act, wider worlds open up within.

Some years later, more deeply read, a lecturer herself, Rachel learned to appreciate this account for what it was. Clear-headed, passionate, a high-school teacher doing his best. At the time, however, it promised much greater things: access to the larger conversations of adulthood, in which vital matters could be openly discussed, the heart's dearest secrets offered up. *People talk about important things.* Still later, as a grown woman, a married mother, she remembered him more sympathetically: simplicity has its place. 'If you refuse to act, wider worlds open up within.' This kind of talk still attracted her. She had supposed such conversations were commonly held; by this time she realized her kinship with Mr Englander was something rarer. (She thought of him whenever she looked over those drafts of her unpublished novel, kept in the storeroom of her house on 82nd Street. She abandoned it after college, quite happily in the end. Like a neglected pasture, covered in clover, they suggested a more general prosperity.)

That night she went home to Park Avenue and began to write, hot in her head in her hands in her heart. Beginning her first serious argument with him:

The play is called Hamlet and not Ophelia because Ophelia really does go mad. Hamlet's father has been killed and Ophelia's father has been killed. So the lovers have a lot in common. But the play isn't about the problem of action – if you look at him clearly

Hamlet does a lot of acting from the beginning – but the problem of going mad. Going mad is the only honourable thing to do in those circumstances: that is, if your mother divorces your father and kills him. That's why Hamlet insists 'I have that within which passeth shew', which is a pun on the word show, which can mean either something displayed on the outside or something demonstrated, something reasoned and proved . . .

All of this seemed tremendously important to her, even with her father dying in the next room.

As soon as she stepped out of the lift, Rachel knew she was there. There were empty bags from Dean and Delucca lined neatly against the wall. A glass of hyacinths on the coffee table gave off meadow odours, a strong undertone in the room, a window letting in a draught of outside air. A rug from home lay folded over the red couch. Cluck-cluck of closed-door talk from her father's bedroom. She knocked, and he answered alone, 'Come in.' Tasha lay back at an angle on the bed, one leg on the floor. She had her hand on her father's hair, lifting up the strands of it, patting them down again. 'Rachel, darling,' she said, rising brightly. 'I'm making coffee. Do you want some?' The manner of someone brushing off an infidelity.

When she was gone, Reuben tried to sit up. 'Help me.' Taking his hand, she shifted him back in the bed, then let go to get pillows to place behind him. 'Now that I'm dying she's collecting me again.'

'That's not fair, you walked out on her.'

'Well, what could I do? And now she's walked in again. I'm in no position.' Rachel's still face was subtly accusative; she felt like a child again, pulling no weight, as her father tried to lift her in his arms. All give; amazing how hard it was to carry someone utterly unresisting. That's how she felt now: slack. And wanted no part of this set-up. 'Hear me out. I'm in no position.' His voice, carefully modulated, betrayed the repetition of his thoughts, a private argument already thrashed out. Even so, an audience inspired him with fresh passion, at a third try. 'I'm in no position to turn down what I can get. I'm scared, Rachel. I have to do this alone. I don't want to. I want to take somebody with me.'

'Don't I sit here? Don't I listen?'

'Believe me, at this stage, if you could take somebody with you, you would. You'd hold on to their hand and drag them after you.' Tasha came in with two cups of coffee, set them down and went out again. She was wearing a flowered dress, light blue; her legs were still good from the knees down, her high lean calves, her arched feet. 'Well,' Reuben said, preparing to drink, leaning his head tenderly forward on his neck, 'You're too young. It isn't fair.'

Afterwards, they all ate supper together. Tasha ordered in; they sat at the kitchen table. 'Isn't this nice?' she kept saying. Rachel felt like a kid again; she wanted to scream, why do we have to pretend to be happy? The opened window looked over the courtyard, and the windows on the far side, unevenly lit. So many private lives. Later, she watched Tasha make her inspection of the apartments. Very approving: there were no marks anywhere of a third party. Rachel read silently on the couch. After Reuben went to bed, Tasha moved to sit beside her, laid her hand on Rachel's thigh. 'I thought you'd be happy,' she said.

'All you two do is fight. It's all you ever did.'

'We haven't fought yet.'

'You will.'

Tasha withdrew her hand and sat back. 'Fighting isn't so bad,' she said. 'You'll learn that.'

Rachel closed her book. 'I'm going to bed.' She didn't move, preparing herself for speech. Even she guessed it sounded over-rehearsed. 'You can't even let him die without nosing in. You always have to take centre stage.'

Tasha, deliberately childish, playing her daughter's game, 'I saw him first. I saw him first.' Rachel knew when she was being talked down to. But she remembered what Frannie had said: 'It isn't only your death.' Well, it didn't feel like hers at all any more. Or rather, this was only her first death; she had all the others to come, the people she hadn't met yet, the lovers, the friends. Also, of course, her mother's. For Tasha, this was the last one that mattered. She had the better right.

In the morning before school, Rachel liked to look in on her father in bed. Mostly in a rush, a glance in the door; the school bus came at a quarter to eight up Madison. When she put her head in the next day, her father lay on his back with his eyes open; Tasha on her belly still sleepy, heavy in sleep, the covers around her rumpled in human shapes, her plump arm sprawled across Reuben's chest and holding him by the neck. He didn't want to move; he didn't want to wake her up. He lifted his eyes and closed them again, one of those gestures, more intimate than meaningful.

She decided to do something about Brian Bobek; in the event, this proved to be relatively easy. They had coffee one night in the diner on First. He smoked a cigarette, the taste of it later strong on her tongue, a little headrush. She told him about her father; consolation quickly turned to something else. With her eyes shut and her face pressed against his, the world seemed close and large; gratefully, she was blind to most of it. They held hands at lunchtime. In the baseball field, in the bright weather, she laid her head on his lap and he tried not to move. Frannie's name never came up. Rachel, looking up through shut lids, saw red. Sometimes, among the bins in the alley behind the cafeteria, they made out; the sun shone hot on the white concrete, their faces sweated and cooled each other, their hands were restless and full of blood. Once Mr Englander discovered them; she was suddenly heartbroken, and ran after him, feeling an urge to . . . confess everything. But there was nothing to confess. And she never told Tasha or Frannie or her father.

Reuben didn't have long left in any case. The nausea got worse. After all this, a lifetime of eating, shitting, pissing, fucking, he couldn't keep anything down, he was sick to his stomach. He was beginning to reject the world, his body wanted no part of it any more. Not that you saw Tasha cleaning up. Mostly it was still Rachel who brought mop and bucket from the kitchen cupboard, who held his hand and lifted heavily upwards when he got off the pot, who counted the pills out for him in her childish palm. When Rachel mentioned this, Tasha cried, 'You have no idea what I've been doing all day, what I've been dealing with. You, you come home after a day of school. Every morning you leave him to me.' In any case, Rachel was glad enough of the work, of doing her bit to help him die. She couldn't share his bed at night, this was what she could do. It also occurred to her that these relations were less painful for her than for Tasha; her mother had known him in his more vigorous days. And Tasha, after anger, very weepy, heavy-nosed, yellow-eyed, leaned also on her daughter. 'What have they done to him?' she said. 'My husband, my lover. When I first met him, you should have seen the way he danced, like a man from the movies. Such light, quick feet. Me, I always had heavy limbs, my breasts alone . . . a woman's sleepiness. Later he told me how much the lessons cost; he could never refrain from mentioning prices. It gave him real pleasure on its own: the best in town, the most expensive.' Now, she didn't say, there were days he couldn't walk unaided from the bed to the bathroom to be sick.

Also, the headaches; the pressure on his brain was growing. His private doctor, a grizzle-headed German who took peculiar pride in his unstained accent, his American manner, prescribed cortisone pills. These relieved him somewhat. There were worse details. Rachel discovered the terrible power of the specific – of things, as she said to Frannie, you could never imagine, and never imagine going wrong. They had inserted a 'line' in his stomach to facilitate the chemotherapy; this became infected, an ugly, bloody mess. Two days in the hospital, a course of antibiotics. Visiting him in his white-tiled room was particularly painful, the journey to his ward alone exposed wide human suffering, the family of suffering, the vast sibling struggle for the parent's attention, to alleviate pain. Money bought Reuben his own room, a view of warehouses. But in this case at least it couldn't buy him what mattered.

Reuben, at his best, managed to keep up the joke. 'Tell me, Doc; how much does a new head cost?'

The doctor was unamused. A conscientious man, also honest: he had little real interest in the pain he could do little to cure. And his sympathies were less tender than his professional curiosity. Still, he was an excellent physician, at the top of his field. His time was in large demand and humour wasted it. Everywhere, everywhere, Rachel thought, we are one among many. (Her language for such reflections had grown richer, subtler; yes, this did in fact soften the blows of reflection, cushion them slightly. She was reading passionately.)

Such a relief after all that to have him home again. It was almost happiness in itself, or very like it, to nurse him in his own bed. To arrange the daffodils on his window sill, and in the pleasure of this arranging, imagine his own.

The German increased his dose of morphine. Reuben swallowed the dry tablet dropped on his tongue in the morning, in the evening. Between times, when the pain grew inhuman, he drank morphine from a coffee mug. Rachel looked up the word in her dictionary: he was drinking not sleep but dreams. His manner was beginning to suffer from this necessary blurring. Rachel knew she was losing him – a loss of focus, a fade not to black but to the colour of ordinary life. When he died, ordinary life could begin again; they could wash the sheets of his bed, open the window, drive his smells from the room. They could go to the movies. Reuben drifted in and out of consciousness; like a man on an airplane, uncomfortable, dreaming of arrival.

Meanwhile, summer came to Manhattan. When she missed the school bus – she was rising later, unhurried – Rachel had to walk across the Park to catch the subway on the West Side. The grass in the Great Lawn blistering thick, thick as fingers. Lines of chalk had been drawn around the softball diamonds; in the early dew, the chalk trails caked and darkened. Pats of dogshit dried in the sun; when the mowers cut, the smells were pungent, humid. Baked earth. After school, she took the subway downtown again and walked back the same way. She didn't want to share a bus with kids; their lives differed so widely from her own, she was losing touch. Also, she took comfort in this extra hour before home. Tasha now had the nursing of him.

Those early summer afternoons. Hot smells rising from the streets. Even at five, sunshine caught the high-rise windows and burned their edges. Boys played ball again on the public courts; fat young men, glad to be out of the office early, took over the softball fields. Air-conditioning units dripped off the sides of apartment blocks. Walking across town, she felt the dirty cool flecks against her cheek, as many, perhaps, as a wet hand shakes loose after washing. The cherry trees on 82nd Street scattered bloom; confetti aftermaths. Petals wrinkled in the heat, then turned grey with pavement dirt. The days grew longer, stretched on loose elastic that had lost its snap. The rich packed up to leave Manhattan to the poor.

Towards the end, his eyesight began to go. The universe was being taken away from him in black spots; these Rachel imagined being given to the survivors, little gifts of unused light. She considered the world from his point of view; it was going out. Her own sight seemed astonishingly rich and clear by contrast. His headaches became unbearable; he stopped bearing them. A morphine drip was plugged into his opened forearm. He had nothing left to tell her. He had nothing left to tell her. Tasha and Rachel discussed only necessary things; they had lost any appetite for the unnecessary. (Later, after his death, these habits were reversed.) Tasha bought a television for the bedroom; less for his sake than for hers. When Rachel came home, she found her mother in bed watching soaps, her hand on Reuben's head, idly tender. Rachel left them to it, she had taken a step back.

Tasha was getting fat on takeaway food; she hardly dressed in the morning after washing. Rachel, for her part, remained meticulous: she spent at least a half-hour making up in the bathroom mirror before facing the day. Her worries about dress were particular, and therefore consoling. The summer brought with it flowers and summer dresses. Rachel wore her short red frock, patterned with hearts and black lines (bought the same day Reuben told her his news); high-heeled shoes. Some days she didn't bother going to school; the silence in her head was almost unbreakable. And then, a day short of her eighteenth birthday, real high weather, the skies blue all the way up to the stars, he died. Rachel came home at lunchtime, and Tasha said, 'It's over. What are you doing home?' Tasha wrapped her dressing-gown tight round; her eyes were black with yesterday's mascara. She was eating toast; the crumbs had fallen in flakes across the silk. Her mother was terribly hungry, her hands like ice.

Rachel had to look. She stepped into his bedroom, the windows now wide open. Even at the tenth floor you could smell summer. Reuben had complained steadily of the cold; it was the last thing he talked about, not money or memory, only how cold it was. No matter how high they turned the heating. Honestly, she found it hard to tell he was dead. They waited a day and a night to call the doctor; they wanted to see if he moved. Tasha had nowhere to sleep and so the two of them, tightly huddled, lay in Rachel's bed together. All night they wondered what he was doing; he had left them alone again, just the two of them, mother and daughter.

The next night, however, after the fuss with doctors and ambulances, Tasha slept at home. Rachel said she had schoolwork to collect from her father's apartment; in the end she spent the night in his bed, in his unclean sheets. Tasha rang of course all morning, worried and needy. 'What should I do?' she complained. 'I give up everything to nurse him. Now what do I do? Come home.' Rachel, sober and responsible, explained she was busy at school, there was a great deal of work to make up. In fact, she dressed in the morning, and went out to walk the streets. Composing thoughts. When she was a young girl, her teacher asked the class to write a poem about their summer holidays. It would begin: The summer I turned seven. The rest was up to them. Her thoughts began: The summer I turned eighteen. She dried off a patch of bench with paper napkins from the hotdog stand, and sat watching softball. The summer I turned eighteen I kissed a boy. My parents fell in love. (The form of words itself suggested this thought, its childishness. She shook her head.) My father died. The summer I turned eighteen.

On Friday Mrs Fuentes came late morning, and Rachel, embarrassed to be caught at home, decided to make her way to school. It was after lunch before she got in. She wanted to talk to Mr Englander, and waited for him in the little office overlooking the baseball field. Her essay was overdue, she had a few notes, she needed to explain. In a white blouse, very summery; she didn't want to make a show of mourning yet. The odour of her armpits, the stink of heavy emotions amid humid blustery weather, rose in her nostrils. She knew she looked perhaps a trifle overheated against the white cotton – discoloured, the blood in her face hectic, uneven. The lights were off and she couldn't bear to switch them on. The weather had turned since the clear heat of her father's death; wind and wet followed the high pressure. In the grey light, the summer skies outside had a sepia tint. She imagined the storage cupboard; here there was only the one door coming in; she couldn't back out.

She heard him enter and didn't turn round, her heart beat like a penny on piano strings; he was at the desk before he saw her. A heavy-shouldered walk, much burdened, even worse: properly unhappy. So he had his own private affairs. 'Well, what am I supposed to do about this?' he said, almost angrily. He clearly hadn't been told of her situation, an awful word. The way this loose talk crept into your own thoughts. 'I give up on you. I give up.'

'Don't say that, Mr Englander.'

'I don't have a choice. I've given you every chance, every encouragement. It isn't up to me; there are rules I can't bend. This isn't the kind of behaviour I can let pass.'

'I tried to write. You have no idea. I've given up on everything else. But I wanted to write for you.'

Don't cry, she thought, whatever you do, don't cry, but she cried anyway, she hadn't cried since her father's death. Almost as if the animal in her had tears and tensions to release; it was her conscious duty to give them vent. He came quickly to her side and sat down. 'Hey, hey, hey,' he said, and then her name, 'Rachel', as she had always imagined it, a word with intimate meanings. A word like Tasha in her father's mouth: with vintage. A heavy man, unlike Reuben, his body and side gave off dissatisfied heats, unhealthy odours. When he stretched his arm across her neck and palmed her shoulder, she smelt him vividly. Still, there were solid comforts there, even warmth, whatever the source of it, bloody nourishment and health. Her father's hand had felt like a glass of cold water.

She stopped crying; her father was dead. It was time Rachel realized she wasn't a girl any more – to acknowledge this fact and behave accordingly. Her body offered certain promises to men, she saw the way they looked at her, what they expected. 'Mr Englander, please,' she said, 'Mr Englander, please.' She had pressed her face against his ribs, with her hand on his leg. Now he held her against his shirt and she couldn't breathe without smelling him. Once she'd caught him looking through her purse after class, fingering a tampon; the shame of it. Later she told him someone was following him round after school. Even to the pharmacy, she said; Frannie had put her up to it, but she was by no means an innocent. 'Two can play that game.' It seemed only silly at the time, a girls' joke: girls were always imagining things, vague threats, especially Frannie. Frannie would say, look at the way that man looked at you, it's disgusting; and what she really meant was, why didn't he look at me. Rachel chastised herself for such egotism; but it didn't mean she didn't think it was true. 'Mr Englander, please.'

His heavy face turned towards her, he looked unhappy. As if happiness and good humour were only a carefully constructed expression, and when you saw a face up close, a few inches away, like a painting, it revealed more basic components. How near and large he seemed; this intimacy in itself was very persuasive. Her hand on his thigh also sensed other urgent pressures. Her eyes narrowed, she was terrified. But for the first time in months she felt the excitement of *what next?* She thought, for a second, implausibly: he could easily fit me inside his shirt, and hold me there. The way Reuben used to when she was a small girl, her face pressed to his undershirt. She reached up an arm; he let her hold on by his tie. One hand under her bottom for support. She breathed only him, wonderful comfort and heat. But then Mr Englander stood up, moving unsteadily towards the door. His manner, when he spoke, correct and formal. 'It's better,' he said, 'for various reasons, we leave that open. Some of them legal, I'm afraid; such are the times we live in. Our powers of comforting are greatly circumscribed. Tell me what's wrong.'

Perhaps she'd misread him. He was nothing like her father; she hardly knew him. 'I'm fine, thank you.' You have to make your own way with grief, nobody can help. There are no replacements, what's lost is lost. When she came home she found Mrs. Fuentes had changed the sheets in her father's room, the smell of him gone. Folded they lay at the foot of the unmade bed, perfectly white and clean.

What was left were two ceremonies, his funeral, her graduation. Later, she remembered, perhaps, more of those weeks than she noticed at the time, living through it the first go round. The course of her thoughts was strong, smooth; undisturbed, it left no mark, but offered clear reflections.

The funeral was a grand affair at the synagogue on 79th Street. Rachel realized, by the time a man gets to the funeral, his family have put on public mourning. Tasha in particular looked pink-faced, radiant, in her costly black dress, specially bought. Men in dark suits, young and old, crowded the service; she didn't know their names. All these people she didn't know were coming to bury her father.

(Only, they didn't bury him there, thank God, on the spot. This was only for *city* people. At the weekend, Tasha and Rachel went up to Port Jervis for a second funeral, a quieter affair. Tasha took it much harder. Whenever she dressed badly, Rachel knew, her mother was unhappy: what Tasha called 'ugly unhappy'. She wore grey slacks, a heavy pullover, rollneck, in spite of the heat; sunglasses. The pressures of nostalgia and grief, so different in nature, combined powerfully; winded her. She was confused. Rachel at one point had to ask for directions. Her mother's shame was awful; Tasha stood ten paces behind, hid her face. Muttering inaudibly, 'I can find it, Rachel. Leave me alone. We'll get there.')

Rachel remembered later seeing Miss Bostick at the service on 79th Street. Her Biology teacher, on the arm of one of the Conways. Miss Bostick was a nervy unripe woman, long-legged, less well liked by the girls than boys. She was wearing a soft grey dress, lined tight around her figure, buttoned up the front; exposing the flat wide pressure of her breasts, very sexual. Her healthy colour, pink, wind-blown; a woman in bloom. Charles Conway, the son of her father's partner, hadn't shaved. The mineral stubble of his cheeks, sandy, silicon-grey, flared in the sunshine coming through the high bank of coloured glass at the top of the hall. At the reception afterwards, among the cups and plates set down, the hum of business talk, he made a point of approaching Rachel. Miss

Bostick never once let go his arm. 'I didn't know him well, he was my father's friend. We played golf sometimes; he played short and straight, never three-putted. Usually took my money. I'd like to kiss you.' Stooping slightly to touch her cheek. She felt the rich abrasion of his beard, smelt his cologne – the breath of scented skin thick in her nose.

'Yes, that's my father,' she said. 'Hello, Miss Bostick.'

Charles continued. 'It's like kissing the bride. At a wedding every man should kiss the bride. Very special.'

'Charles!' Miss Bostick pinched him. And Rachel guessed already the little thrill in the pulse of her guiding hand. To have a man to play with, money! These were high times for her, too; her reach was growing.

'My great condolences,' Charles said, lightly touching her temple where a clutch of hair fell loose. She found him hugely comforting, the cut of his tie, his good looks: so she didn't have to hide, she was the star of the show, the real grief. Miss Bostick apologized for him. 'Why don't you come to my office this week,' she said. 'I want to talk to you.'

There was also the reading of her father's will, at Reuben's law firm on 57th Street. Rachel met her mother in the lobby. She'd taken another afternoon off from school. Together they took the elevator up, in that cool dry inner air. Tasha was going to pieces, her blond hair loose on her head, the grey growing through. Her wide cheeks unmade up, without colour: a simpleton's face. They stepped into reception. Around them, all these busy men behind closed glass doors. Reuben once said to her, 'When you step on a man's foot, after he's done complaining, the first thing he'll tell you is how hard he works. This is what entitles him to suffer.' Rachel thought of this now and smiled. Her father had worked hard; he was entitled.

Mr Conway himself led them into his office. Midtown Manhattan spread wide in the tall window. Rachel caught the fishscale glitter off the Chrysler building. From this distance, nobody's life below mattered much. Bert Conway, a big, bald man, wide-shouldered – even at his age, he could hardly fit into his jacket – carefully explained the will. The dry language reminded Rachel of her father's medical condition: only suffering, it seemed to her, could come from such specific attention to detail.

Reuben had altered it after the divorce. Rachel at eighteen came into the apartment and various portfolios of stock. A cash fund, too. To be managed at her own discretion: she was free to do what she liked. As he said to her that night over dinner: 'Not now, but later, I want you to consider what I've said. What I've worked for all my life offers you real freedoms; do what you want with them, that's all I ask. Don't confine yourself for form's sake.'

She remembered the way she covered her ears. 'I don't want to talk about money, I don't want to talk about money.' But she was growing up: she paid close attention now. An independent woman, if she wanted she could cut herself free from Tasha entirely. That night she made her father's bed herself and slept there. She wondered what to do with her wealth: how could she live, as her father wished, freely, without any attention to 'form'? He can't have been happy, to have worked so hard all his life in order to give his daughter a life without work. Tasha was heartbroken and rang at all hours. Rachel herself was surprised at her own coldness: perhaps she had something to forgive. The way Tasha moved in at the end disgusted her: she couldn't even let him die in peace. She blamed her mother obscurely for Reuben's death.

She did in the end visit Miss Bostick at school. Few of the girls liked Miss Bostick. Not that she flirted too much, though she did, subtly, favour her boys. Rather, she relied too often on certain sisterly appeals: as if she said, you know what I'm talking about, girls. You know what it's like; help me out here. Simple weakness: it did them no honour. Rachel, at least, never warmed to her. But she stepped demurely into the L-shaped office during lunch, and asked to see Miss Bostick. Mr Peasbody, one of the older men, generally loved for his dry manner and easy authority, gestured to the back of the room. And Amy stood up and took Rachel in her arms. Her manner initially tender; her concern oversweet.

'Trust me,' she said at one point, 'I know what a father is to a girl. I know how much he means. I couldn't get any food down at the reception, I was so wound up.'

Later, 'Still, I think we need to have a conversation.' Rachel sat with her hands on her lap and distantly noted these phrases. 'I'm worried about you.' A phone directory held open the window. 'Life goes on.' A little wind went off and on, unsettling the pages of a textbook. She had forgotten the pressures of school, the strong constriction of enforced childishness. 'Women', Miss Bostick explained, 'need to be strong. Even a little cold.' She sat with her legs crossed, leaning forward. Her legs, it's true, were long and elegant: enviable. 'This is an important time for you. The way you're going, I don't see how I can graduate you.' Rachel noted an engagement ring on her finger, a platinum band, the bright clenched fist of a diamond. Yes, Miss Bostick had changed in the course of the year, grown more sure of herself. There were rumours she was leaving the school. Rachel thanked her sweetly, said she would do her best.

In the hallway afterwards, she felt a rough hand on her arm. Mr Peasbody stood there in a sweat; she was shocked to see him, she could still feel his fingers on her skin. 'Take all the time you want,' he said. 'I want you to know that none of this matters, none of this matters at all. Don't listen to any of us.' He loomed over her rather unsteadily, and smoothed his thin hair with a damp palm. He'd put on weight; there was hardly any colour in his face at all. 'None of this matters,' he repeated. And then, more spitefully, 'She's one of those girls, marriage has gone to her head.'

Rachel knew who he was: Frannie's father. Her friend had

quizzed Rachel about him, though she had little to offer: a well-liked teacher, clever, disrespectful. Lately, he'd let himself go: the sour smell of the dissection lab still clung to him. For once, she stood her ground. 'Don't touch me,' she said. 'I don't need to be told any more what matters and what doesn't.' Even she guessed it was the wrong thing to say, and which is worse, not quite true. And the wrong person to say it to. He looked at her, large-eyed, his heavy head tenderly nodding. 'No,' he said laughing at last, 'I don't suppose you do.' She walked slowly her narrow line along the hallway; when she turned at the steps, he was still watching her.

The graduation itself was another grand affair. Bleachers lined up around the baseball field. Rows of blue cafeteria chairs in the middle for the students. A podium at one end, by the road where the school buses parked. Tables under a canopy with squares of cake, punch, plastic cups. Flowers blowing away, a scratchy microphone. A cloudy morning gave way to windy sunshine, one of those days no matter how you dress, you'll end up in a sweat from time to time, you'll suffer a chill. Dr Holroyd, apologizing for Miss Bostick, had promised Rachel an honourary diploma; nobody needed to know, she could make up the work in the summer. Rachel wasn't sure how she felt, but went along. She went along with everything; she was drifting free.

Tasha came, and Rachel's heart, for once, went out to her: the care she took. Her hair cut short, her long mottled neck exposed, unashamed. A simple blue dress and pumps, no shades. Her vivid flat eyes took everything in. Too nervous to gossip with the other parents, she held her purse tightly on her lap.

Rachel sat at the end of a row of Ks. Summer grass underfoot; she took off her shoes. The ground was still a little wet, cold. She could see the back of Brian Bobek's head, the confident crewcut coloured vaguely by the pink of his scalp. A few weeks ago, after a late meal, they'd been caught out in a summer shower. She took him back to *her* place, as she called it, and offered him some of her father's clothes. Nothing would fit, of course, apart from his undergarments. Still, they spent a giggly tearful hour trying things on. Reuben's working suit. The jacket hunched large around Brian's shoulders, his wrists stuck out, he looked like an ogre, a bear. Reuben's ties. In the end he wore only a cravat around his bare neck and a pair of spotted shorts. They slept in her father's bed. Rachel consciously exposed herself to him, taking off her wet blouse, her bra, her shoes, her skirt, her stockings. Looking for her nightgown under the pillows and pulling it over her head in front of him, feeling the play of her breasts under the silk.

She couldn't sleep and turned on her side towards him. Her freedom in the world seemed extraordinary, terrifying; no one was watching them. Whatever she did no one was watching her. Her privacy was enormous. Brian's cheeks, his hairless breast, his strong thighs, were perfectly pink and white. She remembered what she thought was a nursery rhyme: strawberries swimming in the cream. Schoolboys playing in the stream. His voice was thick in his throat, a little burdened, as if by humid weather. And in fact the night air was heavy and oppressive. Childishly, she wanted to put her small hand against his shorts to see if it moved. She didn't yet dare to pull them below his hips. Instead, she held her hands against her belly, and thought of her father's words: *everything inside desires a human touch*. Brian complained he was coming down with a cold; perhaps they shouldn't kiss, he didn't want her to catch it. Really, the smell of sour rainwater between her legs, the little loose hairs he saw as she undressed, appalled him. Years later, he confessed to her: he'd begun to dream about boys. They slept side by side, restless and silent. She had never seen him so cast down; he could barely face her in the morning, over milk and cereal. The sound of him gulping unhappily stuck in her mind all day.

She decided she couldn't go through with another ceremony – put on her shoes and slipped out between the bleachers. The press of people was too great, her insignificance and false position. One among many was the rule of each thing; she wanted to break apart. If only she could get a note to Tasha. They could have a bite to eat instead, the two of them. She hadn't felt so hungry in weeks. Another memory moved her. Once, coming home from school, she found her parents fighting over a piece of carrot cake. Tasha had bought it for him specially from Le Pain Quotidien, a baker on Madison. By such small gestures she used to ornament her love. Tender curls of carrot shred, a thick cream icing. A large wedge toppled and stuck in a paper box. Late in April, Reuben was very bad, but had made it to the sitting room and lay on the red sofa. Tasha was picking at the cake from the wooden chair – licking the frosting off her finger, and breaking a piece in crumbs to put in her mouth. Tears streaming down her face. 'I won't give you any more, you haven't been good to me. You haven't been a good boy.'

'Come to me, Tasha,' he said. 'Sit here. Don't be silly.'

Rachel went to her room; she couldn't bear to watch. Their voices muffled by the wall between. She sat perfectly still, an emblem, it seemed, of her general condition: she kept quiet to hear how other people were living.

'You haven't been a good boy. You left me. You shouldn't have left me. You're leaving again.' Tasha's voice both motherly and complaining; and yet, even so near the end, she couldn't refrain from coaxing a little, at her most womanly. She was an old flirt; even in her grief she played up to him. She wanted him to agree: he had abused her terribly. As if whatever they did to each other, it was her job to suffer. She had the more difficult role.

'But you bought it for me, you bought it especially for me. A gift, a kind thought.' Reuben pleaded with her, as you plead with a child, painfully dependent on his own powers of consolation. He had often fallen short; whereas she could console him, he sometimes thought, at will. Perhaps he overvalued her moments of sweetness, his own affection involved such deliberations. But they did seem very sweet to him, her happy impulses. What moved him most was her own happiness. This had at one time seemed particularly necessary to him, to his interest in life.

Tasha, still licking her fingers, still breaking off crumbs. 'I don't want you to die, you fool. I don't want you to die. What am I supposed to do with myself after? What will I do?'

Rachel couldn't hear what her father said, his tone low and consoling. Even in these circumstances, he tried to comfort.

'It's better I go now,' her mother said, these heavy assumed tones of the matter-of-fact. 'That way I won't be so miserable afterwards.' She inhaled and brushed her hands together and stood up; looked sharply round for her purse. And then hesitated. If she found it, there was nothing left to delay her. The only thing they had left was delay. Rachel could hear her, putting on her ordinary exasperation. 'What have you done with my handbag?' she muttered implausibly. 'I can never find anything when you're around. I remember that much.' She was losing steam. The world had appeared to her in its more durable form: when she had nothing to complain of, no one to resent. When he was dead.

'It's always been this way with you,' Reuben protested. 'We were happy a minute ago. Eating cake. And now you suffer for it. It takes you completely by surprise; as if you forgot you have to pay for everything. I can't bear it.'

'You can't bear it!' Tasha screamed, giving way at last and losing her voice. 'I can't bear it. I can't bear it!'

Rachel put her fists over her ears, sitting in her bed with her shoes on, sitting so her shoes didn't touch the bed. She could never stand the way her mother shouted, her father's calm voice, perplexed. How much of her life had been spent listening to these two bicker? On her own; out of the heat of it; left out. Thank God, at least, they were running out of fight. And then she shivered in the coldness of that thought. Later, when she came out, they'd gone to the bedroom. The box of cake empty on the coffee table. The urgent hush of their privacy next door. It was impossible to ignore any longer, much as she tried to: her parents' love. She was the child of love. In the years to come this fact seemed increasingly significant.

She stood in the outfield now hoping to catch her mother's eye. Let's get out of here, she thought; mother, can we please get out of here. Tasha, her head erect, sitting high up in the bleachers. 'Mother,' Rachel urged into the summer skies, 'mother.' They could go for coffee and eggs at the bottom of the hill, a little Spanish diner. Dr Holroyd squeaked a little on the microphone, testing it. Her magnified voice broadcast in the open air suggested vast distances; the wind caught it. 'Well, we just about got through again. One more year.' The tone false, jolly. Wide applause. Rachel was weeping freely, while Tasha bent to look for something in her purse. 'Mother!' Rachel called, a half-call, into the breeze. You silly woman, she thought, turn around, turn around.

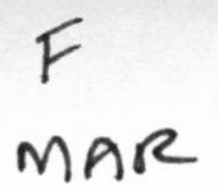
F
MAR

Sussex Downs College
102986

SUSSEX DOWNS
COLLEGE
Putting Students First

by the same author

THE SYME PAPERS